Turnag
Turnage, Leceila
Peony's daughters

Peony's Daughters

Peony's Daughters

LECEILA TURNAGE

URBAN BOOKS

www.urbanbooks.net

URBAN SOUL is published by

Urban Books
6 Vanderbilt Parkway
Dix Hills, NY 11746

ISBN-13: 978-1-59983-073-5
ISBN-10: 1-59983-073-6

First Printing: July 2009
10 9 8 7 6 5 4 3 2 1

Printed in the United States of America

Acknowledgments

Dear God, I thank you first and foremost for grace and mercy, and the blessings you continually shower down upon me each and every day.

To my parents, Ermadine and Garland Turnage, thanks for the lessons you've taught and continue to teach in word and deed to my brother, sisters, and me about perseverance and prayer.

A world of thanks to Priscilla Copeland, Shelia Dodd, Brenda Owens, Jimmy Stuart, Sharon Barrow, and my sisters Anjanette Turnage and Lornita Turnage, for the critiques, suggestions, and support. To Levernard Speight, and cousins Kenny Earl Whitaker, Therman Hunter, and Nein Daniels-Chambers, thanks for the invaluable information you've provided. To Dale Roane, R. C. Chambers, Diane Marti-Lopez, Linda Sanders, Joe Baker, Jeanice Young, my brother McKinley Turnage, and my sister-in-law Valencia Turnage, thanks for the best wishes and support you've given me.

And last, but certainly not least, to my agent, Kimberly T. Matthews, my publisher, Carl Weber, my editor, Nicole Peters, and the entire Urban Books family, thanks!

Leceila Turnage

Sweet flowers alone can say what passion fears revealing.
Thomas Hood, poet

Prologue

Violet

Caroline Rosetta Johnson was born July 17, 1924, in McKinley, North Carolina, to the late Leander and Wilhelmina Sims Johnson. She departed this life Wednesday, May . . .

The tears that filled my eyes made reading impossible. Oddly enough, and in spite of the mournful Mahalia Jackson CD playing and the brief exchanges taking place in Fowler's Funeral Home, I could hear my tears splatter as they trickled down my face onto the obituary in my hand. I shook my head and wiped my eyes. The women from Dean's Florist were leaving. They'd delivered the peony, daisy, lily, ivy, jasmine, and violet arrangements Mama ordered yesterday. My grief momentarily gave way to joy. The arrangements were beautiful, and if Aunt Caroline was looking down from heaven, she was smiling. Caroline Rosetta Johnson loved flowers.

"Violet, everything look okay?" Bertha Fowler, the

mortician's wife, asked, walking up to me with a box of tissue.

I nodded and looked back down at the obituary.

She leaves to cherish her memories a loving and devoted sister, Peony Vernester Shaw of McKinley, North Carolina . . .

I closed the obituary and suppressed the wail rising up inside me by clearing my throat. I wanted to walk over and join Mama, but my feet wouldn't move. She and the mortician were standing in front of the bronze casket where Aunt Caroline was lying, dressed in the lilac Anne Klein suit my sisters and I gave her for Easter. The words *May the Work I've Done Speak for Me* were etched into the casket's lining in bold, gold script letters.

"She was a fine lady. A pillar of this community. She will be missed," George Fowler said.

"Yes, she will be missed. No one's going to miss her more than me," Mama said.

"Yes, yes," George said solemnly.

I looked down at the picture of Aunt Caroline on the front of the obituary and whispered, "Why, Lord?" one more time.

"Peony, we'll print two hundred copies like you asked," Bertha Fowler said.

Mama looked back at Mrs. Fowler and said, "Thank you." Mama was thankful that the Fowlers were able to accommodate her on such short notice, given it had been less than twenty-four hours since the hospital had released Aunt Caroline's body to them.

"Everything looks just fine, George," Mama said, running her hand down the satin lining of the casket. "Caroline looks just like she's sleeping."

I couldn't contain my grief any longer. "Mama! I miss Aunt Caroliiiine!" I cried. My outcry ripped through the heavy, oppressive air. I followed it with "Lord, why did you have to take her!"

Mama hurried over to where I stood weeping uncontrollably. Bertha Fowler stepped aside and shoved a handful of tissue to her.

"My daughters loved my sista, and she loved them. Yes, she did. God knows she did," Mama said, consoling me.

"She was a fine woman," Bertha Fowler said. "So, so sweet." That comment caused me to give way once more to the grief inside me.

"Let them tears flow! Let 'em flow!" Bertha Fowler said, handing Mama more tissue.

"Yes, yes," George Fowler said with a clap of his hands.

"Peony, when will your other daughters get here?" Bertha Fowler asked.

"Sometime tonight or early tomorrow," Mama replied, smiling.

"I see," Bertha Fowler said, clearing her throat.

"Daisy, my oldest," Mama said, "won't be able to make it."

"Oh?" Bertha Fowler asked.

Mama shook her head. "Her son, Cedric, got hurt pretty bad fightin' over there in Iraq. He's in the hospital." Mama paused and shook her head. "He might lose both of his legs."

"My Lord!" Bertha Fowler exclaimed.

"Daisy's in Arizona with him and his family. I told her when I talked to her this morning, not to stress herself over trying to come."

Bertha Fowler nodded and said, "My Lord!" again.

I burst out crying once more.

"So, the other three will be here for the services?" Bertha Fowler asked.

Mama nodded.

"You—you just call us when they get in, all right?" Bertha Fowler said, smiling weakly.

"I will," Mama said.

George Fowler was looking at us, scratching his balding head. His brows were creased together. He looked worried; so did Mrs. Fowler. Worried, no doubt, that one of my sisters—Lily—would not be pleased with what they'd done. Lily had given the Fowlers such a hard time when Daddy died sixteen months ago. Mama had yet to call her, Ivy, or Jasmine to inform them of Aunt Caroline's death and committal service. They would be devastated upon hearing the news from Mama that Aunt Caroline was dead and mortified that Mama hadn't called sooner. Mama didn't want to be stressed out any more than she already was. But there was no getting around that my sisters—namely Lily and Jasmine—were stressors. Mama hadn't called them or Ivy, because she didn't want Lily coming in and taking over like she did when Daddy died. She even made me promise not to call them; she wanted to personally see to Aunt Caroline's final arrangements herself.

"We've reserved three family cars for the service Sunday. You sure that'll be enough?" George Fowler asked, walking over.

Mama nodded.

"We can get another one if you—"

Mama interrupted Mr. Fowler with a wave of her hand. "Three is more than enough."

George Fowler nodded slowly and looked at his wife.

"We'll have a fourth one on standby, just in case," Bertha Fowler said with a smile and a nod.

Mama nodded. "All right, Bertha."

I prayed then that Lily would find everything to her liking.

"Let's go, honey," Mama said, placing an arm around my waist.

"If there's anything more that we can do for you and your daughters, Peony, please don't hesitate to ask, you hear?" Bertha Fowler said.

Mama nodded again and smiled. "Thank you, Bertha."

The Fowlers walked us outside. When I drove off, they were still standing outside, looking worried.

Chapter 1

McKinley, NC

Violet

I could hear the phone ringing as I made my way up the steps onto the front porch of the big two-story house where my four sisters and I were raised. "Father, *please* help Mama and me get through this," I prayed for what could have been the thousandth time since Aunt Caroline's death. Fumbling with my keys, I managed to unlock the front door. I ran inside and grabbed the phone in the kitchen. Before answering, I took a deep breath and prayed my prayer again.

"Hello."

"Is this the Shaw residence?"

I took another deep breath and silently prayed, *Strength now, Lord!* "Yes, it is," I said pleasantly.

"Violet, that you?"

"Yes, ma'am."

"Let me speak to Peony."

"Miss Emma, Mama's busy right now." Mama was outside talking to seventy-seven-year-old Sadie Copeland, the next-door neighbor and neighborhood news reporter, aka gossip, who walked over when we pulled into the yard.

"Busy doin' what?" Miss Emma asked loudly.

"She's outside. Talking to Miss Sadie."

Miss Emma grunted. I imagined she made a face too. She didn't like Miss Sadie and Miss Sadie didn't care for her either. "Is Ca'line's body out yet?" she asked.

"Yes, ma'am."

"What time Fowler put her out?"

"At three o'clock."

"I rode by there a little after two o'clock and saw yo' car. I didn't stop 'cause I didn't know if her body was ready for viewin'."

Thank you for being so respectful, I said to myself.

"How Ca'line look? Lord knows she'd fallen off some. Does she look like herself?"

I inhaled deeply and prayed my short prayer again. Miss Emma thought I was crying.

"Go 'head on and cry, chile!" she said soothingly. "Don't hold it in. That way, you won't be so filled up at the wake or funeral. You and yo' sisters gone have to hold Peony up. Y'all can't cut up and carry on like you did at yo' daddy's funeral. Knockin' over pews and rollin' round on the flo'."

My sisters and I were the talk of Charity Chapel Missionary Baptist Church for quite some time after Daddy's funeral. We loved our father, and yes, we did take his passing very hard. We didn't apologize then, and we weren't about to apologize now, to anyone for our behavior.

"Them two sistas and that niece of yours tryin' to pull Augusta outta his casket. My, my, my!" Miss Emma exclaimed. "In *all* my seventy-seven years of livin', I ain't never witnessed anythang quite like yo' daddy's funeral. Whew! Lord, Lord, have mercy!"

I kept praying my short prayer over and over again.

"Yes, indeedy, y'all cut up some. So go 'head and cry now. You wants me to pray for you?"

My eyes popped open and I blurted out, "No, ma'am!"

"I don't care what nobody say, though," Mrs. Harris said adamantly, "Ca'line would still be with us if she hadn't gone on that cruise!"

I started humming to myself one of Mama's favorite spirituals, "Lord, Help Me to Hold Out."

"She didn't have no business, none *whatsoever*, goin' to Mexico. Hmph! She nor Peony. I heard somewhere that the water over there ain't fit to drink. When Ca'line got back here off that trip, she was sick as a dog. Looked right puny! Why y'all send her and Peony on that trip anyhow?"

If anyone had the nerve to say my sisters and I were responsible for Aunt Caroline's death, it would be the uncouth, opinionated, surly Emma Harris. Aunt Caroline, Mama, I, and quite a few others at Charity Chapel didn't care for the boisterous widow I nicknamed Mother Loud and Wrong.

"Violet!" Miss Emma yelled. "You still there?"

"Yes, ma'am." My grief had given way to anger and I had to bite my bottom lip to keep from saying something disrespectful. Mama and Daddy taught my sisters and me at an early age to respect our elders *and* church leaders. Emma Harris sat on the Mothers' Board at Charity Chapel alongside Mama. When word got out at church that my sisters and I were sending Mama and Aunt Caroline away on "another trip," Miss Emma had nothing but negative things to say. She was jealous of Mama and Aunt Caroline. Jealous of Aunt Caroline mostly, because seventy-five-year-old Odell Jackson, a widower and church deacon, had the hots for Aunt Caroline and wouldn't give her so much as the time of day.

"Peony decided what she gone do with Ca'line's house?" Miss Emma asked.

I gasped. *I know she didn't just ask me about Aunt Caroline's house!* I thought angrily to myself.

"Huh? Has she?" Miss Emma asked again.

"No, ma'am."

"Oh, so you ain't gone move in it?"

Miss Emma didn't give me time to answer her. Not that I would have anyway, because what Mama decided to do with Aunt Caroline's house was none of her business.

"I figured you'd move in it," Miss Emma said, clearing her throat. "Unless you too scared to live by yo'self now. Is you?"

"No, ma'am."

It had been two months to the day that my house, a two-story, four-bedroom, three-and-a-half bath I'd purchased four years ago, was destroyed by fire. I was on my way home from my book club meeting when I saw the flames from a distance shooting up to the sky. According to the fire marshal, the cause of the fire was an unattended burning candle. I questioned the fire marshal's findings, because even though I often burned scented candles in my home, I always made sure I extinguished them before going to bed or leaving home.

"Were you planning to build again?" Miss Emma asked, interrupting my thoughts. "I don't know why you wanted to live out there in that big house in the first place. I can't understand you young, single women. No children, no husband, why you want to stay in sump'n that big? You remind me"—Miss Emma chuckled—"of my granddaughter Sandra in Raleigh. You what she call 'an independent woman.' And she's just like you," Miss Emma said, chuckling again, "independent."

"Is that right?" I said, hearing a hint of sarcasm in my voice.

"Uh-huh," Miss Emma replied. "I'm sure Peony 'preciates you bein' there with her, Violet. And if you don't move in Ca'line's house, I know somebody that would love to rent it. My son Nub. He and that wife of his talkin' 'bout gettin' back together again."

I laughed to myself. Nub, his loud, brawling wife, and those delinquents they called children, uh-uh, moving into Aunt Caroline's house—that would never happen.

"How you say Peony holdin' up?"

"Fine, Miss Emma. Considering," I snapped.

"When yo' sistas comin' home? I thought they'd been here by now."

"Miss Emma, I have to go."

"Okay, okay, chile. I'ma go on over to Fowler's to see Ca'line. You and yo' sistas be strong for yo' mama now, you hear?"

"Yes, ma'am."

"Her husband dead and gone, now her sista."

Tears fell from my eyes. "Miss Emma, I got to go."

"Okay, go on now. Tell Peony I called, and I'll call her later."

I slammed the phone down and looked out the kitchen window. Mama and Miss Sadie were walking across the street to Aunt Caroline's house: a small, vinyl-siding rancher that bore a fresh coat of yellow paint. Potted planters with red ivy geraniums sat on the front porch and below in the immaculate front yard, azaleas, dogwoods, pansies, daffodils, and daisies basked in the sunlight. Just four days ago, Aunt Caroline was out in her yard planting those daisies.

My thoughts drifted two hundred fifty miles away to Washington, D.C., where my oldest sister, Daisy, lived, then to Phoenix, where she was attending to her son. It would break Mama's heart to know her firstborn had become a compulsive gambler. Daisy's gambling was just one of many things my sisters and I kept from Mama. My one-month relationship with Warren Jackson—Deacon Odell Jackson's grandson—was another thing. When Mama overheard Warren ask me out a week after he joined Charity Chapel, she couldn't wait to tell me after he'd walked off that she forbade me to see him. Warren was still a married man, she said. Even though Warren and his wife of twelve years were separated and divorcing, Mama said it wouldn't look right, it wouldn't be right, and she wouldn't think much of us going out together. The "proper, respectable thing" for me to do, she said, was to wait until Warren's divorce was final before I started "swapping spit" with him.

While not wanting to disobey my mother and be branded an adulteress by the church, or deny myself Warren's company, I resorted to sneaking around to see him. The extent of our moments together didn't go beyond hugs and kisses. Thoughts of the ten minutes we spent in his Denali the night before filled me with joy.

In small-town McKinley, well, anywhere for that matter, Warren was considered a "good catch." Four years shy of my forty-one years, he was not only tall, bald, and fine, but degreed—he had a bachelor's in criminal justice. He also had an impressive fifteen-year career in law enforcement. And Warren wasn't hurting for money either. His family made a small fortune when they sold some of the family's land to developers building the town's first strip mall that would be home to a Super Target and a Golden Corral.

Two months after Warren moved to McKinley from Durham to begin work as a detective with the police department, he joined Charity Chapel. To the dismay of Miss Holier-than-thou, pretty, forty-three-year-old, cat-eyed Colette Worrell—Emma Harris's twice-divorced daughter and mother of four—and a slew of other single women at the church, Warren sought after my affections. I welcomed Warren's advances because at the time, the only man hot on my heels was Willie, a homeless man who frequented the library where I worked as librarian.

Colette approached me one Sunday after worship service in the fellowship hall. She had rarely said two words to me prior to Warren's arrival at Charity Chapel, so I figured something was up and it involved Warren.

"So, Violet," she said, smiling broadly. "What're you and yo' little book club reading now?" she asked loudly. Before I could answer, she said, "I'm thinkin' 'bout starting a book club myself."

"Oh, really?" I replied.

"Uh-huh," Colette said with a nod. "We won't be

reading any smutty books like you and yo' book club members."

Several people were standing nearby and overhead Colette's derogatory comment. They looked at me disapprovingly.

"We don't read 'smutty books,'" I countered loudly.

Colette smiled. "If you say so."

I shot Colette a phony smile, while fighting the urge to get into a testy exchange with her in, of all places, the Lord's House.

"We will be reading *Christian* material," Colette continued, "books by T. D. Jakes, Juanita Bynum, Paula White. Folks like that."

"Wonderful," I said with another phony smile.

"Warren, by the way, is reading one of my T. D. Jakes books."

"Oh?" I said.

"Yeah," Colette said, smiling broadly. "And it's autographed. It's one of many I got when I went to the Woman Thou Art Loosed Conference some years back."

A smile and an "uh-huh" were all I could muster up. Warren hadn't mentioned to me that Colette had given him a book to read.

When the people standing near us walked off, Colette's entire disposition changed. "What's going on between you two?" she asked, glaring at me with her hands on her hips.

"What do you mean?" I asked with a big smile.

"You know *exactly* what I mean. Are you and Warren seeing each other?"

"Why didn't you ask him, when you gave him your book?"

Colette narrowed her eyes at me, sighed heavily, and walked away.

The following weekend at the church's single women's retreat at the Grove Park Inn in Asheville, her sister, the equally self-righteous Evangeline Harris, stood and said she'd had a reoccurring dream about Colette standing at the church altar, dressed in a beautiful wedding gown. The man she was marrying was tall, bald, and dressed in a dark blue uniform. Colette jumped up and started shouting.

I looked back out the window. Mama and Miss Sadie were standing in Aunt Caroline's yard. I pulled my cell phone out of my pocket and dialed Warren's mobile. He answered on the second ring.

"Hey, darling."

"Hi."

"How are you?"

"I'm hanging in here."

"You and your mother back from the funeral home?"

"Yes."

"Did that go okay?"

"Uh-huh. My aunt looks like she's resting. She looks so peaceful. I looked down at her lying there in that casket, and had the hardest time believing she's gone." I burst into tears. "I can't believe she's gone, Warren!"

"Oh, honey, I know."

"I'm trying to be strong for Mama. I'll be so glad when she calls Lily, Ivy, and Jasmine, and they get here."

"I have all of you in my prayers."

"Thanks, and don't stop praying."

"Baby, I won't. And don't you worry too much about your sisters being upset with you for not calling them."

"I'm not. Mama was *determined* to see to Aunt Caroline's arrangements by herself. And she didn't need or want Lily stressing her out. Besides, Aunt Caroline had said long before she died that when that day came, she wanted George Fowler to have her body. And despite how Lily feels about itty-bitty Fowler's Funeral Home, Mama honored Aunt Caroline's wishes."

"She has to respect that," Warren said.

I grunted. "She will. It will take some time for her, though. Lily holds grudges."

"I'll say an extra, *long* prayer for her," Warren said, laughing.

I laughed too and wiped my eyes. "I don't think I told you that when Daddy died, she gave poor Mr. Fowler a fit, because his wife had mistakenly ordered the wrong casket, which, when Mama saw it, said it was okay. But noooo, uh-uh, Lily won't having none of that. So Daddy's funeral was delayed *two* days until the casket we had originally ordered arrived. And it was just one thing after another after that! Mr. Fowler's limos weren't new enough. The obituary didn't look professionally done. Warren, Mama was so stressed out. And if she had called Lily right after Aunt Caroline died, Lily would have been here in no time barking out all sorts of demands to Mr. Fowler."

"Sounds like your sister Lily is a force to be reckoned with," Warren said, chuckling.

"She can be," I said.

"I have heard," Warren cleared his throat, "that *all* of you Shaw girls are something to contend with."

"Nooooo!" I exclaimed.

Warren laughed. "I'm just teasing, baby."

Warren had a great sense of humor. I liked that about him.

"I'm so glad you didn't move away from McKinley," he said.

"You are?" I replied demurely.

"Yeah."

"Tell me why?" I asked, knowing the answer because Warren had said it to me many times before.

"You know why," he said, laughing.

"Yeah, but I want to hear you say it again."

"Because," Warren said softly, "I would never have met you."

"Let's see, if I'd taken that librarian position in Charlotte years ago," I said dreamily, "you're right. We probably would never have met."

Warren groaned. "Please, don't torture me."

"Oooooh, poor baby. Now—"

"Violet! Where is your mother?" Warren asked, interrupting me.

I burst out laughing. "Warren, calm down. Mama's not here. She's across the street at Aunt Caroline's."

Warren exhaled.

"Do you think I would be carrying on like that if Mama was nearby?"

Warren laughed. "Your mother is one of the sweetest women at the church. I'm trying to get on her good side. I want her to like me."

"Mama *likes* you Warren, she just doesn't want us to date, not until your divorce is final."

Warren exhaled again. "June fifteenth, and it can't come soon enough."

"No more sneaking around!" I said, laughing.

"Yeah," Warren said, "no more sneaking around!"

"You have to admit, though, there's an element of excitement to that," I said, glancing back out the window. Mama was still across the street, standing in Aunt Caroline's yard with Miss Sadie.

Warren laughed. "There is. But I have all the excitement I can handle, keeping McKinley free of crime."

"And you're doing a *marvelous* job of that, Detective Jackson."

"Why, thank you for that vote of approval, Miss Shaw."

"You're welcome."

I liked Warren a lot, and was looking forward to the next time I saw him. "I won't see you until tomorrow evening at the wake."

"You will see me before then, suga."

"Huh?"

"How does this evening sound?"

"Warren! There's no way I can get away!"

"You don't have to. I'm coming there."

"What?" I yelled.

"Some of the church members are coming by to pay their respects around six o'clock. I'm bringing Uncle Odell. He wants to come by for a little while."

"Oh, okay."

"I know how your mother feels about my uncle," Warren said, sighing. "We won't stay too long, I promise. Just long enough to pay our respects."

"I don't know who Mama dislikes the most, your uncle Odell, Emma Harris, Ulysses Robinson, or Odessa and Eugene Humphrey."

Warren sighed again. "My uncle is grieving. I think he was in love with Miss Caroline."

Tears filled my eyes. "Poor Deacon Jackson."

"She could have been the next Mrs. Odell Jackson."

I laughed. "Oh, really?"

"'Really?'" Warren chuckled. "Girl, you better recognize. My uncle has a way with women."

"Women like Emma Harris."

"Ooooh, low blow."

"Sorry."

"Don't apologize."

"She wants him like Colette wants you."

"Wanting and having are two entirely different things."

"Am I as pretty as Colette?"

"You're *prettier*," Warren replied, "and sexier."

I smiled, then giggled. Colette, like her sisters, was not only pretty, she was voluptuous and exuded an air of sensuality. Even though I wasn't as shapely as Colette, I was a far cry from being a plain Jane. Truth be told, I wasn't getting any younger and neither was Colette, but still I felt threatened by her, and she pissed me off with the way she threw herself at Warren at church. And in light of the string of suitors that wined and dined me following my appearance in *Ebony* as a bachelorette five years ago, not one date had blossomed into anything comparable to what Warren and I had. So I was excited about my budding relationship because I'd been in a dating drought for two years before Warren arrived on the scene and was desperately hoping things would work out between the two of us and wishing Colette would back off.

"Did Miss Caroline dislike my uncle too?" Warren asked, interrupting my thoughts about my rival for his heart.

"No. I think she was a little sweet on him. Whenever Mama would complain about him, Aunt Caroline would jump to his defense."

"That's good to know."

"Mama thinks Deacon Jackson is . . . wimpy," I said.

Warren said nothing.

"I'm sorry."

"No, no. Don't apologize," Warren said hurriedly. "If that's how she feels, there's no need for you to apologize."

"She can't understand nor does she support his and Deacon Humphrey's decision to side with Deacon Robinson against considering Reverend Cherry for pastor."

"I see."

"Sorry."

"There you go again, apologizing."

"Sorry."

"Violet?"

"What?"

"I'm crazy about you."

I smiled.

"And I miss you."

"I miss you too."

"Violet!"

I looked out the kitchen window. Mama and Miss Sadie were back in the yard. "Violet!" Mama yelled again.

"Warren, I gotta go!"

"Okay, bye!"

I stuffed my phone back in my pocket and headed outside.

Chapter 2

75 Miles Away

Lily Shaw-Davenport sat in her spacious fifth-floor office contemplating the eight conference requests before her. As program manager for the Child Welfare Division of the county's Department of Social Services, she had to make the decision on who would attend the all-expense-paid weeklong Social Work Conference in Chicago. The registration deadline was rapidly approaching, and she needed to submit the names to the Accounting Department no later than Tuesday morning when the agency reopened after the Memorial Day holiday. Since her announcement at last week's staff meeting that she would be sending five social workers, several hopefuls, with the exception of Charlene Powell, had been kissing up to her big time. The thought of Charlene kissing up to her made Lily laugh out loud. Charlene wouldn't give her so much as a drink of water if her life depended on it, and she had the nerve to submit a conference request. Lily tossed Charlene's request aside. She didn't like the outspoken veteran social worker, and Charlene didn't hide the fact that she didn't like Lily either. Charlene had told her once in a staff meeting that she was "unapproachable" and "demanding" and she didn't appreciate the "condescending tone" Lily often used when addressing her and some of the other social workers.

In spite of her feelings for Charlene, Lily admired her boldness. Charlene was also a darn good social worker, who had willingly taken up the slack in the foster care unit more than once when they were short-staffed. Lily's failure to hire the intern from Fayetteville State University that Charlene thought deserving of a recent vacancy bred further resentment in Charlene. Charlene verbalized her disapproval of Lily's hiring decision in a unit meeting and even took matters one step further; she complained to the Human Resources director.

Lily didn't defend her decision to hire the inexperienced Sandra Harris to Charlene or the HR director. Hiring Sandra was her way of reaching back. Reaching back to help someone who just happened to be from the same small town as she: McKinley, North Carolina. Peony called her at her office one morning and asked if she could help one of Emma Harris's granddaughters. "Emma say the girl is having a hard time finding a job," Peony had said to Lily. "Can you help her, honey? Are there any openings where you work?" she had asked. Always ready to do her mother's bidding, and to be thought highly of by others, Lily didn't hesitate to call Sandra in for an interview and offer her a job.

Lily had never met Sandra, not until the day of the interview; however, she knew Sandra's mother and aunts. They were a family of pretty women; hailed the prettiest black women in McKinley. Men were attracted to the infamous Black Beauties like bees to honey. Lily and Sandra's aunt, Evangeline, were classmates, rivals once over the same boy. Evangeline eventually won out, because Lily didn't put out. Unlike Lily, who graduated from high school and went on to college to earn a bachelor's in social work and a master's in public administration, Sandra's mother and aunts barely finished high school. Sandra's mother quit school in the ninth grade and went on to have seven children by seven different men. Sandra, the youngest, was a freshman in college when her mother died. She tearfully told Lily over lunch one day that she didn't know who her father was.

Sandra didn't strike Lily as being "common" like her mother or aunts. There was an air of refinement about her. Lily also surmised that the long-legged, twenty-four-year-old had plenty of men vying for her attention. She was pretty. If Tyra Banks had a twin, Sandra was it. With a bachelor's in social work, Sandra verbalized plans to pursue her master's in the same field.

Thumbing through the conference requests, Lily was surprised to see that Sandra didn't submit a request. She probably figured, Lily thought, being the new kid on the block she didn't have a chance of getting selected anyway, and if she did, Charlene would raise sand.

The thought of pissing off Charlene amused Lily. She wasn't going to wait until she got back from the Memorial Day holiday; she was going to make her decision today and submit the names to Accounting. Lily looked at her watch; it was 5:13. The agency closed at five o'clock. It was a holiday weekend, and by now for sure, Lily assumed, many of the agency's employees had left or were in the process of leaving for the weekend.

Lily opened her in-box and e-mailed the Accounting Department supervisor and cc'd the five social workers she'd approved to attend the conference and their supervisors. After she sent the message, she picked up her phone and dialed the only supervisor at the agency she regarded as a friend, Marilyn Carmichael. Marilyn was the supervisor of the Child Protective Services unit one floor down from Lily.

"Marilyn Carmichael, may I help you?"

"It's me."

"Hey, me, make it quick. I'm on my way out the door."

"I just cc'd you an e-mail. I've decided who I'm sending to Chicago."

"Oh, good. Who?" Marilyn asked excitedly.

"Deborah, Anita, Rhonda, Kendra, and Melanie," Lily replied indifferently.

"Lily?"

"What?"

"You're not sending Charlene?"

"No," Lily replied flatly.

Marilyn sighed.

"After the way she addressed *me* last month in the staff meeting. Uh-uh! She canceled out any chance she had of going then."

"Lily, come on now. That's not right. And if I may be brutally honest, you both need to learn how to be a bit more civil to people."

"Oh, shut up. And she has *one* more time to talk to me like she—"

"And what? You gone write her up? Huh?"

Lily rolled her eyes. "Marilyn, you're frustrating me."

Marilyn laughed. "Well, excuse me, Your Highness, for distressing you so."

Lily ran a hand through her long dark brown hair, which she had highlighted with honey-gold streaks hours ago, exhaled, and sat back in her leather desk chair. "I hope *Russell* likes my hair," she said, glancing over at the eight-by-ten picture of she and her husband along with their three children in a heart-shaped gold frame on her desk.

"I'm sure he will."

"Yeah, he will," Lily said, blushing. "I'm looking forward to our trip to the beach this weekend."

"And I'm sure Charlene is looking forward to going to Chicago in July."

"Give it a rest, Marilyn."

"Please rethink your decision," Marilyn pleaded.

Lily spun around in her desk chair and looked out her office window up at the sky. She and Russell were heading to Myrtle Beach first thing tomorrow morning. Even though the weekend forecast was sunny and warm, Lily planned to spend the majority of the time indoors making love to her husband.

"Lily?"

"What?"

"Let Charlene go to Chicago. She deserves to go, and you know that."

Lily exhaled loudly and spun back around in her chair. "I've made up my mind."

"You need to stop being so *vindictive*."

"I'm not being 'vindictive,' Marilyn."

"Oh yes, you are," Marilyn asserted.

"Whatever!" Lily sang.

Sandra Harris walked slowly past Lily's office and waved.

"Marilyn, I gotta go! Have a great weekend!"

Lily hung up the phone and yelled for Sandra to come in.

"Hey," Sandra said, walking in.

"How do you like"—Lily tossed her head from side to side—"my hair?"

"Oh, nice!" Sandra said admiringly.

"And," Lily said, opening a side desk drawer, "what about this?" She pulled out a Victoria's Secret bag from the drawer, and out of the bag a red silk teddy.

"Oh, that's nice too," Sandra replied with a smile.

"Sit down," Lily said, waving her hands. "Tell me, what're your plans for the holiday?"

Sandra smiled. "I'm going home to see Grandma. I haven't seen her in a while."

Lily's brows creased together. "Is Miss Emma okay?"

"Oh yeah," Sandra said with a wave of her hand. "Grandma's fine."

"Tell her and everyone in *McKinley* I said hello," Lily said, laughing.

Sandra opened her eyes wide. "I'm not spending the entire weekend home," she said, laughing too. "Maybe I'll join you and Russell at the beach."

Lily laughed. "No!"

Sandra stuck out her bottom lip.

Poor thing! Lily thought, laughing to herself. *She idolizes me.*

Most women, Lily believed, did. A tall, pecan-complexioned, attractive, classy-looking woman at forty-nine, Lily had it all: beauty and brains; an adorable husband; three smart, healthy children; a tastefully decorated four-thousand-square-foot home; a luxury car; and money in the bank. Lily was happily living her dream life, a fairy-tale existence that many women dreamed of having, but were never able to attain.

Lily Shaw-Davenport didn't have one care in the world. She often marveled at how good she had it. Marilyn and many of the married women at the agency didn't have it as good. They openly spoke about how unhappy they were. Combating the overwhelming demands of the social work profession and personal woes on the home front had, over time, taken a toll on some of the women, physically and emotionally. Marilyn was fifty pounds overweight. So it was no surprise, according to the grapevine, that Marilyn's and a few of the other women's husbands were cheating on them. Lily pitied her unhappy colleagues, and sometimes went out of her way to avoid them.

Pretty, vibrant Sandra, on the other hand, was a breath of fresh air. She called Lily "mentor," and Lily found her obsequious behavior flattering. Hiring Sandra was a good move on her part, she believed, given how the folks back home in McKinley admired her family. She and her sisters—the Shaw girls were well thought of. Lily looked over at the picture of her and her adorable sisters on the bookcase in her office. Of her mother's five daughters, three were college educated beyond the bachelor's level and doing quite well. Ivy, the prettiest of all the girls, was an attorney in private practice in Durham, and engaged to wed a man from a prominent family who happened to be a superior court judge. Violet was a librarian back home. Daisy, the oldest, was a registered nurse at Walter Reed Medical Center, and Jasmine, the youngest, was a single, unemployed mother of two. As guest speaker for the upcoming Women's Day Program in June at Charity Chapel—thanks to Miss Emma, who invited her to speak after she hired Sandra—Lily would bask in the accolades the folks at Charity Chapel were sure to shower upon her for giving Emma Harris's granddaughter a job.

Lily had expected Charlene and the other foster care social workers to treat Sandra cool, and to her surprise the first three months of Sandra's employment, they did not. They were kind and helpful. However, things had changed in the last month. Sandra hadn't said anything to her about the change, so Lily thought she would question her about it. "Are things still okay downstairs?" she asked.

Sandra frowned. "What do you mean?"

Lily narrowed her eyes at Sandra. "Are you and Charlene getting along? That's what I mean."

Sandra grunted and rolled her eyes.

"So what's happened?"

"I don't know, and frankly"—Sandra crossed her legs—"I don't care. It doesn't bother me that Charlene and her *friends* treat me cool now."

"Well, I'm pretty sure it doesn't, but I didn't know if you had a run-in with one of them or not. They're close. If you piss one off, you piss all of them off."

Sandra scoffed. "I can survive without their 'good mornings' and 'have a nice days.'"

"Y'all seemed to be getting along so well," Lily said, shaking her head.

Sandra sighed. "Things change."

Lily raised her eyebrows. "You haven't stolen somebody's man, have you?" she asked, laughing.

"Please," Sandra said, rolling her eyes.

"Correct me if I'm wrong, but this change came about after Gladys's birthday party last month. I told you not to go."

"What was I supposed to do?" Sandra asked, hunching up her shoulders. "Janice gave me an invitation."

"Just because you were given an invitation didn't mean you had to go, Sandra. Goodness!"

Sandra dropped her shoulders. "I like Gladys. She's cool."

"'Cool'?" Lily remarked, opening her eyes wide. "That motormouth is one of the biggest gossips at this agency. How do you think I heard that Charlene and the others had fallen out with you? She told Marilyn's secretary, who told Marilyn, and Marilyn told me."

Sandra pursed her lips together.

"You shouldn't have gone to that party. Attractive women like us," Lily said, wagging a finger at Sandra, "aren't welcomed in social gatherings where there are a bunch of *homely*, married women."

Sandra sighed.

Lily hunched up her shoulders. "So *what* if somebody's man eyeballed you at the party? You couldn't help that. Gee. I've had this problem *all* my life, men lusting after me."

"I won't trying—"

"'Won't'?" Lily said, interrupting with raised eyebrows.

Sandra smiled. "Excuse me. I *wasn't* trying to steal anybody's man at that party."

Lily laughed. "I know you weren't. Don't sweat it, dear. Just know that unattractive women feel insecure and threatened by beautiful women. Your beauty, Sandra, is a blessing and a curse. You won't ever have many female friends."

Sandra nodded.

"I wonder if the day will ever come," Lily said, sighing, "when women will garner more self-respect."

Sandra's brows creased together. "I'm not following."

"When it comes to relationships."

Sandra continued to look puzzled.

"What I'm saying, Sandra," Lily said with a dramatic wave of her hands, "if a woman's man chooses to be unfaithful to her, that woman should not take her anger out on the other woman. It takes *two* to tango!"

Sandra pressed her lips together and bobbed her head. Whenever Lily started in on one of her all-knowing, sanctimonious spiels, she, like others in the unit, said very little or nothing at all.

"Once a woman's man steps out on her," Lily said, with another wave of her hands, "the trust in their relationship is gone. Gone! The woman needs to walk out of the relationship with her dignity intact. Too, too many women have such low self-esteem. They'd rather stay with their unfaithful spouses or boyfriends and be treated like garbage. It just *amazes* me how some women are so pathetically needy."

"What about you?"

"Huh?"

"What would you do if Russell stepped out on you?"

"Russell would *never* do that!" Lily said smugly, shaking her head. "We have a rock-solid marriage." She stretched out her left hand and eyed her three-carat diamond ring. "My husband loves me. He respects me. He worships the ground I walk on."

Sandra scoffed, then laughed. "Yeah, that's what all married women want to believe. Any man will cheat, if given the opportunity."

"Not my Russell," Lily said defensively.

When Sandra failed to respond to Lily's remark, Lily pressed her lips together and shook her head at Sandra. "I'm not surprised to hear a comment like that from you, Sandra. I don't expect you to have a favorable opinion of men."

Sandra's eyes grew large and round. "You don't?"

Lily shook her head. "No, I don't. You wouldn't know a good man if he walked up to you and said hello."

Sandra's eyes grew wider and rounder. "No kidding?" she said facetiously.

Lily leaned forward in her chair. "How could you? Your childhood was marred—"

"'Marred'?" Sandra asked, eyeing Lily sharply.

"Yes, marred. Your father abandoned you—you have no idea *who* he is. Your aunts and *mother*—may God rest her soul—paraded man after man before you, your sisters, and your female cousins. Men with one-track minds, who thought of them as nothing more than good-time girls."

Sandra sighed loudly and looked off.

"I don't mean to upset you, Sandra. I'm just stating hard facts, reasons for your negative opinion of men."

"Okay," Sandra muttered.

"You aren't like your mother and her sisters," Lily said, softly.

"Thanks for pointing that out, Lily."

Lily smiled. "You're welcome."

For a brief moment, neither Lily nor Sandra said anything. Sandra finally interrupted the tense silence by yawning.

"Sleepy?" Lily asked, sitting back in her chair.

Sandra nodded. "Yeah, and I've been dragging *all* day."

Lily raised her eyebrows and smiled. "Late date last night?"

Sandra smiled back. "Something like that."

"I went to bed early last night. Russell, poor thing,

had to work late again. I don't know what time he came in."

Sandra yawned again, then glanced at her watch. "Well, I'm going to call it a day," she said, standing up.

"Wait a minute! Is that a new watch?" Lily asked, leaning across her desk.

Sandra smiled. "Yeah."

"Let me see!" Lily ordered, extending her hands with the palms up.

Sandra stretched out her left arm.

Lily gasped. "A Movado? You can't afford this on your salary!"

"It's a gift."

"From?"

Sandra smiled again and winked. "Someone with *very* good taste."

"And money, no doubt," Lily said.

"No doubt!" Sandra said, laughing, as she headed for the door. Just as she was about to exit Lily's office, she looked back and said, "Don't wear Russell out at the beach."

Lily laughed. "I intend to ravage every inch of his body."

Sandra smiled and waved good-bye.

"Bye! Have a great weekend!" Lily yelled after her.

Just as she closed her office door behind her, Lily remembered she'd forgotten to respond to an e-mail from the Family Support unit's supervisor. She reentered her office, went to her desk, and scribbled a response to the supervisor's e-mail on a sticky note. She exited her office and headed toward the elevator. She pressed the Down button and when the elevator stopped on the fifth floor she stepped on and pressed the number 4 button. The Family Support unit was on the same floor as the Child Protective Services and Foster Care units. Each unit was sectioned off into three separate wings on the fourth floor.

When the elevator door opened on the fourth floor, Lily heard laughter and people talking. "They're still working?" she muttered. It was 5:43. Gladys, the gossipy Foster Care unit secretary, was laughing loudly. Laughing and talking to Gladys were Lily's nemesis—Charlene—and two other Foster Care social workers: Anita and Janice. Except for the women's laughter and chatter, it was quiet on the floor. Lily quickly and quietly made her way down the Family Support unit's wing with the sticky note in hand. As she hurried back up the hallway toward the elevator, she stopped dead in her tracks when she heard Gladys say, "She's ain't gone stop till she gets ole girl's husband naked and in her bed. Provided she ain't already done it!"

Although she didn't fraternize with people in the agency like Marilyn and some of the other supervisors, Lily was not above hearing their gossip.

"I can't believe she's that *heartless*!" Anita cried.

"Believe it!" Charlene said.

"They had lunch *together*?" Anita asked, sounding horrified.

"Yes!" Gladys replied loudly. "Just the two of them. Delores in Family Support saw them. And when Miss Thang came back from lunch, she asked me if I knew a good florist. Naturally, I told her about Capital Florist."

"Naturally," Charlene said, laughing.

"I called my cousin later, to see if they'd gotten a call from her, and sure enough, she called and ordered a dozen red roses."

"What?" Anita yelled.

"Had them sent to ole boy's office," Gladys said. "The card said 'Thanks. Much love, Sandra.'"

"You satisfied now?" Janice asked.

"You know how Anita is," Charlene said. "She tries to give everybody the benefit of the doubt, including that hateful bitch upstairs."

Lily dismissed Charlene's disparaging comment with a grunt. She was trying to figure out whom the women were talking about. "Miss Thang"? *Could that be Sandra Harris?* she wondered.

Beside herself with curiosity, Lily strained to hear more.

"Maybe she's just being friendly," Anita said.

"Friendly, my ass!" Charlene yelled. "If some woman sent your husband flowers, Anita, would you think she was just being 'friendly'?"

"Well, I—"

"Hush, Anita!" Charlene said.

Gladys and Janice burst out laughing.

"Then she spent the rest of the afternoon—doing no work as usual, just sitting at her desk doodling," Charlene said.

"Yeah!" Gladys said loudly. "Writing her name and his on pieces of paper with hearts around them."

"Shut up!" Anita yelled.

"And before you ask me how I know *that*, Anita," Gladys said, "when she left yesterday to go home, I went in her trash can and got the pieces of paper out."

"Gladys, you didn't?" Anita said.

"Yes, I did," Gladys said.

Charlene burst out laughing.

"I showed 'em to Charlene and Janice."

"You still got them?" Janice asked.

"I threw 'em back in the trash can."

"I'm glad you did," Anita said. "This is awful! Just awful! I don't know what to say!"

"Ain't nothing for you *to* say," Charlene said dryly. "The girl is a skank!"

"I knew she was nothing but trouble when I first saw her," Gladys said. "I told y'all that. Remember?"

"Yeah, you said she was trouble," Janice said.

"I know trouble when I see it," Gladys said.

Lily had begun to perspire. Her deodorant had finally clocked out, and she was having a severe case of dry mouth.

"She hasn't done *any* dictation in almost a month!" Gladys exclaimed. "*Nor* has she made all of her site visits for the month. If she's not yakking on the phone to her girlfriend over at the Health Department, she's on the Internet shopping at eBay."

"I just can't believe she would do something like that," Anita said.

"You don't *want* to believe she would do something like that," Charlene said. "You saw how she was smiling all up in your cousin's husband's face at Gladys's birthday party."

"She was just being friendly, that's all," Anita said.

"She's a femme fatale, a flirt, a tease," Gladys grumbled. "I wouldn't trust her around my man. And I don't know why you invited her to my birthday party in the first place."

"She saw the invitations on my desk," Janice said. "I couldn't not give her one. I didn't think she would come."

"So, *Sandra*, this is why they're treating you cool," Lily muttered sadly. "You're just like your mammy and aunts! The apple doesn't fall from the tree, or as Aunt

Caroline often said, 'The wood chip doesn't fly far from the woodpile.'"

But why would Sandra get involved with somebody's husband? Lily wondered. There were so many single, professional men, Sandra often told her, pursuing her. Why couldn't she make herself satisfied with one of them?

"So Delores saw them at P F Chang's yesterday?" Anita asked.

"Yes, Anita!" Gladys said. "They went way 'cross town, I guess to make sure they didn't run into *wifey*."

"They could have saved themselves some gas *and* time, and gone two blocks over to Peking's," Charlene said, laughing. "Lily doesn't eat Chinese food!"

Gladys burst out laughing.

Lily's stomach knotted and she fell up against the wall. *"Lily"? Lily who?* she wondered.

"I guess they're trying to be discreet," Gladys said.

"It's a shame!" Janice cried. "A shame!"

"That's one backstabbing tramp!" Gladys said.

"She can't have a conscience," Janice remarked bitterly. "To mess around with Lily's husband, and grin in her face every day!"

Lily who? Lily wondered, as she began to hyperventilate.

"Yeah, yeah, Janice, we agree," Charlene said, laughing loudly. "Miss Sandra Harris deserves the Brazen Huzzy of the Year award and her *homegirl*, Mrs. Lily Shaw-Davenport, deserves the Fool of the Year award."

Gladys burst out laughing.

Lily turned and staggered to the exit. The last thing she heard before the stairway door closed behind her was Anita saying, "It's not funny, y'all. It's not funny."

Chapter 3

Respects

Violet

"I don't understand it! I just don't understand it!" I heard Mama exclaim from her bedroom. Since coming inside from talking with Miss Sadie, she had been in and out of her bedroom returning and making phone calls.

I walked into her room and sat down beside her on the bed. "What's wrong, Mama?"

Mama looked over at me with a distressed expression on her face. "Jasmine's phones should be back on," she said.

I sighed and shook my head.

"I sent her *five* hundred dollars!"

"Mama! You did what?" I exclaimed, standing up. I stood up so fast I got dizzy. And the shock of what Mama said along with my outburst caused the throbbing pain in my head to intensify.

Mama exhaled and threw up her hands.

"Please tell me you didn't," I said, slowly sitting back down.

"She needs phone service, Violet!" Mama yelled at me.

"Surely she didn't need five hundred dollars to turn her phones back on, Mama?"

Mama sighed and looked off.

I took a deep breath and started massaging my temples. The last thing I wanted to do was get into an argument with Mama about her irresponsible youngest child. Besides, then wasn't the time anyway; we had guests. People had stopped by to pay their respects.

"And don't mention this to Lily," Mama said, looking back at me.

"I won't. Don't you worry about that," I said.

I took the phone out of Mama's hand and dialed the last home and cell numbers we had for Jasmine. After dialing each number, I heard the same message Mama had heard: "The number you've dialed is no longer a working number."

"When did you send Jasmine the money, Mama?" I asked, handing her back the phone.

"Last week! And she called me from Tina's when she got it. Told me she was going to the bank to cash the check, and when she left there, she was going to get her phones turned back on. It don't take this long," Mama said, shaking her head, "to get a phone turned back on. What do you think she did with all that money?"

I was seething by this point and sweating bullets. I had some ideas about what my ghetto-fabulous, bling-blinging baby sister did with five hundred dollars, but

I wasn't about to share them with Mama. "Your guess is as good as mine," I said, getting up to raise the window next to the bed.

"*Five hundred* dollars!" Mama cried. "And don't you tell Lily," she said again.

"I said I wouldn't, Mama."

"I should have paid the phone bills myself!" Mama said, looking at me like she wanted me to say, Yeah, you should have.

A car pulled up outside. I watched the occupants exit the vehicle and make their way into the yard. "Deacon Humphrey and Miss Odessa just pulled up," I said. Mama didn't hear a word I said.

"I just don't understand why she won't do right. And don't mention this to Lily," she said.

"I *won't*, Mama." There would be enough going on once everyone got home without getting Lily riled up about Jasmine.

According to Lily, not only was it Mama's and my fault that Jasmine was a burden to taxpayers, but it was Aunt Caroline's, Daisy's, and Ivy's too. Lily had told us more than once that by having given Jasmine everything she wanted since she took her first step, we had in essence done her a disservice. And instead of being her personal ATMs, we needed to dole out tough love.

Sadly, I'd come to accept some responsibility for how Jasmine's life had turned out. I was the youngest— twelve at the time—when Mama, who thought all her childbearing days were behind her, discovered she was pregnant at forty-three. The cute brown bundle of joy she and Daddy brought home from McKinley General twenty-nine years ago has never had to want for anything. We spoiled Jasmine, or as Aunt Caroline often said, we "ruined" her. With Jasmine being a single, unemployed mother with two daughters, living in public housing in Charlotte, I'd overheard Mama say to Aunt Caroline many times, "That girl keeps me on my knees, talking to Jesus!" Jasmine had never held a job, never voiced plans to get one, and she seemed quite content living in a two-bedroom apartment in the projects. And despite how frustrated we were with her, whenever she called saying she needed money to reconnect her phone or utilities services, to buy food and clothes for the children, we—with the exception of Lily—came to her rescue.

"Have you called Tina's?" I asked.

Mama nodded. "Several times! No answer."

"Well, we keep trying until we get her."

"Suppose we don't get her?" Mama said, her voice cracking at the end.

"We will, Mama," I said reassuringly. If it meant me having to get Warren to intervene. He could call the Charlotte PD and request that an officer go to Jasmine's apartment.

Five hundred dollars! I couldn't wait to tell Ivy. When Ivy and I had gone to Charlotte two weeks ago, we told Jasmine not to call Mama or Aunt Caroline for any more money. She promised us she wouldn't. *That lil' lying sneak!* "She say how she and the girls were doing when she called?" I asked.

Mama smiled. "She said they were fine." Her smile grew wider. "She said Kenya and Shaunda were doing real good in school."

I could never understand why Jasmine wasted time lying to Mama about anything, because the lies she told always came back to bite her in the butt. I had spoken to the school social worker at Rashaunda's school when I was in Charlotte two weeks ago; she told me Rashaunda would be retained. How Jasmine thought she would keep that from Mama—who always asked to see the girls' report cards at the end of each school year—baffled to me.

"She say anything else, other than 'I need some money'?" I asked.

Mama shook her head.

Thank you, Lord! Not that I thought she would, as Jasmine was on probation for assault. Lily told her if she breathed a word of that to Mama she was going to make a trip to Charlotte and make her wish she hadn't. It looked like Jasmine had taken Lily at her word.

Jasmine's most recent brush with the law occurred three months ago. She had been arrested and jailed for trespass, communicating threats, and assault and battery on her current boyfriend's—who according to the Charlotte PD is a small-time drug dealer—babies' mama. I flew with Ivy to Charlotte to bail her out of jail, and was back in Charlotte with Ivy when she defended Jasmine in court two weeks ago. Thanks to Ivy's courtroom suaveness, the trespass and communicating threats charges were thrown out, the assault and battery charge was reduced to simple assault, and Jasmine was placed on unsupervised probation for one year. To make sure our baby sister wouldn't end up in jail for having violated her probation for failing to pay her monthly probation fee, Ivy and I assumed the responsibility for making that payment.

Mama pressed the Talk button on the cordless phone.

I took the phone out of her hand. "Mama, go on back and sit with our guests. I will handle the phone, okay?"

"Okay," Mama said, slowing rising to her feet. "If Lily calls—"

"I will give you the phone."

"I've left a message for her to call me."

"Okay, Mama."

My cell phone started vibrating in my pocket. I reached in and pulled it out.

"Who is that?" Mama asked.

I looked at the display screen. "It's Floyd Jr." He was my sister Daisy's oldest child.

Mama sighed heavily and walked out of the room. When the door closed behind her I flipped open my cell phone and said, "Hello, nephew," into the phone.

"Hey, Aunt Vi. How are you?"

"I'm hanging in here," I replied.

"I'm still in shock!" Floyd Jr. said. "I can't believe Aunt Caroline is *dead*."

"Honey, I'm right here and can't believe it."

"How's Grandma really doing?"

"Yesterday was not a good day. She spent most of the day over at Aunt Caroline's, walking around and crying." I could hear my great-nephews, Rakeem and Brandon, making noise in the background. "You're at Daisy's?"

"Uh-huh."

"Daisy told Mama that Niecee's moved back. She's been back two weeks now?"

"Uh-huh," Floyd Jr. muttered.

I sighed heavily and looked out the window.

"She needs to have her butt here taking care of these boys of hers."

"Where is she?" I asked.

"Your guess is as good as mine," Floyd Jr. replied.

My sister Daisy's only daughter, Niecee, was eight

months pregnant and, like Jasmine, the mother of two children by two different men.

"Is Floyd there?" I asked.

"Yeah. Pop's here," Floyd Jr. said. "And he's already had a few, so he's in his recliner, passed out."

"Poor Floyd," I said.

"And I've told Niecee, Aunt Vi, not to leave the boys here with Pop when he's been drinking. They're three and five! Ooooh," Floyd Jr. muttered angrily, "she's so damn irresponsible!"

"Sweetie, I understand."

"How's Aunt J doing?"

I scoffed.

"That good, huh?" Floyd Jr. said, sighing.

Floyd Jr. was a D.C. cop. My sisters and I often confided in him about Jasmine. Sadly, his sister Niecee's life mirrored Jasmine's in many ways. I was about to tell him about the five hundred dollars Jasmine had conned out of Mama when a black Denali pulled up outside.

My heart started racing and I swallowed dryly. "Fl-Floyd Jr., I—I ne-need to go," I stammered.

"Aunt Vi, you all right?"

I swallowed dryly again. "Yeah," I said, fanning myself with my hands. "Just feeling a little overwhelmed, that's all."

"Many folks there?"

"Oh yeah, a houseful. Two church members just pulled up."

"I told Grandma when we talked earlier that we will be there tomorrow around six o'clock."

"Okay, honey."

"Aw'right, Aunt Vi. I'll call back later and check on you and Grandma, okay?"

"Okay. Thanks, honey."

"Love you."

"Love you too."

My heart went out to Deacon Jackson as I watched him step out of Warren's SUV. In spite of his wimpiness, I liked him, not because he happened to be Warren's uncle, but because he loved my aunt and I believed she loved him. Before leaving Mama's bedroom, I closed my eyes and prayed my short prayer again, "Father, *please*, help Mama and me get through this."

"Yes, the good Lord knows what's best," Eugene Humphrey said, shaking his head.

"Yes, he does," his wife, Odessa, said, sorrowfully. "Yes, he does."

"It's a comfort, I know," Miss Odessa said to Mama, "to have Violet here with you."

"It is," Mama said.

"When your other daughters comin' home?" Miss Odessa asked.

"I expect them soon," Mama replied.

Miss Odessa looked up at me. "You decided whether you gone rebuild?"

"No, ma'am," I said.

"She might move in Caroline's house," Mama remarked.

"Uh-huh," Miss Odessa said, bobbing her round head.

"Now, if she don't," Mama said, "Daisy and her husband will just as soon as he retire from his job."

"How soon you reckon that'll be—your son-in-law retiring?" nosy Miss Odessa asked.

Mama shook her head. "Don't know."

"He a city bus driver, right?" Deacon Humphrey asked.

"That's right," Mama said.

The telephone rang. Mama looked at me. I had the phone in my hand and looked at the display; it was a local call. I looked at Mama, shook my head, then stepped into the hallway and answered the phone.

The volunteer coordinator with the Meals-on-Wheels program was the caller. Aunt Caroline had been a volunteer with the program for five years. The coordinator wanted to know if Mama and I needed anything. She had come by the house the day before with several boxes of food. I told her we did not need anything and thanked her for calling. Before our conversation ended, the phone beeped. I looked at the display. I placed the phone back to my ear and told the lady someone had beeped in I needed to speak to. Before saying good-bye, she hurriedly said she would see all of us tomorrow evening. I thanked her again for calling and pressed the Flash button.

"Hey, Auntie," I said, expecting to hear Aunt Louise answer back. Instead I heard, "It's me, girl, Cheryl." Cheryl was my aunt Louise's middle daughter. Aunt Louise was one of my paternal aunts who lived in McKinley.

"Mama and I just back from the funeral home," Cheryl said, smacking loudly into the phone. "Aunt Caroline looks good."

Tears filled my eyes. "Yeah, she does," I managed to say.

"Mama wants to know who's over there."

"Church folk, mostly," I said, wiping my eyes.

"Church folk, Mama!" Cheryl yelled.

"What time y'all getting here?" I asked.

"Hold on, Violet. She said, 'church folk'!"

"Okay!" I heard Aunt Louise yell.

"Aunt Peony got in touch with Lily and 'em yet?" Cheryl asked, still smacking loudly in my ear.

"No," I replied, "and what're you eating?"

"Cabbage. Mama made a big pot. Ho-hold on. Say what, Mama?"

I could hear Aunt Louise talking in the background, but couldn't make out what she was saying.

"Mama said," Cheryl began, "tell Aunt Peony she's on her way with dinner. She's taking the ham and roast out of the oven now."

"Okay. When are you coming over?"

"After I rehearse with the group. Girl, I haven't sung 'I'm Free' in years!"

Cheryl was a gifted singer. She was also the founder and lead singer of a local gospel group called Cheryl and the Gospelettes. They had cut two CDs that were doing marginally well and spent many weekends traveling and singing on programs with many renowned gospel artists. They would be singing at Aunt Caroline's wake and graveside service. "I'm Free" was one of two spirituals to be sung at the graveside service.

"How're you and Aunt Peony doing?" Cheryl asked.

"We're hanging in here. We'll be a lot better when everybody gets home."

"I know. Hold on, Violet. Whatcha say, Mama?"

"Ask Violet if any of the hospitality committee members are there," I heard Aunt Louise say.

"Tell her yes," I said, before Cheryl asked the question.

"She said yeah, Mama!" Cheryl yelled to Aunt Louise. Cheryl cleared her throat. "Violet, let me go help Mama get the food in the car. I'll see you later."

"Okay."

"Bye."

I went back to the living room and relayed Aunt Louise's message to Mama. I was heading for the den, where Warren and several other church members were gathered, when the phone rang again. Mama yelled, "You got the phone, Violet?"

I looked at the caller ID display and stepped back into the living room. "It's Miss Emma."

"Tell her I got company," Mama said.

I nodded, stepped back into the hallway, and pressed the Talk button.

"Hello."

"Violet?"

"Hey, Miss Emma."

"Ca'line sho' looks good. George Fowler did her justice, considerin' how sick she was."

"We got company, Miss Emma."

"I know y'all got company. I rode by there on my way home from the grocery store."

I'm sure you did, I thought to myself.

"I saw Warren's truck parked on the street. Odell with him?"

"Yes, ma'am."

"Uh-huh," Miss Emma said real slowly. "I woulda stopped, but Colette ain't home yet, and I don't want to leave them chil'ren of hers at the house too long by themselves. So tell Peony I called. I won't disturb her since she got company. If I don't talk to her before the wake, I'll see her then. You hear?"

"Yes, ma'am."

"Good night."

"Good night."

I took a deep breath and headed to the den.

* * *

Throughout the throng of visitors, whenever the phone rang, I jumped and Mama yelled asking me if I had it. A few times I tried to reach, without success, Lily and Russell. Allen, Ivy's fiancé, told Mama and me when we called him that Ivy, like we thought, was at the prison with her client. For the last two days, she'd been in the news on all the local channels. She was feverishly trying to get a stay of execution for a young woman scheduled to be executed at midnight. Allen told us Ivy had left for the prison after they had dinner at five o'clock. He volunteered to go there and inform Ivy of Aunt Caroline's passing; Mama told him not to do that. She didn't want to distress Ivy with the news of Aunt Caroline's death, given that she was under a tremendous amount of stress trying to save someone's life. Mama told Allen if the governor granted Ivy's client a stay of execution, then he was to contact Ivy immediately. If no stay was granted, Allen was to tell Ivy after her client's execution to call home, regardless of the time. Allen promised to do as Mama instructed. After Mama ended the call with him, she and I held hands and prayed for Ivy and her client.

"Blessed are they that mourn, for they shall see the Lord," Deacon Robinson said solemnly.

I cringed and prayed that lightning wouldn't strike the house. I'd learned the beatitudes as a child, and here sat one of my deacons, unable to recite Matthew 5:4 correctly. Ulysses Robinson was illiterate. It was for that reason Mama and others had voiced objection to the sixty-eight-year-old becoming a deacon. "According to the Word," Mama had argued in the church business meeting before the nomination was made and the vote cast two years ago to add Ulysses Robinson to the Deacons' Board, "one requirement of a deacon is that he be apt to teach. And Ulysses Robinson," Mama boldly asserted at the business meeting, "does not meet that requirement!"

I looked over at Mama. Her brows were creased together and she was shaking her head. I figured she was hoping Deacon Robinson would soon leave before he opened his mouth again and misquoted more of God's Word.

"Yes, yes," Miss Odessa said with uplifted hands. "The good Lord is a comforter to those who are grief-stricken."

"We all got to go one day," Deacon Jackson said, dabbing at his eyes with a handkerchief.

"Sho 'nuff!" Deacon Humphrey asserted.

From where Warren and I stood in the doorway, I counted the number of people in the living room. There were sixteen people—church members and a few neighbors—standing and sitting. Many were seated in the gray folding chairs Mr. Fowler brought over from the funeral home.

"We gone get ready to go," Miss Odessa said, struggling to get to her feet.

"Yes, Sista Peony. We gone head home," Deacon Humphrey said. "'Fore we leave, I would like to pray for you and your family, if that's all right."

"That would be fine, Eugene," Mama said.

"Everybody join hands," Deacon Humphrey said, rising to his feet.

Once everyone had joined hands and bowed their heads, Deacon Humphrey started praying. "Dear Lord, please stop by here and have mercy on Sista Peony and her daughter Violet in this, their time of need."

"Pray, son, pray!" Deacon Robinson shouted.

"Give 'em strength in this, their hour of b'reavement," Deacon Humphrey prayed.

"Yes, Lord!" Deacon Jackson shouted.

"We know," Deacon Humphrey continued, "that Sista Caroline is in a better place, 'cause she's resting in your loving arms."

"Yes, Lord!" several folks shouted.

"Jeeeee-sus! We pray," Deacon Humphrey said, clapping his hands, "that our dear sista here's children arrive home safe."

"Yes, Lord!" Mama cried. "Lord, please let my children and grands and greats get here safely!"

I burst into tears. "Please, Lord!"

Warren gave my hand a gentle squeeze.

"And please, dear Master," Deacon Humphrey prayed, "look in on our sista's grandson lying in a hospital bed out there in Arizona unable to move his legs!"

"Please, Jesus!" Mama shouted.

"The doctas say they've done all they can!"

"Have mercy!" Miss Sadie cried out.

"But we know you to be a docta in the sickroom unlike any other."

"Pray, Eugene, pray!" Deacon Robinson shouted.

"When man say 'no' you say 'yes'!" Deacon Humphrey prayed.

"Yes! Yes!" several people shouted, including me.

"We callin' on you, Father, to heal, heal Sista Peony's grandson!"

"Please, dear Lord, heal my grandson!" Mama cried.

"And, dear Master," Deacon Humphrey said,

clapping his hands again, "please look in on the sista's daughter, Ivy, there in Raleigh tryin' to save a life."

"Be with her, Jesus!" Miss Odessa cried out.

"Please, Lord!" Mama shouted.

"We count it all done," Deacon Humphrey said, "in Jesus' name, we pray. Amen."

When Deacon Humphrey finished praying, Miss Odessa said as she wiped her eyes, "Caroline look mighty pretty lying there in that casket. Weatherman speaks of rain Sunday. I sho' hope it hold off till after the service."

"Them weathermen don't always know what they talking 'bout," Deacon Jackson said, dabbing at his eyes again. "It's gone be good weather come Sunday."

"I sho' hope so, Odell," Mama said.

"It ain't gone rain," Deacon Jackson asserted. "Wanna know how I know that?"

"Yes," Miss Odessa replied.

Deacon Jackson smiled. "'Cause an angel's being laid to rest."

I burst into tears again. Warren grabbed my hand and led me through the kitchen out the back door. Once outside, he embraced me and held me tightly. When he kissed me, I grew weak in the knees, and had it not been for him holding me I would have slid down to the ground. "It's going to be all right," he whispered in my ear.

I heard the house phone ring.

"Violet!" Mama yelled.

I stepped out of Warren's arms and ran inside the house to answer the phone.

Chapter 4

Distraught

As she sped down the beltline in her Mercedes sedan, Lily kept asking herself as she wept, "Why?" Russell, the love of her life, the man who gave her goose pimples every time he touched her, tall, handsome Russell Mitchell Davenport—the father of her children, well-respected figure in their church, their community, assistant school superintendent—had broken their marital vows. "Ha!" Lily yelled as she gripped the steering wheel tighter. One thing for sure, Sandra Harris could kiss her career with the Department of Social Services good-bye. As she slammed down her foot on the accelerator, Lily vowed to make sure of that. The first thing she intended to do when she returned to work was head to HR with Sandra's termination papers.

After hearing the news about Sandra and her beloved, Lily sat in the agency's parking lot slumped down in the driver's seat of her car crying and waiting for

Charlene, Gladys, Anita, and Janice to leave the building. When they did, she reentered and returned to the fourth floor. She removed a stack of files from Sandra's desk and took them to her office. She discovered, like Gladys had said, that Sandra hadn't done dictation in weeks. And there was no evidence that she had made any foster home or group home visits in a month, or even made contact with three new cases referred to her two weeks ago.

"Now *I'm* the talk of the agency!" Lily cried, wiping her eyes and runny nose with the back of her hand. *Has Marilyn heard?* she wondered. *She's my friend, surely she would have said something to me!*

Blinded by the tears in her eyes, Lily almost sideswiped a YMCA activity bus filled with children. Several of the children stuck their heads out the bus windows and yelled at her. The young driver honked the horn and gave her the finger.

"Why, Russell, why?" Lily cried. "Why did you do this to us?"

Lily and Russell were to be celebrating their twenty-fifth wedding anniversary in August. They were planning to celebrate in a grand way: a formal dinner party with relatives and friends followed by a weeklong vacation in Italy. The closer their wedding anniversary got, the more elated Lily had become. Now all her exuberance had turned to unimaginable sorrow and despair.

Lily reached for her cell phone and called Russell's mobile for the tenth time: still no answer. She threw the phone down and hit the gas again as her thoughts shifted to Sandra.

Beautiful Sandra Harris, her *homegirl*, the girl from McKinley whom she'd befriended and taken under her wing. *After all that I've done for her, why would she do this to me?* Lily wondered. "You're gonna pay, Sandra!" she snarled. "You're gonna pay!"

Lily retrieved her cell phone again and dialed her home number.

"Hey, Mom. Where're you?"

"Out."

"Real funny," Russell Jr. said, laughing. "Where've you been?"

"I had to work late, honey. Is your dad there?" Lily asked, praying her son would say yes.

"No."

"He's not?"

"No, Mom, he's not. You try him on his cell?"

"No," Lily lied. "I'll do that."

"If he comes in before I leave, you want me to tell him to call you?"

"And where're you going?"

"To the movies, remember?"

"Oh yeah," Lily said, sniffling.

"You coming down with a cold or something?" Russell Jr. asked.

Lily chuckled. "Nooo, my allergies are flaring up again."

"Are you on your way home?"

"Not yet. I have a few errands to run."

"You've had a few phone calls."

"Who from?"

"Grandma Peony. She wants you to call her when you get home. Mrs. Whitfield called. She said the sorority meeting scheduled for next Wednesday night will be at her house, not Mrs. Brown's."

"Okay. Is that it?"

"Yep. Oh, I like the new housekeeper."

Lily chuckled again. "You don't say?"

"Yeah. She fixed me some burritos *and* tacos."

"That was nice of Martina."

"She seems nice."

"You go straight to your sister's after you leave the movies."

"I will. You and Dad have fun at the beach."

"Thanks, honey."

Lily lowered her cell phone from her ear. *Where is Russell? Is he with Sandra?* she wondered. That thought not only sickened Lily, it angered her also. "How long has this been going on?" she muttered, while hoping what she'd heard would prove to be nothing more than an ugly, malicious rumor.

Lily tried to think back, trying to recall the slightest change in Russell's behavior. Her head was hurting so badly she couldn't think clearly. What she did know, she had believed her husband when he told her he had to work late many evenings with the superintendent and school board on student reassignment plans for next year. More tears filled Lily's eyes and streamed down her cheeks. She hit her brakes seconds before running a red light. Her cell phone, her purse, and the Victoria's Secret bag slid out the front passenger's seat onto the floor. Lily fished around on the floor of the car for her phone. When she had it in hand, she dialed Sandra's cell. Her call went straight to Sandra's voice mailbox. She ended the call wondering, *What would I have said to her if she had answered?*

A honking horn from behind snapped Lily out of her dazed, distressed state. She eased through the intersection and made a sharp left turn.

Sandra's candy-apple-red Nissan 350Z wasn't parked out front of the town house she and her roommate shared, nor was Russell's black Lexus. Lily circled the lot to see if their cars were parked in other spaces. They were not. Lily sped out of the lot and headed back across town to P F Chang's. Sandra and Russell weren't at the restaurant. The hostess told her that no one resembling them had been in that day. Lily then made a mad dash to the school district's administration building. The parking lot was empty. Lily went back to Sandra's. To her dismay, the 350Z and black Lexus were nowhere to be seen. "Aha!" she exclaimed, speeding out of the complex lot toward the business and retail district. *Maybe they're couped up in some hotel room!* she thought angrily as she began to weave in and out of hotel parking lots. *Will I go mad if I see them and run over Russell like that woman in Texas ran down her husband?* she wondered, while reflecting on the question Sandra had posed earlier to her: "What would you do if Russell stepped out on you?"

It was approaching 9:00 p.m. when Lily started her car and backed out of the parking space in front of Sandra's town house. When she pulled into her driveway, she pressed the garage door opener and prayed that Russell's car would be parked inside. She closed her eyes and didn't open them until the garage door was fully open. What she saw caused her to slump forward. Russell's parking space was empty.

Lily lost track of how long she sat in the driveway crying. Her ringing cell phone abruptly ended her crying and maddening, murderous thoughts. She couldn't make out the number on the phone display for the tears in her eyes. She flipped open her phone. "Russell?"

"No, Lily. It's me, Violet."

"Violet? Oh, hey, girl. What's up?"

"You all right?"

"Yeah. Allergies. You and Mama okay?"

Violet sighed. "Hold on, Mama wants to talk to you."

"Hey, baby!" Peony soon yelled into the phone.

"Hey, Mama."

"Y'all doing okay?"

"Yes."

"You need to come home, honey."

Lily flinched. "Why? Is something wrong?"

"Your aunt Caroline is dead."

Lily lurched forward. "Huh?"

"Caroline is dead. Sh—"

"Mama, uh-uh! No!"

"She's gone on, baby. She passed away—"

Lily didn't hear the rest of what Peony said. Her wails spilled out the windows of her car into the driveway.

"Lily. Talk to Mama now."

"I—I just ta-talked, to Aunt Caroline, Tues-day night. Ma-Mama wh-what hap-pened?"

"The doctor said it was a heart attack."

"Mama, nooooo! No, Mama, no!"

"She's gone on, baby."

"When she diiie?"

"Wednesday night."

"No, no, no!" Lily cried, shaking her head.

"The wake's tomorrow and the graveside service is Sunday."

"Huh?"

"The wa—"

"Mama! Why're you just calling?"

"Well—"

"You know I would have come home and—and taken care of everything."

"I know, baby. I know. But this was something *I* wanted to do. Besides, Violet's here with me."

"Mama?"

"And y'all know Caroline always said when she died, she didn't want her body laid out for days."

"Mama?"

"Everything's been taken care of."

"Mama?"

"What, honey?"

"Where was Aunt Caroline when she—she died?"

"At the hospital."

"Ooooooooooh!" Lily cried.

"Wednesday around noon she started complaining of chest pain. She thought it was indigestion."

"Oh, Jesus!" Lily cried.

"She didn't feel any better after she had dinner, so Violet and I took her to the hospital. They ran a few tests. Her heart was beating kinda fast, her pressure was up, so they decided to keep her overnight. She was resting real good when Violet and I left. No sooner had we got home than the hospital called and said she'd slipped away."

"Ooooooooooh!" Lily cried.

"Where're you now, honey?"

"I—I'm home."

"Is Russell there?"

"Yes," Lily lied, placing her forehead on the steering wheel.

"When can I expect y'all?"

"Tonight! I'm going by Reid's first thing in the morn—"

"Caroline's body is at Fowler's."

"Fowler's? George Fowler's?" Lily spat out.

"Yes, and he's done a very good job."

"Mama!"

"Lily, Caroline wanted George Fowler to have her body and I'm not gone argue with you about that. I have a houseful of people here who stopped by to pay their respects."

"Oh, Mama!" Lily moaned.

"Violet and I have had the *hardest* time reaching you."

"It wasn't a good day at the office, Mama."

"I'm sorry, honey."

Lily burst into tears. "Mama, how're you doing?"

"I'm holding on."

"You ta-talked to Daisy and Ivy?"

"I've talked to Daisy. Haven't been able to get up with Ivy, or Jasmine. Now, when you say I can expect you?"

"As soon as I pack, I'm on the road," Lily said, wiping her eyes.

"You and Russell drive safe."

"Okay."

"Bye, baby."

"Bye, Mama."

After saying good-bye to her mother, Lily clasped her hands together and said, "Dear God, please help me."

Chapter 5

Domestic Disturbance

So busy pulling clothes out of the Samsonite Pullman, Lily didn't hear Russell enter their bedroom. When she realized he was present, he was standing next to her with an incredulous look on his face. "Honey! What're you doing? I'm taking those," he said, referring to a pair of blue swim trucks Lily had taken out of the suitcase.

Lily spun around and answered Russell with a slap across his face.

"Hey!" he yelled, jumping back, nursing his cheek.

"You *bastard*!"

Lily lunged at Russell, knocking him onto their king-size bed.

"Lily! Wh-what—'"

"You, lying, cheating, whorish bastard!"

"Lily! Stop it!" Russell yelled, struggling with his wife.

Lily clawed at Russell with all her might. They rolled

across the bed amid the clothing. The Pullman slid to the floor; the Davenports rolled off the bed on top of it.

"How could you?" Lily screamed.

Russell grabbed Lily's hands, rolled on top of her, and pinned her arms to her side.

"Get off me! Let me gooooo!" Lily screamed, squirming about, trying to free herself.

"What is wrong with you?" Russell demanded, looking down into his wife's tear-streaked face.

"Get off me!" Lily shouted.

"Not until you tell me what's going on!" Russell shouted back.

Lily let out a sarcastic chuckle, then burst into tears. Russell stood up and reached down to help her up off the floor. "Get away from me!" she yelled, rolling over onto her side.

Russell sat down on the edge of the bed. His tired eyes large with confusion, he asked, "Lily, what's wrong?"

"My aunt Caroline is dead."

"Oh, honey! I'm sorry."

Lily burst into sobs. Her sobs filled the huge room. Russell knelt down to comfort her and she elbowed him in the face. He jumped back.

"Why are you attacking me?" he screamed.

Lily sat up and faced him. "I know."

"You 'know'?" Russell asked loudly. "What are you talking about?"

Lily smiled. "About you and *Sandra*."

The bewildered expression that covered Russell's face gave way to one of surprise.

"So it's true? You are screwing that sneaky, backstabbing bitch!"

"What? No! Where did you hear that?"

"It doesn't matter where!"

"Lily—"

"Where're you coming from? From a tryst with your mistress?"

Russell shook his head and chuckled.

"I don't see anything funny!" Lily screamed.

Russell sighed. "Lily, you can't be serious?"

"I've been trying to reach you for *hours*!"

"Honey, don't you remember," Russell said softly, with outstretched hands, "me telling you this morning that the guy we want for Cookman High was flying in from Philadelphia this afternoon to be interviewed?"

Lily didn't answer Russell.

"After the interview," Russell continued, "some of us took him out for dinner."

"You're lying," Lily snapped.

Russell shook his head. "I am not."

"You didn't answer your phone."

Russell sighed and shrugged. "I forgot to recharge it last night."

Lily stood up and slapped Russell.

Russell flinched, then ran a hand down his stinging cheek.

"I can't recall the number of times," Lily muttered, shaking her head, "that she's been in our home, for family dinners and—"

"Lily, listen to me," Russell pleaded.

"You two do it in here?" Lily asked, glaring at Russell.

Russell narrowed his eyes at Lily. "You're serious, aren't you?"

"I heard about the roses she sent you yesterday."

Russell sighed and shook his head. "She wants me to help her get a job, honey. She doesn't like what she's doing at Social Ser—"

Lily picked up a sandal off the bed and threw it at Russell. It hit him on the top of his head.

"Stop it!" he yelled.

"Pack your clothes, adulterer. I told Mama we would be home tonight."

Chapter 6

Watching and Waiting

Violet

By ten o'clock, all the visitors who'd stopped by to pay their respects with the exception of Cheryl, Aunt Louise, Reverend Cherry, and Miss Sadie were gone. Reverend Cherry and Miss Sadie were sitting in the den with Mama, and Cheryl and Aunt Louise were in the kitchen helping me tidy up things.

"Guess who got hired at the Nursing and Convalescent Center?" Cheryl said to me.

I was placing dishes in the dishwasher. I stopped and asked, "Who?"

"Dimples. Nub's wife," Cheryl replied, laughing.

"What?" I said, shaking my head. "Uh-uh!"

Cheryl nodded. "Hired yesterday and *fired* today."

I burst out laughing.

Cheryl worked in the housekeeping department at the Nursing and Convalescent Center in McKinley.

"Why would y'all hire somebody like her in the *first* place," I said, "to work around the infirmed? Y'all that desperate for help?"

Cheryl sighed. "We are short-staffed. We've had two people retire this month, and one girl just went out on maternity leave."

"But to hire someone like mouthy, temperamental Dimples!" I said, laughing and shaking my head. "Y'all must be *desperate* for help."

"My supervisor is placing an ad in next week's paper. So if you come across somebody in need of a job, tell them we're hiring."

"What y'all think gone happen?" Aunt Louise said, turning to look back at Cheryl and me.

"What're you talking about, Mama?" Cheryl asked.

"With Ivy's client," Aunt Louise replied.

Cheryl sighed and shook her head.

I sighed and shook my head too. Mama had asked Allen that same question when he called to check on us an hour ago. He told Mama the chances of the governor overturning Ivy's client's death sentence were fifty-fifty. With a reputation of being tough on crime, the governor had surprisingly approved two of the last four stay of execution requests that had come across his desk, and overturned several death sentences in the three years that he'd been in office.

"Looks like we won't know anything until the eleventh hour," I said softly.

"Yeah, it looks that way," Aunt Louise said.

* * *

I was rushing upstairs to shower when my cell phone rang. Mama had already showered, and was sitting up in her bed in her nightclothes with the phone in one hand and the TV remote in the other. The number on my cell phone's display screen had a 602 area code. The call was from Phoenix. I pressed the Send button and said, "Hey, Daisy."

"Hey," Daisy said back. "Calling to check on y'all."

"We're doing okay," I said.

"Y'all still got company?"

"No, everybody's gone now."

"What Mama doing?"

"Resting."

"Has she gotten in touch with Jasmine yet?"

"Nope."

"I just talked to Lily. She and Russell are about to leave Raleigh. What's the latest with Ivy?"

"She's still at the prison, waiting to hear from the governor," I said.

Daisy sighed heavily or blew out some cigarette smoke. I couldn't tell which. Smoking was another vice of hers. She smoked up to three packs of cigarettes a day. With her having seen firsthand as a registered nurse people die from lung cancer because of smoking, I couldn't understand why she smoked. At fifty, she was financially strapped, overweight, and had more gray hair than Mama. She cried the last time she was home after someone at church mistook her for one of Miss Sadie's sisters from South Carolina.

"What you think gone happen?" Daisy asked, sighing or blowing out cigarette smoke again.

"That's been the question of the night around here," I replied. "I'm hoping we'll know something at eleven o'clock."

"Eleven o'clock?" Daisy asked.

"The news will be on then."

"Oh yeah. I keep forgetting; I'm on Pacific time."

"That being said," I said, chuckling, "let's say good night. I wanna shower before it comes on."

"Okay. Tell Mama I called. I'll talk to y'all first thing tomorrow morning."

"Okay."

"Bye-bye.

"Bye."

I closed my phone and looked at my watch; it was 10:37. I dashed up the stairs. Once in the bathroom, I stripped off my clothes, jumped in the shower, adjusted the Waterpik showerhead to the pulsating position, and turned on the water. With my back to the showerhead, I rolled my head from side to side and moved my shoulders up and down in an effort to release the tension that had built up there. I then prayed for Ivy and her client.

Chapter 7

Charlotte, NC

Jasmine Shaw and the people leaning up against DeAngelo Morris's overly accessorized black Nissan Maxima heard the popping sounds coming from the direction of the Laundromat. They all glanced over at the Soap 'n Suds. Satisfied it was nothing more than neighborhood kids shooting off firecrackers again, they returned their attention to the courtyard. It was jam-packed with dancers keeping beat with the rap music blaring from the Bose speakers on the roof of Q-Tip's Yukon. Githens Court's Memorial Day Weekend Block Party was well under way. The only thing likely to ruin the festivities was rain. Jasmine took another sip of her Corona and searched the crowd for her daughters.

Twelve-year-old Rashaunda, dressed in a pink crop cotton tee and a pair of tight, low-riding jeans, was over by one of the grills. She was sandwiched between two boys dancing. A seventh grade D student with a string of in-school suspensions, she was sneaky, "boy-crazy," and rumored to be part of a gang. She had denied such involvement when her aunts Ivy and Violet questioned her about that two weeks ago. Her goal in life, she told them, was to quit school when she turned sixteen and become a "video honey."

Unlike her adorable baby sister, Kenya, Rashaunda didn't have the good fortune of having a positive male presence in her life, and she resented Kenya because she did. Kenya's father, Lorenzo, a city sanitation worker, loved Kenya not just in word, but in deed. Not only did he pay child support and shower Kenya with gifts, but he spent quality time with her. Kenya spent many weekends with him and her paternal grand-mother. Rashaunda rarely saw her father, even though he only lived a short city bus ride away.

Jasmine smiled when she spotted eight-year-old Kenya, the apple of her eye. She was standing a few feet away with a group of children slurping on a Sno Cone. A straight-A student ever since she'd been in school, Kenya had not given Jasmine one minute of trouble. She prided herself on excelling in school and making her parents proud of her. Lorenzo—fearful of Kenya's safety in the projects—had threatened Jasmine on more than one occasion with plans to gain custody of her. Jasmine had dismissed Lorenzo's latest threat with a grunt and a "Whatever!" She figured the chance of him making good on it was nil. Lorenzo had recently gotten married, to a woman who had no children of her own. Even though Lorenzo's wife, Yolanda, and Kenya got along wonderfully, Jasmine figured Yolanda would want to start a family of her own with Lorenzo.

Just as the dancers started in on a funky rendition of the electric slide, a spine-chilling scream erupted from the melon-colored lips of SaShay Jenkins, Q-Tip's girlfriend. Jasmine flinched and her Corona slipped from her hand. The dancers froze. All eyes were on SaShay, who was looking down in horror at the red spot growing on the front of her yellow midriff-baring halter top. Q-Tip was on his knees gagging. It looked as if he was about to puke all over his girl's white espadrilles, while she stood over him twitching and babbling expletives.

"SaShay and Q-Tip been shot!" someone yelled.

Mayhem erupted and more popping sounds rang out. Jasmine ran toward the courtyard screaming for her daughters. "Kenya! Rashaunda! Run!" A shove from behind sent her to the ground. Over the screams and stampeding footsteps, she could hear Kenya calling out for her. Scrambling to her feet, Jasmine limped toward her cries. Kenya was standing in the living room door of their apartment holding on to Rashaunda.

Jasmine pushed her daughters into the apartment and slammed the door shut. Like a week ago, and the other times prior, they fell to the floor and crawled to Jasmine's bedroom. Kenya was trembling and sobbing loudly.

"Girl, will you shut up!" Rashaunda yelled at her.

"Mommy, pray that we don't get shot!" Kenya cried.

Jasmine grabbed Kenya and kissed her on the top of her head. "I will, baby."

"Q-Tip done got shot!" Rashaunda exclaimed, rocking her head from side to side. "It's gone be *on* up in here!"

Jasmine shuddered at the thought of what the days ahead would be like if Q-Tip had indeed been shot. She closed her eyes and rocked Kenya in her arms. For months, the rumor had been spreading through

Githens Court that another crew—a gang out of Brooklyn, New York, headed by brothers Money and Pharaoh Seabrook—had moved into town and were taking steps to rid Githens Court of its current drug lords, Sir Charles and Q-Tip.

"Yeah! Yeah! Yeah!" Rashaunda yelled out. "Money and Pharaoh best get to steppin'!"

"I know that's right!" Jasmine muttered.

Unlike with Kenya, the violence in the projects didn't frighten Rashaunda.

"Mommy, can I sleep in here with you tonight?" Kenya asked.

"Sure, baby," Jasmine replied.

"Good!" Rashaunda snarled, rolling her eyes.

It would be another sleepless night for Kenya and days before she felt comfortable enough to venture out in the courtyard to play with the neighborhood kids. Since the surge of violence in the projects, Kenya had begun to wet herself and have nightmares: nightmares of them being killed. The social worker and the guidance counselor at her school had suggested to Jasmine that she consider counseling for Kenya. Jasmine had yet to do that, even though the social worker gave her the names and numbers of several child therapists who accepted Medicaid not far from where they lived.

"Can I go stay with Grandma Lois tomorrow?" Kenya asked.

"Sure, honey," Jasmine replied reluctantly. Jasmine knew Kenya's frequent trips to her father's and paternal grandmother's homes were nothing more than her attempt to get out of "the hood." Their apartment had been broken into three times in the last two years. The last break-in had occurred a week after Christmas. The bikes that Violet had given Rashaunda and Kenya as presents were stolen.

Githens Court was the only place Jasmine had lived since leaving McKinley a little more than twelve years ago. She was a lovesick eighteen-year-old with a colicky infant, running behind a man. Her parents and sisters voiced disapproval of her behavior and begged her to come back home. Jasmine wouldn't heed her family's pleas. She followed Rashaunda's father to the housing project to his grandmother's apartment, where he left her three months later to join the army. His first year in service, he married a woman he met in a club off post. Ashamed, and not wanting to hear her sisters' "I told you so's," Jasmine stayed in Charlotte and got an apartment of her own. Despite its problems, Githens Court was the place she considered home now, and being one of the "flyest shorties" in the projects, she planned to stay there, despite her family's insistence that she leave.

"Mommy, why can't we move someplace else?" Kenya asked, whimpering.

Here we go again! Jasmine thought. *Move where? From one housing project to another one?* She laughed at the thought. Most, if not all, of the other projects in the city were no different from Githens Court. And the four hundred and twenty-five dollars that Lorenzo faithfully sent her every month in child support—the only steady income she had—wasn't enough to cover rent and utilities someplace nice. Sure, Maniac, her boyfriend of one year, gave her money from time to time and so did her doting mother, aunt, and sisters Violet, Ivy, and Daisy. Only thing, their money wasn't steady like Lorenzo's and she had to go through changes sometimes to get it.

"Huh, Mommy?"

"Someplace like where, Kenya?" Jasmine asked, hearing irritation in her own voice.

"Where they don't be shooting and breaking into people's apartments," Kenya replied.

"It costs a lot of money to live someplace like that," Jasmine said.

Kenya looked up at Jasmine. "You have money. Don't Daddy give you money for me?"

Jasmine looked away.

"Don't he, Mommy?"

"Yes, Kenya, he does."

"So why can't we use that money and move someplace else, someplace safe?"

Because it's not enough, Jasmine wanted to say, but couldn't bring herself to. Lorenzo was providing more than what the state required in terms of financial support for Kenya, and despite her issues with him, Jasmine couldn't and wouldn't make him look bad in Kenya's eyes. "We'll see, baby," she finally said. "We'll see."

Rain started falling outside and police and ambulance sirens wailed in the distance.

"I'm going to my room and call Ariel," Rashaunda said, jumping up and exiting the room.

From where she and Kenya sat on the floor, Jasmine could see the clock radio on her nightstand; it was 10:42. *Another violent, bloody night in the projects*, she thought with disgust. She got up, walked over to the window, and peeped out. Several police cruisers were already in the courtyard. Jasmine wondered, like she had every time a shooting occurred in the place she now called home, if she and her children would be so fortunate the next time, or if they would incur the same fate as SaShay, Q-Tip, and the others who had fallen victim to the senseless violence around them. The mere thought of burying her children brought tears to her eyes. She blinked them back, took a deep breath, and looked back at Kenya. "Everything's okay now," she said, smiling.

Kenya climbed up on Jasmine's bed into the fetal position. Jasmine went into the kitchen to get Kenya something to drink and was heading back to her bedroom when she heard heavy pounding on her front door. She ran to the living room door and yelled, "Yes!"

"Charlotte PD!"

Jasmine cracked open the door.

"Ma'am, I'm Sergeant Lloyd with the police department, I'd like to ask you a few questions. Can you tell me anything about the shooting that occurred here this evening?"

Jasmine shook her head.

The officer sighed heavily, thanked Jasmine for her time, and walked away. Jasmine figured he'd probably gotten that same answer from everybody else he'd questioned.

"Look at *all* them people," Jasmine muttered. She was lying across her bed staring at the TV screen. Kenya was lying beside her. Rashaunda was across the hall in her and Kenya's bedroom talking on her cell phone. The Asian female reporter with WBTV News 3 who interviewed Ivy last week in her office, was standing in front of Central Prison, the state's maximum-security prison where executions were carried out. Off at a distance was a huge crowd of people marching and carrying signs opposing the death penalty.

"Governor Flowers still has not made a decision on whether Mia McWilliams's death sentence will be overturned," the reporter said. "Ms. McWilliams's lawyer, Ivy Shaw, reportedly has been here at the prison since seven o'clock this evening. If executed, Mia McWilliams will be the first woman put to death in this state since 1997."

"You think they gone kill aunt Ivy's client?" Kenya asked.

"I don't know," Jasmine said, shaking her head.

Kenya clasped her hands together and closed her eyes. "Jesus, please don't let them kill my aunt Ivy's client," she prayed.

"Amen," Jasmine said, picking up the TV remote and changing the channel. "Let's see what's on HBO Family."

Kenya nestled up closer to Jasmine. *Shrek* was on the HBO Family Channel. Fifteen minutes later, Jasmine and Kenya were laughing hysterically at the antics of Shrek and Donkey when heavy pounding on the living room door occurred for a second time that night. Jasmine slid off the bed, hurried to the door, and peered through the peephole. Tina, her best friend and neighbor, was standing out on the stoop, frowning and holding a magazine over her head from the rain.

"Jazz! Open the door!" Tina yelled.

Jasmine threw open the door and Tina rushed inside.

"You got a phone call," Tina said hurriedly. "It's your mama."

"My mama?" Jasmine asked, looking back at the clock display on the stereo in her living room. It was 11:21.

"Yeah!" Tina answered.

"She all right?"

"She sound okay to me."

"She don't sound mad, do she?"

"She sound like she normally do, Jazz, when she call my apartment looking for you, okay?"

Jasmine sighed.

"She said she didn't have your new house or cell numbers."

"Damn! I forgot to call and give them to her."

"I told her I didn't have them either, and that I'd stopped tryin' to keep up with you and your numerous, forever-changin' phone numbers!"

"I wouldn't have to keep changing my numbers if it wasn't for—"

"Girl, c'mon!" Tina yelled, turning to leave. "I got a card party goin' on, and I got a good hand!"

"Tell my mama I'll call her."

"I ain't telling your mama nothin'!" Tina yelled, running out of the apartment.

Jasmine darted back to her bedroom and grabbed her robe. She told Kenya and Rashaunda that she was running over to Tina's and would be right back. As she hurried down the walkway to her friend's apartment, Jasmine played over in her mind how the conversation between her and her mother would go. She even rehearsed the lies she was going to tell her mother regarding the five hundred dollars she'd sent her.

Peony would start off the conversation by scolding her on how important it was for her to keep a phone, considering she lived four hours away and if there were ever a family emergency she would need to be able to contact her right away. Then she would tell Jasmine she needed to call home at least once a week to let her know that she and the girls were doing okay.

When Jasmine got to Tina's, she went into Tina's bedroom, closed the door, and picked up the cordless phone on the nightstand. She listened to Peony breathe and sigh for several seconds before finally saying, "Hey, Mama."

"Hey, baby," Peony replied. "How you and the girls?"

"We're fine. Mama, it's kinda late. Are you okay?"

"I know what time it is," Peony snapped. "I've been trying to reach you for the longest! I thought you were getting your phones turned back on with the money I sent you."

"I did, but I got new numbers."

"Why didn't you call and give them to me?" Peony yelled.

"It slipped my mind, Mama. Honestly, it did."

"Lord, have mercy!"

Jasmine fingered the eighteen-inch gold herringbone chain around her neck. Two hundred dollars of the money her mother sent went toward buying it. Eighty dollars was spent at the Nail Boutique for her and Rashaunda's manicures and pedicures, and the balance—two hundred and twenty dollars was used to reconnect her mobile and landline phone services. "Mama, hang up. I'm gonna run to my apartment and call you back from there."

"Let me just tell you why I'm calling now, since I got you on the phone," Peony asserted.

Jasmine sighed. "Okay, Mama."

Peony sighed heavily and muttered, "Lord, have mercy."

Jasmine rolled her eyes and sat down on Tina's queen-size water bed.

"Well, baby, like I said, I've been trying to reach you to—to let you know that your aunt Caroline has died."

Jasmine chuckled. "Mama, say what?"

"Honey, your aunt Caroline is dead."

"Mama, stop."

"Caroline has gone on to be with the Lord. Her wake is tomorrow evening, and her graveside service is Sunday afternoon."

"Ma-ma!" Jasmine cried, springing up.

"I want you and the girls to come home."

"Ma-ma! Uh-uh! Aunt Caroline's dead?"

"Yes, honey."

Jasmine's wails filled Tina's musk-scented bedroom. And had it not been for the music blaring from the stereo in the living room, Tina and her drinking, card-playing guests down the hall would have heard Jasmine's cries.

"I know, baby. I know," Peony said in an effort to calm Jasmine.

"Ma-ma, Aunt Caroline is d-dead?"

"Yes, baby, she is."

"No, no, no!" Jasmine cried.

As Jasmine cried, stomped her feet, and pounded the wall behind Tina's bed, Peony prayed, "Lord, have mercy." When Jasmine's sobbing subsided a bit, Peony said softly, "Come on home, baby, and say good-bye to your aunt. Okay?"

"All—all—all right, Mama," Jasmine whimpered.

"Where're the girls?"

"Th-they're home."

"You go on back to your place now. You can call me when you get there, I'll be up for a while."

"Where's Violet?"

"Across the street at Caroline's."

"What she doing over there?"

"She took some food over. Some of you will be staying there."

"Who?"

"You and the girls along with—"

"Why I gotta stay over there?" Jasmine asked loudly. "I wanna stay with you."

Peony sighed. "Ivy and Allen are staying here and so are Lily, Russell, and their children."

"Why Lily and her family get to stay there? Why can't me and my kids stay with you, Mama?"

"Honey, ple—"

"As usual, Lily's running thangs!"

"Jasmine!"

"I know it was her idea, Mama. Won't it? You just let her *have* her way!"

"Jasmine Aster Shaw! You calm down, and you calm down right now!"

Jasmine pursed her lips together and started pacing the floor in Tina's bedroom.

"I don't know *whose* idea it was that you stay at Caroline's. And if you think, two days before my sista's body is laid to rest, that *I'm* gone argue with you about that, think again!"

"I'm not arguing with youuuu, Mama," Jasmine cried. "I apologize if you think I am."

"The way I see it, whoever gets here *first* gets to choose where they stay."

"Okay, Mama. That sounds good."

Jasmine heard Peony sigh and mutter, "Sweet Jesus!"

"Ain't nobody home yet?" Jasmine asked.

"No. Lily's on the way. Daisy's not coming. She's still in Phoenix, but Floyd, Floyd Jr., Niecee, and her children are coming. I suspect Ivy will get here just as soon as she can."

"Poor Ivy," Jasmine said softly. "I don't think the governor's gone spare her client's life."

Peony sighed and said, "Lord, have mercy."

"Mama," Jasmine whimpered, "what time is Aunt Caroline's wake?"

"Seven o'clock."

"O-okay."

"You spent all that money I sent you?"

"No, ma'am," Jasmine lied.

"That's good, honey. Is there enough left for you to get bus tickets?"

Jasmine inhaled, squeezed her eyes shut, exhaled, and opened her eyes. "Yes, ma'am."

"Good."

Jasmine could hear the smile in Peony's voice. "Mama, I'm gonna go on back to my place. I'll call you later. Will that be all right?"

"Yes, honey, of course it will be."

"How're you doing, Mama?"

"I'm holding on."

Jasmine closed her eyes and shook her head. "Okay, bye, Mama."

"Bye, honey."

When Tina strutted into the bedroom, Jasmine was sitting on the edge of the water bed, rocking back and forth with the phone in her hand. "What's wrong with you?" Tina asked.

"My aunt Caroline is dead."

Tina gasped out loud. "Oh, Jazz! I'm so sorry," she said, reaching down to embrace Jasmine.

"She's gone be buried Sunday."

"Sunday!" Tina yelled, jumping back.

Jasmine nodded.

Jasmine last saw her mother and aunt in December, when she and her daughters went home for Christmas. Peony and Caroline were disappointed with her when she failed to come home for Easter and Mother's Day.

They had, as usual, brought Jasmine and the girls outfits for Easter. Jasmine would have gone home for Mother's Day, had it not been for NeShell Scott: Maniac's three-week-old twins' mama. She'd gotten into another fight with NeShell, and even though she got the better of her, she didn't walk away from the fight unharmed. She incurred a small gash down her left cheek and another one across her forehead. She didn't want to go home and have to explain to her mother and Aunt Caroline why she had scratches on her face.

"Damn!" Tina exclaimed, sitting down on the bed next to Jasmine. "I mean, that's some shit! Why yo' mama just callin' you now?" Without giving Jasmine time to respond, Tina rambled on. "Girl, how you gettin' home? I know you ain't got no money."

Jasmine looked over at Tina.

Tina threw up her hands and stood up. "Don't look at me. I ain't got none either. I just lost fifty dollars!"

"How am I gettin' home?" Jasmine cried.

Tina shook her head. "Damn if I know."

"I gotta get home, Tina!"

Tina clapped her hands then popped her fingers. "I know how!"

Jasmine wiped her eyes. "How?"

"Maniac."

"No!" Jasmine yelled as tears filled her eyes again. "I don't want Maniac takin' me home!"

"And why *not?*"

"Why do you think, Tina?"

"Your family ain't never met him. They don't know *nothin'* about him, so I don't see what the problem is."

Jasmine sighed and smiled. "You right."

Chapter 8

Central Prison

Forty-two-year-old Ivy Shaw stared out into the darkness. The tears in her eyes distorted the size and shape of the moon and twinkling stars. In an effort to cool her fevered body, she began to fan herself with her hands. A sudden movement to the right of her startled her, interrupting her distressing thoughts. Mia had rushed to the window, and in the manner of an awestruck child was peering and pointing out into the darkness.

"Is that a falling star?"

Ivy wiped her eyes. "Where?" she asked, pressing her face close to the window.

"Over there! See?" Mia said as her brown eyes danced with excitement.

Ivy narrowed her eyes. She couldn't see the falling star, but didn't want to spoil the moment for Mia. "Oh, I see it," she lied. "Are you going to make a wish?"

Mia scoffed. "Naw. I used to do that." She turned and

faced Ivy. "I don't believe in make-believe anymore. Do you?"

Ivy shook her head. "I don't know what I believe in anymore."

"That's too bad," Mia said softly. "There're still lots of things and people worth believing in."

Ivy grunted and walked away from the window. Each step she took in her two-hundred-dollar BCBG navy pumps intensified her self-hatred. "I'm going to be sick," she muttered, holding her stomach. Ivy's stomach was in knots, and she hadn't been able to eat anything all day, despite her fiancé's earlier efforts to get her to do so.

Ivy was afraid, and couldn't recall a time that she had felt more afraid. Never had she been in a predicament like this, agonizing over what could be the final hour of someone's life, while wondering how it would all ultimately affect her personally. She also feared that her coveted reputation as one of the best criminal defense lawyers for women in the Raleigh/Durham area was at stake.

Pride goeth before destruction, and a haughty spirit before a fall. How many times had her mother recited that scripture and others about pride and arrogance to her? But as always, Ivy was quick to defend her pretentious and narcissistic ways to be nothing more than self-assurance. Her ability to skillfully deploy know-how in the courtroom while manipulating people around her amazed her most adamant critics. Her uncanny brilliance and numerous political connections had never failed her. The fact that she was engaged to a superior court judge only made things better. But now here she was, for the first time, she feared, facing defeat.

Ivy sighed loudly and glanced down toward the

floor. A cockroach scurried across the cement floor behind the commode. The sight of the insect made her more nauseated.

"It sure is a beautiful night, isn't it?" Mia asked, staring out the window.

Ivy couldn't bring herself to answer. She found Mia's behavior unnatural and bizarre. And the thought that DA Colin Michaels was in his posh home laughing at her infuriated Ivy. She clenched her fists and sighed loudly.

Ivy had faced the blond-haired, pompous district attorney several times in court. He lacked the charisma she had and seemed unable at times to connect with jurors. But as fate had it the fifteenth day of June eleven years ago, he had the good fortune of being blessed with a judge and jurors who believed in an eye-for-an-eye system of justice. Thus making Mia LeShelle McWilliams, Ivy's only client to date, sentenced to death.

"I have something for you," Mia said, walking over to the narrow bed in the room.

Ivy watched Mia retrieve a book from underneath the mattress.

"Here," she said, extending her hand.

"No," Ivy said, shaking her head. "I can't."

Mia sighed and hunched up her shoulders. "Why not? I don't need it anymore."

"You don't know that!" Ivy yelled. It angered her that Mia was so calm, so unafraid.

"Miss Shaw, I won't be needing it anymore."

"There's still time, Mia!" Ivy's outburst sounded more like a plea than a declaration of faith.

"No," Mia said softly, "there isn't. And it's time you realized that too."

"Uh-uh, not yet!" Ivy asserted, her voice rising to a feverish pitch.

"You're suffering from what psychiatrists call 'denial.' You're in denial, Miss Shaw."

Ivy rolled her eyes. "Call it what you want!"

"I *will be* executed tonight," Mia said, her brown, oval-shaped face yet to show signs of worry. She reminded Ivy of her sister Jasmine.

"Don't talk like that," Ivy said, choking on the words. She was an emotional wreck and quickly falling apart. She glanced at the gold Cartier watch on her wrist, a recent gift from her fiancé, and wished she could make time stand still. "Don't talk like that," she said again.

Mia ignored Ivy's pathetic pleas and continued. "In less than one hour, I will no more be a part of this world."

"Stop it, Mia! Stop it! The governor—we still haven't heard from the governor!"

Mia scoffed. "Please take the book."

Ivy snatched the book out of Mia's hand and threw it across the room. It crashed into the right wall, then landed loudly on the floor.

The correctional officer sitting outside the prison cell jumped up. "Is everything all right, Miss Shaw?" she asked, peering through the bars.

"Everything's fine!" Ivy snapped.

Mia turned and resumed her gaze out the window. Ivy stared in disbelief at her and became envious. She was facing death and doing it without fear, without having once begged for her life. And she, Ivy Shaw, who prided herself on being the epitome of coolness under pressure, was an emotional wreck. In all of her seventeen years of law practice, she'd never dreamed that she, who vehemently opposed the death penalty, would see this day. She firmly believed that she would get Mia's sentence overturned. Feelings of incompetence and guilt replaced the envy Ivy had for Mia. She hung her head in shame.

"It's a philosophy book," Mia said, without turning around. "The chaplain gave it to me along with a Bible, when I first came to death row."

"Nice," Ivy managed to say.

"Some philosophers say man is essentially evil."

"I don't believe that."

"They also say that humans are not that different from animals living in the wild."

Ivy looked up. "What?"

"When animals are afraid or angry, they strike out and inflict harm."

"You're no animal, Mia!"

"I committed a horrible crime at a time when I was afraid and angry. Since that time, eleven *long* years, I've been cooped up in a cage *like* an animal."

"Killing you won't solve anything!" Ivy shouted.

Mia turned and faced Ivy. "A jury of my peers say I must die. I've accepted that. Why won't you?"

"Because I can't," Ivy whispered as tears formed once more in her eyes. "I can't. Can you, *really*? Huh? Re-remember your dream?" Ivy saw disappointment cloud Mia's eyes before she looked away. "I'm sorry."

Mia picked up the book from the floor and returned to the window.

"I'm sorry, Mia," Ivy mumbled.

Mia had shared with Ivy five years ago that she would no longer discuss the life she had before her imprisonment. "It's too painful for me to keep discussing," she had said. The only good thing she recalled ever happening to her was the praise her third grade teacher showered on her for a poem she had written. Mia had dreamed from that moment until the day she was incarcerated that she would become a renowned poet like Maya Angelou.

When Ivy first met Mia, Mia would cry for hours and spew hatred at those she felt responsible for her incarceration. Abandoned by her parents at age five, she grew up in a series of foster and group homes. At the age of sixteen, she quit school and ran from what she described as an abusive situation and married a man eighteen years her senior. She thought she had finally found somebody to love her, until that cold winter day she made an unexpected, early trip home from her cashier job at the 7-Eleven across town. To her horror, she found her husband in bed with another—a girl, two years younger than her, who also worked at the 7-Eleven. They were asleep, snuggled underneath the afghan Mia had spent hours knitting. Beer cans and an empty Pizza Hut box were on the floor next to the bed. Mia quietly exited the bedroom. She closed the door and went back into the living room. She doused the bedroom door, the hallway, and front door with the kerosene she had purchased on the way home for the space heater, before exiting the apartment. When the police and firefighters arrived, she was sitting across the street at the bus stop watching flames shoot out the second-floor windows with the empty kerosene can next to her on the ground. The fire killed her husband's lover—her coworker—and two other tenants. Scarred for life with second- and third-degree burns to his face and upper body, Mia's husband told the judge during the trial that he hoped "the stupid black bitch rots in hell for what she'd done." Mia was just eighteen years old.

"Those people I killed, what about their lives?"

"We don't have to discuss this," Ivy whispered, fighting back tears.

"I killed, now I must be killed," Mia said, running a hand across the book.

"It doesn't have to be this way! Your life is sacred too! To execute you is immoral, inhumane!"

"This is the world in which we live, Miss Shaw."

"Is that more wisdom from *philosophers*?" Ivy asked angrily.

Mia laughed and shook her head.

Ivy looked away.

"What time is it?" Mia asked softly.

Ivy looked at her watch. "Eleven forty-six."

"You thank those protestors praying and marching outside for me, okay?"

"They believe in you, Mia, like I do."

"So believe me when I say I don't want to live the rest of my life in prison."

Ivy closed her eyes and exhaled loudly.

"The governor's not going to call."

"Don't be so pessimistic!" Ivy said with outstretched hands.

Mia shook her head at Ivy. "It would comfort a troubled soul to know that even during the most trying and difficult of times," she said poetically, "one must acquire the courage to live with pain and disappointment." She smiled at Ivy. "You can't win 'em all," she said, turning to look back out the window.

In the distance, Ivy heard footsteps. She rushed to the cell door. "Officer! Is someone coming?"

"No, ma'am," the woman said, shaking her head.

"Ooooh, I see another falling star!" Mia yelled.

Ivy staggered to the window. She grabbed Mia's hand. "Help me, help me be strong now, like you."

Mia smiled. "Here," she said, "take this book—open it. If you don't want it, give it to Jasmine, along with my diary."

"Your diary?"

"Yes, it was mailed to your office yesterday. And tell Jasmine I said she's lucky to have a big sister like you."

Ivy burst into tears. She unashamedly let them flow down her face. She took the philosophy book in her hands. It was entitled *Ethics, Morality and the Philosophy of Man*. On the inside cover were the following hand-written words:

From the darkest hour of the night,
my wretched soul cries,
how I wish I could reverse the hands of time,
to blot out this sin of mine.
For when night becomes day,
and the sun shines its brightest,
the injustice that I've committed,
presses on me ever more tightly.
Soon no more this world,
shall bear the sight of me,
for I have long since accepted,
what must and shall be.
When death at last consumes me,
and swallows me whole,
I pray that forgiveness and peace,
awaits my sin sick soul.

Mia

"Miss Shaw." The correctional officer was standing at the cell door. "The warden and chaplain are coming."

Ivy swallowed dryly and clutched the book to her chest. When the warden and the chaplain entered the cell, she straightened her back, cleared her throat, and ran a sweaty palm down her navy suit.

"I'm sorry, Mia," the warden said, "the governor is not granting a stay of execution."

"Would you like to pray?" the chaplain asked.

Mia smiled. "No, Chaplain, I prayed my last prayer a long time ago."

Ivy could feel Mia's, the warden's, the chaplain's, and the correctional officer's eyes on her. *I don't believe this is happening!* she screamed to herself.

Mia walked up to Ivy and placed her hands on Ivy's shoulders. "Thank you. Besides my third grade teacher, you're the only other person who has ever genuinely cared about me."

Ivy burst into tears. "I'm so sorry."

"You have nothing to be sorry for," Mia said. "Don't follow us. I don't want you to see them put me to death."

The officer tugged at Mia's arm.

"It's time to go," the warden said.

Ivy threw her arms around Mia and sobbed loudly.

"Miss Shaw, please," the officer said, patting Ivy on the back.

Mia pulled away and walked out the cell door. The warden and the chaplain followed. Ivy ran to the window and looked out up into the starry sky.

"Mia LeShelle McWilliams was pronounced dead at 12:13," the warden announced. Ivy didn't hear anything else he said. As Mia had requested, she went out and thanked the death penalty opponents. She was heading for her car twenty minutes later and saw someone leaning against it. Ivy started running toward her car.

"Oh, honey, I'm sorry," Allen said, when Ivy jumped into his arms.

"She's gone, Allen!" Ivy cried. "She's gone!"

"I know," Allen said, holding Ivy tightly.

"I didn't expect to see you here," she said, pulling back.

"C'mon, let's go," he said, taking Ivy's car keys and unlocking the doors to her BMW. "I'll drive."

Ivy slipped into the front passenger seat of her car and Allen started the engine. When he pulled out of the prison parking lot, he sighed heavily.

Ivy looked over at him. "Allen? Are you okay?"

Allen sighed again.

"Allen, what is it?"

"Baby, call your mother."

"What's wrong?"

Allen pulled over and cupped Ivy's face in his hands. "Your aunt Caroline is dead."

Ivy moaned loudly and slumped forward.

Chapter 9

Lily Arrives

Violet

I peeped in on Mama after talking to Ivy. She was lying across her bed in her pink robe and slippers, snoring. I quietly closed the bedroom door and tiptoed down the hall toward the kitchen. Lily had phoned ten minutes ago. She and Russell were a few miles outside town, and Ivy and Allen were not that far behind them. Poor Ivy. The only thing she said when she called was "I'm on my way."

My cell phone vibrated in my pocket. I pulled it out and hurried to the kitchen. "Hey," I said into the phone.

"Hey, sweetie. Calling to check on you."

"Thanks. I'm good. Lily and Ivy are on the way."

"That's great," Warren said. "So, Mrs. Shaw has gotten in touch with everyone now?"

"Yes."

Car lights crept through the kitchen curtains and I heard a car pull into the driveway. I hurried to the window and peeped out. "Warren! I gotta go. Lily just drove up."

"Okay. I'll check on you later."

"Bye."

"Bye."

I ran to the front door and flung it open. Lily had already emerged from the passenger side of the Mercedes. Her diamond loop earrings were sparkling in the moonlight and her face was wet with tears.

"I'm so glad you're here," I cried, running down the porch steps to embrace her.

"I would have been here sooner, had you or Mama called me," Lily cried, hugging me.

"I know."

I released Lily and wiped her face. "Go on inside. I'll help Russell with the bags."

Lily ran up the walkway and soon disappeared into the house. Russell was still sitting in the driver's seat of the car. I walked around and opened his door. When he stepped out, I gasped. There was an egg-size knot on his forehead, and he looked exhausted.

"I'm so sorry to hear about Miss Caroline," he said, embracing me.

"Thank you. Are you okay?" I asked, stepping back, staring at his forehead.

"Oh!" Russell pointed to his head and laughed. "I tripped and fell getting out of the shower this morning, can you believe that?"

"Oh, wow! I bet that hurt like the dickens," I said, frowning.

Russell laughed again. "Yeah, it did."

"Violet!"

I looked back. Lily was standing on the porch with her hands on her hips. "Mama wants you. Russell can get the bags!"

"Yeah," Russell said, "I got it, Violet. You go inside."

I followed Lily back into the house. Mama was coming up the hall.

"Where're you going?" Lily asked.

"To make coffee," Mama replied.

"No, you're not! Go back to your room and lie down!" Lily ordered.

"I'm not sleepy, Lily. Where's Russell?"

"Outside," Lily replied blandly.

The way Lily said "outside" made me wonder if she was upset with Russell about something. She removed her earrings and tossed them in her shoulder bag.

"When did you get *that* done?" I asked, admiring her hair.

"This morning," she replied with a smile.

"It looks good! Don't it, Mama?" I said.

"Yeah, it does. I might get mine done like that," Mama said, laughing.

Lily and I burst out laughing.

"Violet, do you know what I did with that obituary I had? I remember Odessa reading it. I hope she didn't take it with her!"

"Mama, Mrs. Fowler gave me ten copies. They're on the chest in your room."

Lily grunted. "I pray there are no misspelled words or grammatical errors."

"There *aren't*," I said.

"George Fowler has done right by Caroline. Everything is real nice, just like Caroline wanted," Mama said, eyeing Lily sharply.

"Yes, everything is real nice," I added.

Tears filled Lily's eyes and her lips started quivering.

"I'll make a pot of coffee, Mama. Go lie back down," I said. "When Ivy gets here we'll wake you."

"How soon will that be?" Mama asked, glancing at the clock on the mantel in the living room.

"A hour, maybe less," I said.

We heard Russell slam down the trunk on the Mercedes. Lily ran to the front door and yelled, "Good Lord, Russell! Will you be quiet?"

"Don't yell at your husband like that," Mama said, walking up to Lily.

"He doesn't need to wake up the neighbors, Mama!" Lily said, scowling.

Something other than grief over Aunt Caroline had Lily all hot and bothered. The knot on Russell's head, the offhanded way she responded to Mama when Mama asked her where he was, and now her yelling at him got me to thinking. Dating a detective had sharpened my sixth sense. I closed my eyes and prayed that there wasn't trouble in what I considered a rarity: a happy marriage.

"Let's go make that pot of coffee," Mama said, tugging at Lily's arms.

"All right," Lily said, smiling down at Mama.

I went to the front door and held it open for Russell. Upon closer inspection, my brother-in-law didn't only look exhausted, he looked troubled. I liked Russell and it pained me to see him like this. "You want something to drink? Want an ice pack maybe?" I asked, when I closed the door behind him.

He laughed. "No, thanks."

I grabbed one of the garment bags and as I walked past the kitchen to the stairs, I overheard Lily grilling Mama about the details of Aunt Caroline's wake. When Russell and I reached the upstairs bedroom he and Lily always slept in when they came home, he told me that their children—Russell Jr., Sabrina, and their oldest, Augustus, named after Daddy, would be arriving tomorrow afternoon.

"Russell!"

I jumped and looked back. Lily was standing in the doorway, glaring into the room. Her chest was rising and falling and her fists were clenched.

"Will you go downstairs and speak to my mama! And *where* is my makeup case? You did put it in the car, didn't you?"

"Yes, Lily, I *did*," Russell said.

"Well, where is it?" Lily snapped.

"I guess I left it in the car," Russell said, storming past me out of the room.

"I guess you did," Lily said, following Russell downstairs.

I wanted to stop Lily and ask if everything was okay, realizing full well if I did ask, her pride wouldn't let her admit to me or anyone that there was trouble in her marriage.

I went to the linen closet in the upstairs hallway to get towels for Lily and Russell. "Russell! What in the world happened to you?" I heard Mama ask.

"I walked into the bathroom door this morning, Miss Peony," Russell said, laughing.

I gasped. Russell had told me minutes ago he fell getting out of the shower. From where I stood at the top of the stairs, I saw Lily exit the kitchen and stalk down the hall to Mama's bedroom.

Yes. Something was definitely going on, and I was bound and determined to find out what it was.

Chapter 10

What Lily Wants, Lily Gets

Violet

"There will be peeeeace, in the vaaalleeey for meeeee, my Lord! There will be peace, in the valley for meeeee, someday!" Mama sang as the old spiritual played on the radio. Like most mornings since I'd returned home following the fire to my house, I woke up to the blaring sounds of Gospel 680 AM, Mama's favorite radio station. I could also smell bacon and sausage cooking. The aroma hovered over the bed where Ivy and I were lying. Dealing with Aunt Caroline's death, and having to keep it a secret from my sisters until after the arrangements had been made, had taken a toll on me. I'd been unable to eat and had suffered one migraine after another. I sat up in bed, threw up my hands, and exhaled. I didn't have a headache and my appetite had returned.

"Good morning, my dear radio listeners! Rise, shine, and give God the glory!" Mr. T, Gospel 680's popular radio personality, said loudly and fervently.

"Thank you, Lord!" Mama shouted.

I looked over at the clock on the nightstand. It was 7:36. I threw back the bedcovers and got out of the bed. "Ivy, wake up."

Ivy moaned and stirred underneath the covers.

"Get up, girl," I said, nudging her. "Mama's fixing breakfast."

Ivy's eyes popped open. "Sounds like she has that radio turned up as loud as it can go," she said groggily.

I crept to the door and opened it, straining to hear over the booming radio and Mama's off-key singing if Lily was downstairs with Mama. It didn't sound like she was, and that was out of character for Lily. She always helped Mama cook breakfast whenever she came home.

"What're you doing?" Ivy asked.

"Shhh!"

"Whatcha think is going on?" Ivy whispered.

"I don't know," I said, closing the door. "Whatever it is, I hope they can work through it."

Ivy smacked her lips. "You know how Lily holds grudges."

"Ahhh, poor Lily. Her perfect marriage may turn out to be not so perfect after all," I said, returning to the bed.

"Is there such a thing, a perfect marriage, a *soul mate*?" Ivy asked with creased brows.

"I don't know," I said, sighing. "I want to believe so."

Ivy kicked back the covers and sat up in bed.

"Don't you believe there is?" I asked, smiling.

Ivy shrugged.

"In two weeks! Two weeks," I said excitedly, "you'll be married. Can you *believe* that?"

Ivy rolled her eyes. "Believe me when I say this, this wedding hasn't been high on my list of priorities *lately*."

"Well, you've been busy. With Mia's case especially."

Ivy sighed and rolled her eyes again.

"Now that that's behind you, you—"

"Do you know the bill for this wedding is close to three hundred thousand dollars?"

"What?" I yelled.

"Thanks to Allen's mother! No lie, Violet. Beatrice Hayes is about to drive me insane!"

I burst out laughing.

"You know what she had the *nerve* to say to me at the bridal shower my sorors threw for me last Saturday?"

"What?"

"That I was lucky to get her son."

"No, she didn't!"

"Yes, she did. Girl, I was fit to be tied."

"I'm sure you were!"

"The Hayeses *are*," Ivy said with an exasperated sigh and eye roll, "one of the most *prominent* black families in Durham. And it seems to be snobbish Beatrice Hayes's mission in life—meddlesome fart—to make sure everybody knows that!"

"Now, now, Ivy. You must not talk like that about your future mother-in-law."

Ivy burst out laughing.

"Well, it's about time y'all got up!" Lily yelled, barging into the room. She was dressed in a light blue sweatsuit and white sneakers. Her hair was pulled back into a ponytail.

"Well, good morning to you!" Ivy said, smiling.

"Is my brother-in-law still sleeping?" I asked.

"He's up," Lily replied dryly.

"He feeling okay?" Ivy asked.

"What?" Lily asked, squinting.

"He didn't look like he was feeling all that well last night," Ivy said.

Lily rolled her eyes. "He'll live. I'm going downstairs to help Mama with breakfast. Our baby sister called. She'll be here around two o'clock."

Before Ivy or I could comment, Lily had exited the room, slamming the door behind her.

"Looks like she's still in rare form," Ivy said.

"I sure hope she doesn't stress Mama out. Ivy, you gotta help me see to it that she and Jasmine don't."

"I will," Ivy said, nodding. "I will."

After breakfast, Ivy and I cleaned the kitchen, and Russell and Allen went up the street to Mr. Carwash to have the Mercedes and the BMW detailed. Mama went into the living room and called Daisy to see how Cedric was doing. Floyd beeped in while she was talking to Daisy. She put Daisy on hold to talk to him. When she ended her call with Floyd she complained of having an earache. She said while she and Floyd talked, Niecee listening on another phone, "wailed sump'n awful."

When Ivy and I finished cleaning up the kitchen, we went into Mama's bedroom and watched Lily rummage through Mama's walk-in closet perusing the numerous dresses and suits hanging there—many of them she'd purchased herself—in an effort to pick out an outfit for Mama to wear to the wake tonight. She'd already settled on Mama wearing the black Evan Picone crepe suit Ivy had given her from Saks a year ago to the graveside service. It still had the five-hundred-dollar price tag on it. Lily had also taken steps toward changing what was to have been nothing more than a viewing of Aunt Caroline's body tonight to a full-blown memorial service. Before Ivy and I got downstairs for breakfast, she had already contacted several people about making remarks at the "program." Even though Aunt Caroline had said many times before she died that she didn't want a lot said over her at her wake and graveside service, Mama didn't protest Lily's plans. "Just don't make it too long," was all she said to Lily regarding the memorial.

I picked up the copy of the *McKinley Messenger*, the town newspaper, lying on Mama's bed. It was opened to the obituary section. There was a picture of Aunt Caroline smiling up at me from the paper. Mr. Fowler had called earlier while we were having breakfast to say he would meet us at the funeral home at eleven o'clock so Lily and Ivy could privately view Aunt Caroline's body.

"So, what's up with you and Russell?" I asked.

"I like this," Lily said, pulling a jade-colored Christian Dior dress from the closet. "Green is, well, *was* one of Aunt Caroline's favorite colors."

"Mama might want to wear something darker tonight," Ivy said.

"Naw, I think not," Lily said, still not answering my question.

Ivy cut her eyes at me.

"Lily, is everything okay between you and Russell?" I asked.

"Yes, Violet," she replied quite unconvincingly.

Clearly hearing a hint of annoyance in her voice, I pressed her further. "So why were you so short with him last night?" I asked.

Lily exhaled loudly and looked back at me. "Girl, yesterday wasn't one of my better days at the office. Just before leaving I found out I needed to terminate an employee."

"Oh, sorry," I said.

"She's only getting what she deserved," Lily asserted, batting her eyes.

"You got to do what you got to do," Ivy said.

"It comes with the job," Lily said with a heavy sigh.

"How's Miss Emma's granddaughter, Sandra, working out?" Ivy asked.

"That's who I'm firing."

"Whaaaat?" I exclaimed.

Lily pursed her lips together and nodded.

"Oh no!" I shrieked. "Uh-uh!"

What Lily was planning to do would send shock waves through the Mothers' Board at Charity Chapel, and would be one more thing for Colette Worrell to sit in church and roll her eyes at me for. "Why, Lily?" I asked.

"She's not working out," Lily answered.

"What do you mean she's not working out?" I asked.

"She's not a team player, the workers in the unit are fed up with her, and there're some doggone good workers in that unit. I don't intend to lose any of them because of Sandra Harris!"

"Why not call her in and talk to her?" I suggested.

Lily sighed loudly and rolled her eyes. "No! I'm not wasting my time doing that. I shouldn't have hired her in the first place. I don't know what I was thinking!"

"You hired her because Mama asked you to, as a favor for Miss Emma, remember?" I said.

Lily exhaled and rolled her eyes again.

"I don't think you're being fair," I said.

"Think what you want, she's outta there!" Lily yelled.

"Okay," I said, with a wave of my hands. "Don't bite my head off." I looked at Ivy for support. She shrugged.

"And since when have you cared about the Harrises?" Lily asked, frowning at me. "You can't *stand* Colette."

"Regardless of how I feel about Colette—"

"And if Emma Harris has the nerve," Lily said, interrupting me, "to get in *my* face and tell me that we're responsible for Aunt Caroline's death, I'm gone tell her a thing or two."

"Lily, uh-uh, don't do that," I said, shaking my head. "Mama's not going to like that."

"That's right, Lily," Ivy said. "You know Emma, I mean *Mother* Harris, is as uncouth as they come. We shouldn't be surprised by anything that comes out of her mouth."

I shook my head. "You can say that again," I said, recalling the countless number of times I'd sat in church and hung my head in embarrassment after Emma Harris had stood before the congregation and made some outlandish comment.

"Lily. I'm confused, surprised actually, to hear this about Sandra," I said. "Everything I've ever heard you say about her, up until now, has been favorable. What has she done to make you want to *fire* her?"

"Violet, I really don't feel like discussing this, but if you must know, Sandra reports to work late, her dictation is behind, she hasn't maintained regular contact with many of her clients, she abuses agency property. I—I," Lily said, waving her hands, "have to let her go. Talking to her is not going to change a thing."

"'Abuses agency property'?" Ivy asked, frowning.

"Yeah," Lily replied with a nod. "When she should be typing reports and logging in her daily activities, she's on the Internet shopping at eBay."

Ivy and I looked at each other and burst out laughing.

Lily narrowed her eyes at us.

"You're joking, right?" I asked, still laughing.

Lily sighed and rolled her eyes.

"So your mind's made up?" I asked.

Lily nodded. "Yes, it is."

"Lily, I must admit, I'm surprised too," Ivy said. "I recall you saying once how proud you were of Sandra. That she was different from the women in her family."

"The only girl from that family that's gone to college," I added, remembering hearing Miss Emma tell Mama that on more than one occasion.

"Big deal!" Lily said facetiously.

"It is a big deal," I said.

Ivy nodded in agreement.

"Well, I was wrong about her, okay?" Lily snapped. "She's no different from them other *whorish* women in her family!"

"Will you watch your mouth!" I said horsely, looking back at the door. Mama, the devout Christian woman that she was, didn't tolerate name-calling in her house. She believed it was insulting to God, who created everybody in his image.

"Skanky," Lily whispered. "Does that sound better?"

"No," Ivy said, laughing.

"Mrs. Shaw-Davenport, I'm shocked! Did I hear you say"—I lowered my voice—"'skanky'?"

A slight smile formed at Lily's mouth and she rolled her eyes.

"So, was she messing around with somebody's man?" Ivy asked, wide-eyed.

"I did hear that she came on to somebody's husband at a party."

Ivy exhaled. "That's not good."

"Like I said," Lily began, "she's sk—"

I threw up a hand. "We heard you the first time," I said.

"And *you*," Lily said, pointing at me, "better watch your back."

"Whatcha mean?" I asked.

"Watch Warren around Colette."

I scoffed. "Warren doesn't want Colette."

"Violet, don't get stupid now, now that some man's taken an interest in you," Lily said, shaking her head at me. "You know Colette don't mind dropping her drawers. And don't *ever* forget what Mama used to tell us."

"What?" I asked.

"'A stiff peter ain't got no conscience,'" Lily replied.

"I don't believe Warren would be that low-down *or* desperate," I said.

Lily shook her head at me. "For your sake, sister, I hope he's not."

"Well, sis," Ivy said, clapping her hands, "I admire you, for reaching back, trying to help someone from home."

Lily smiled. "Thanks."

Ivy sighed and opened her eyes wide. "What you're about to do will piss off Miss Emma and her kinfolk."

Lily shrugged and rolled her eyes.

"You can kiss that guest speaker invitation good-bye," I said.

Lily flinched. Judging by her reaction, that hadn't crossed her mind. "Emma Harris ain't but one person on the Mothers' Board at Charity Chapel," she asserted with a bob of her head. "Mama's the president."

"And that's all so true, dear sister. But need I remind you," I said, "of what Evangeline and Colette told me one Sunday morning, 'Whatever Mama wants, Mama gets'?"

Lily grunted and made a face.

I continued. "Miss Emma bullies her way around Charity Chapel and more times than not, tends to get what she wants. If she chooses to oust you as guest speaker, and she will when you fire Sandra, you're out. Because Miss Odessa, Miss Edna, and a few others on the Mothers' Board won't open their mouths to object."

Mama entered the bedroom. "What y'all talking 'bout?"

"What you're wearing tonight," Lily said, smiling broadly.

Ivy and I looked at Mama and smiled too.

"How about this?" Lily asked, removing the green Christian Dior dress from the closet and holding it in front of her for Mama to see.

"That's fine," Mama said. "Green was Caroline's favorite color."

"Who's all staying over at Aunt Caroline's?" Ivy asked, looking out the bedroom window across the street.

"Daisy's family and Jasmine," Lily said.

"I just finished talking to Jasmine," Mama said. "It might be closer to three o'clock before she gets here now."

"What's going on?" Ivy asked. "Is she catching a later bus?"

Mama shook her head and smiled. "Her friend is bringing her and the girls."

"Who?" Lily asked.

"Her boyfriend," Mama said.

"'Boyfriend'?" Lily, Ivy, and I asked in unison

Mama nodded. "Somebody named Elroy."

My sisters and I looked at each other.

"I didn't realize she was dating," Mama said, smiling again. "From what she told me, this Elroy sounds like a right nice fella."

My sisters and I looked at each other again. I'm sure they were thinking the same thing I was. Surely Jasmine wasn't bringing Elroy, aka Maniac, her thugged-out, "alleged" drug-dealing boyfriend to Mama's house.

"Is he dropping her off?" Ivy asked, her nostrils flared.

Mama shook her head. "He's staying for the services."

"We'll see about that!" Lily muttered.

"Say what?" Mama asked.

"Nothing, Mama," Lily replied.

"When was the last time you talked to Jasmine?" Mama asked Lily.

"Two weeks ago," Lily replied.

Mama nodded and smiled. "That's good. I want y'all to stay in touch with your baby sister."

"I wanna touch her right now," Lily muttered.

"What you say, Lily?" Mama asked.

Lily shook her head. "Nothing, Mama."

"Jasmine can learn a lot from all of y'all," Mama said, sitting down on the bed, "if you would just take up some time with her and help her."

"We try more than you know, Mama," Ivy said.

"She's just so irresponsible!" Lily asserted, clenching her fists. "No kind of example what-so-ever for those girls of hers. And I know you're not going like what I'm about to say, Mama, but I'm going to say it anyway. Lorenzo needs to go on and petition the court like he's forever threatening to do, for custody of Kenya."

Mama threw up her hands. "How dare you say sump'n like that, Lily!"

"You want Kenya to end up like Jasmine?" Lily asked, peering down at Mama. "Rashaunda is already heading in that direction."

It never failed. Whenever we were all together, any mention of Jasmine was cause for dissension, and Lily could go on for hours griping about her.

"Mama, it's almost eleven o'clock. Didn't you say Mr. Fowler would meet us at the funeral home at eleven o'clock?" Ivy asked.

"Yes," Mama replied.

"We can't leave until Allen and Russell get back," I said.

"Oh yeah," Ivy said, sighing.

"With the money Caroline left her, I hope Jasmine spends it wisely," Mama said.

Lily scoffed. "Yeah, right, Mama."

Aunt Caroline had a hefty life insurance policy totaling one hundred thousand dollars. In a will she had drawn up years ago, my sisters and I would each receive ten thousand dollars. The remaining money would go to Mama.

Mama sighed and stood up. "I never would have thought," she said softly, as tears filled her eyes, "that Wednesday would have been the last time I saw my sister alive."

Lily was the first to burst into tears. She ran over to Mama and embraced her.

"I hate mighty bad I wasn't with Caroline when she slipped away."

"Mama, please!" Lily cried.

"I've wondered so many times since she died about her last moments," Mama continued. "If she called out for me."

"Mama, don't do this to yourself!" Ivy cried as tears spilled from her eyes.

"I wasn't there to answer her, if she did," Mama said. "I wasn't there to grab hold of her hand, or wipe her fevered brow."

"Oh, Lord!" I prayed. "Please, please help us!"

"I miss my sista, the good Lord knows I do," Mama said.

"We know, Mama. We miss Aunt Caroline too," Lily cried.

"Don't think for one minute you let her down," Ivy said.

"I pray she didn't suffer. That she slipped away quietly like your father did."

When Allen and Russell walked into the house, my sisters and I were huddled around Mama weeping. Our crying had subsided when we left the house for the funeral home. "Lily, I don't want you acting up at Fowler's. You hear me?" Mama said, when Russell backed out the driveway and pulled off behind Allen.

From where I sat behind Russell, I saw Lily roll her eyes.

"You hear me, Lily?" Mama said, leaning forward.

"Yes, Mama," Lily replied with another eye roll.

"George Fowler has done right by Caroline."

"Good," Lily said, looking back smiling.

Mama sat back and looked out the car window. "I sho' hope it don't rain tomorrow."

It was a good thing Mr. Fowler had folks on hand when we arrived at the funeral home. Russell and Allen needed help getting weeping Lily and Ivy up the steps into the funeral home. They were so overcome with grief, Lily started hyperventilating and Ivy collapsed in the foyer.

I heard Mama say, "Lord, if I ever needed you, I need you now."

Despite my efforts to keep it together, I couldn't. I fell apart too, wondering how my sisters and I were going to hold Mama up, "be strong," like Miss Emma told me we would have to be, when we were emotional wrecks ourselves. One thing I knew for sure, Miss Emma would be watching us, and so would several others, to see if we failed our mother in what was another deep hour of sorrow.

Chapter 11

Peeved

Jasmine stopped pacing the living room floor in her apartment. She went back to the window and looked out again into the courtyard. The plainclothes police officers were still milling about. A young black male reporter from WBTV News 3 was in the courtyard earlier reporting on the previous night's deadly shooting. Seven people had been shot; four fatally. If the Seabrook brothers were responsible for what had happened last night, they were pleased. According to the news reporter, "Small-time hood and reported drug dealer Dwayne Reynolds, aka Q-Tip, was one of last night's murdered victims."

From where she sat in the living room, teary-eyed Kenya watched her mother. "Is he coming, Mama?" she asked softly.

"He said he was," Jasmine replied.

"If he don't, call Grandma or Aunt Violet. They'll send us money."

"No!" Jasmine yelled. "Maniac's gone take us!"

"Well, where he at?" Rashaunda asked, walking into the room. "Grandma gone be real mad at you if you don't make it home," she added with an eye roll.

Jasmine swelled with anger. Where was Maniac? He had told her he was on his way an hour ago. It was almost twelve o'clock now; she had told her mother she would be home around three o'clock. That wouldn't be the case now.

Jasmine flipped open her cell phone again and pressed the Send button. Just like before, her call to Maniac went unanswered. "Bastard!" she muttered, pressing the End button. She called Maniac's mother's home; that call too went unanswered.

"I wanna go see Grandma and Aunt Violet!" Kenya cried.

"We're going, Kenya! Now stop crying!" Jasmine yelled.

"And how we gone do that?" Rashaunda asked. "We sho' can't walk to McKinley."

Jasmine yanked open the front door and stalked outside.

"Where you going?" Rashaunda yelled, running behind her.

"Go back inside!" Jasmine shouted. "If Maniac calls or comes by, tell him to call me!"

"Where you going?" Rashaunda asked again.

Jasmine didn't answer Rashaunda or look back. She hurried down the walkway in her four-inch gold stilettos to the bus stop. Tina spotted her when she walked past her apartment.

"Girl, I thought you was halfway home," she said, running outside.

"I'm waitin' on Maniac's ass! The bastard ain't showed up yet! He ain't even answering his phone, and I done paged him I don't know how many times!"

"Girl, naw! So what you gone do? How you gone get home!" Tina asked, frowning.

"He taking me," Jasmine said, hurrying down the walkway. "I'm *not* missing my aunt Caroline's wake or graveside service!"

"Go handle yo' business, girl!" Tina yelled with a wave of her hands.

Jasmine caught the express bus to the downtown terminal and waited ten minutes for a bus that carried her across town. She got off at the bus stop a street over from NeShell Scott's house. Not wanting to risk getting in trouble, at least not today when she was so desperately trying to get home, she stayed what she figured to be fifteen hundred feet from the blue Section Eight house NeShell and her five children resided in. After NeShell had taken out a restraining order against her two weeks ago when they were in court, Jasmine responded in kind. As Ivy sat next to her at the defense table trying to get the charges against her thrown out, and Violet sat behind her praying, the only thought that ran through Jasmine's mind was not that she could end up with a criminal record, but what she was going to do to NeShell the next time she saw her. Even as the judge hauled her and NeShell over the coals for "acting the fool over some sorry thug" and sentenced them each to a year of unsupervised probation, Jasmine couldn't forgo her vengeful plans of getting NeShell. Fully aware that a criminal infraction of any kind could land her in jail and back in court, Jasmine had calmly walked up to NeShell outside the Concord Mills Mall the day after being convicted of assault, and smacked her squarely in the face. Maniac had taken NeShell to the mall to buy clothing for the twins. He broke up the fight, but not before Jasmine bloodied NeShell's nose and blackened her right eye.

Jasmine grunted when she recalled the injuries she'd incurred to her face during the fight. Her frown quickly turned to a smile after she ran a hand down her cheek and across her forehead. The gash marks had healed and with a little makeup, no one would have known they were ever there.

Before turning the corner onto NeShell's street, Jasmine sighed and prayed that Maniac wouldn't be at her house. *What if he is?* she wondered. "I'll jump his ass this time, if he is. That's what!" she muttered angrily, hurrying up the street.

Parked in NeShell's driveway were a ten-speed bike and a tricycle. Jasmine breathed a sigh of relief. She walked back to the bus stop and sat down. She called her apartment to see if Maniac had called or come by. Rashaunda told her he had not, but Violet had called wanting to know when they would be leaving for McKinley. Jasmine sighed and shook her head. It was 12:40 and according to the bus schedule, the next bus wouldn't be by for another twenty minutes. Jasmine thought about calling Violet, but decided not to in light of how things were going, because she didn't know when she would be heading home. So instead of calling her sister, she tried Maniac's number again; her call again went unanswered.

When the city bus pulled up Jasmine hopped on and headed to the only other place she thought Maniac could be: his mama's house. During the bus ride, she called Maniac's mother's house several times. Her calls, like before, went unanswered. Fifteen minutes later, Jasmine exited a city bus on Thurgood Marshall Lane. She exhaled as tears filled her eyes. Maniac's black Chevy Impala was parked on the street in front of the run-down, one-story house that he, his mother, and his adult siblings called home. Jasmine ran across the street, up on the porch, and without bothering to knock reached for the doorknob; the door wasn't locked. Maniac's mother was lying on the tattered sofa in the living room in a floral-print housedress snoring loudly. Debris was everywhere. Empty food containers, dirty dishes, cigarette butts, empty beer cans, liquor and wine bottles were strewn across the living room floor and piled on top of the coffee and end tables. Maniac's mother's house was the party house on the block, and it stank like it always did from alcohol, cigarettes, garbage, and general uncleanliness.

Jasmine made her way through the litter and funk to a back bedroom where Maniac and an older brother generally slept. A Snoop Dogg CD was playing in the room. She ran over and snatched back the covers on the twin bed where Maniac was lying. "Get up! Get up!" she yelled.

Maniac's brother, Wesley, sleeping on a futon across the room, groaned and pulled the bed covering over his head.

"Jazz, wh-what's up?" Maniac said groggily.

"Get your ass up!" Jasmine yelled down at him. "You supposed to be taking me home!"

Maniac turned onto his side away from Jasmine and fell back to sleep.

Jasmine started kicking the bed. "Get up! Get up!" she screamed as tears streamed down her face.

"Girl, what's wrong with you?"

Jasmine looked back and saw Maniac's mother standing in the doorway looking at her like she was crazy. "My auntie has died, and I ain't got no way home!" she cried. "I ain't got no way home!"

Maniac's mother staggered over, farting along the way. "Elroy!" she yelled, kicking the bed. "Get your ass up and take this girl home! Elroy! You hear me? Get up!"

"Aw'right, damn!" Maniac grumbled.

"Sorry to hear 'bout your auntie, baby," Maniac's mother said, patting Jasmine on the shoulder.

It took Maniac all of thirty minutes to shower and get dressed. After swinging by Jasmine's apartment to pick up Kenya and Rashaunda, he rode around Charlotte making one stop after another. Fuming, and fearing she'd miss her aunt Caroline's wake, Jasmine cursed and pummeled him with her fists while they sat at a red stoplight. It was approaching 2:00 p.m. Kenya covered her ears with her hands and yelled for Jasmine to stop. Rashaunda turned up the volume on her MP3 player and stared out the window.

Despite Jasmine's tears, curses, and pleas, Maniac made more stops in the Queen City before hitting I-77, forty minutes, later for McKinley.

Chapter 12

The Wake

Violet

"She knows how to get to the funeral home, Mama," Lily said. "It's ten minutes to seven! We got to go!"

From where she stood in the living room looking out the window, hoping and praying that Jasmine would ride up any minute, Mama sighed and said, "All right, let's go." Daisy's family was already in their car and parked along the street waiting on us to leave the house. Niecee hadn't stopped crying since they'd arrived an hour ago. From where I sat in the backseat of Ivy's car, I silently prayed, *Lord, please let everything go okay tonight. Please don't let Mama get too stressed, and, Lord, wherever Jasmine is, please let her and the girls be okay.* When Allen pulled out the driveway and headed down the street behind Lily and her family, I reached over and grabbed Mama's hand.

The memorial service for Aunt Caroline was a moving tribute to a woman who had touched many lives during the course of her seventy-nine years. The funeral home was packed with relatives, church members, neighbors, friends, and former coworkers of Aunt Caroline's, all with kind things to say about her and with words of comfort to us. Interspersed between the remarks and tributes, cousin Cheryl and the Gospelettes sang Aunt Caroline's favorite hymns and spirituals. They brought down the house with their rendition of "Give Me My Flowers" by the Consolers. I was at the podium tearfully talking about Aunt Caroline's favorite things, when Jasmine appeared, rushing toward the front, bumping into people seated in folding chairs in the aisle. It reminded me of that last scene in *Imitation of Life* where grief-stricken, penitent Sarah Jane barged through the crowd of mourners gathered outside the church where her mother's funeral had just ended, up to the horse-driven hearse. Like Sarah Jane, Jasmine was crying and yelling, "Let me through, please, please let me through!"

By the time Jasmine made it up front—with Kenya and Rashaunda running behind her—Mama and my sisters were standing. And had it not been for the male employees Mr. Fowler had flanking Aunt Caroline's casket, Jasmine would have knocked it over. She flung herself across the open casket screaming, "Get up, Aunt Caroline! Get up! Please, please get up!"

As people gasped and stared in horror, Miss Odessa started singing "I'll Fly Away."

"I'm sorry!" Jasmine cried. "I'm so, so sorry! Aunt Caroline, I love you. Dear Lord, give her back to me. Please, Lord, give her baaaack!"

"My Lord!" I heard Miss Emma exclaim.

In the midst of Jasmine's screams for Aunt Caroline to get up, Niecee passed out. Thirty minutes later, we were all seated and able to resume the service.

Kenya surprised us all when she went up front and read a poem she'd written during the drive from Charlotte about Aunt Caroline. Dressed so cute in a blue shift and low-heeled black patent leather sandals, she didn't look like she belonged to my ghetto-fabulous sister. Maybe Lily was right, she was the professional in the family on child welfare matters, maybe Kenya's father should get custody of her, "rescue her" before she became what Lily called her mother and big sister "hood rats."

Jasmine was dressed in a snug-fitting wraparound black dress and gold stilettos. At five feet five inches tall and weighing not more than one hundred twenty pounds, she looked stunning; however, her outfit was more fitting for a party than a wake. Miss Ghetto Fabulous was accessorized in gold necklaces of various lengths and gold rings, earrings, and bracelets of various sizes. Her oldest daughter looked like a miniature version of her. Rashaunda was wearing a white top with spaghetti straps and a short black skirt. She had on a pair of three-inch white sandals—her mother's, I surmised—and dangling from her ears were gold personalized hoop earrings.

Shortly after Kenya's poem and remarks from the area Meals-On-Wheels coordinator, I began to feel something vibrating against my left side. Instinctively I reached down for my cell phone and soon realized

I didn't have it with me. Rashaunda, who was seated between Lily and me, reached into the right pocket of her skirt and pulled out a vibrating pink cell phone. Before I could take the phone from her, Lily reached over and grabbed it. She shoved the pink cell phone in her suit jacket pocket, stood up, and exited the sanctuary.

Chapter 13

Smack-Down!

"Lily! Oh, Lily! I'm so sorry to hear about Miss Caroline!"

Lily flinched and pulled back. Sandra was rushing up to her with outstretched arms. Lily threw up her hands. "Well, if it isn't Miss Thang!"

"Hey!" Sandra said, slowly dropping her arms.

"Or do you prefer *mistress*?" Lily asked.

"Huh?" Sandra asked, looking puzzled.

"I got another one for you: brazen slut!"

Sandra narrowed her eyes. "Lily, why are you calling me names?"

The door to the bathroom opened and two women walked in. They were volunteers with the Meals-On-Wheels program. They walked over to Lily, hugged her, and told her how sorry they were for her loss. Lily thanked the women and shot Sandra a murderous look as she brushed past her out the door. Sandra followed.

In the vestibule Lily turned and faced Sandra. "All that I've done for you. Why?"

"What are you *talking* about?" Sandra asked.

"Don't play dumb with me. You know damn well what I'm talking about." Lily glanced over at the only other person standing in the vestibule, a disheveled, middle-aged black man peering into the crowded chapel holding a red rose.

"I *don't* know what you're talking about!" Sandra said quite innocently.

For a brief moment Lily couldn't speak. All she could do was stare at the beautiful young woman before her, who could easily have any man she wanted, including, Lily believed, her husband.

Sandra reached out to touch Lily.

Lily recoiled like a snake. "Don't touch me!"

Instinctively Lily wanted to reach out and touch Sandra in the worst way, rip through her youthful, flawless skin and yank plugs of hair out of her head.

"What's wrong with you, Lily?" Sandra asked, inching closer.

Lily threw her head back to respond with a sarcastic chuckle. Instead, what slid across her tongue, out her mouth through her full lips sounded like the outcry of a tortured, wounded animal. The dirty man in the lobby looked over at her.

Amid loud applause, Cheryl and the Gospelettes made their way back up front. Lily covered her mouth with her hands to muffle the wails emanating from her troubled soul when the group started singing "May the Work I've Done Speak for Me."

Sandra reached into her Prada bag and pulled out tissue. "Here," she said, offering Lily a Kleenex.

Lily shook her head. "My husband's not leaving me for *you*," she finally said, as tears filled her eyes.

Sandra burst out laughing. "What?"

"You heard me!"

"Wait a minute!" Sandra exclaimed. "Hold up! Is this all because Russell and I had *lunch* the other day?"

"Shut up!" Lily yelled.

"Oh my goodness!" Sandra exclaimed, chuckling.

Lily wiped away the tears streaming down her face with her hands. "Let's see if you're laughing next week."

Sandra shot Lily a surprised look.

"I guess I should tell you now, no need putting it off until next week."

"Tell me *what?*"

"I'm letting you go."

"You—you're what?"

"*Firing* you, for poor job performance."

"What?" Sandra yelled.

"You're fired!"

"You got to be kidding."

"Do I look like I'm joking?"

"You insecure, vindictive bitch," Sandra sneered. "I will file a grievance for unlawful termination."

"You're on probation, dumb ass, you can't do that. And don't bother coming by the agency to pick up your things, I'll have them sent to you."

Lily turned and looked into the chapel. She started singing along with Cheryl and the Gospelettes. "May the service I give speak for meeee."

Sandra laughed out loud. "You need to quit. 'Cause that's one song you ain't got *nooo* business singing. Knowing you like I do, you ain't never done anything for anyone that didn't benefit you in some way."

"I thought you were different. Not like them home wreckers in your family," Lily said without turning to look at Sandra. "Stay away from my husband."

"You don't deserve him."

Lily flinched and looked at Sandra. "What?"

"You heard me. He deserves better."

"Stay away from him, or you'll be sorry."

Sandra scoffed and stepped back. "Are you threatening me?"

Tears filled Lily's eyes again and she looked away. Angry and embarrassed, more embarrassed than angry, she wouldn't answer Sandra or look at her, for fear Sandra would mock her for the tears in her eyes.

"You're pathetic! You really are. And all this time I thought you, Mrs. Lily Shaw Davenport, was a confident, strong black woman. You're far from it, I see! You're no different from any other woman I've met. Oh yeah, you try to act like you are, but deep down inside you're no different. You make me sick!"

"You're not welcome here, so leave, before I have you thrown out," Lily said, her voice cracking at the end.

"I see why nobody at the agency likes you," Sandra continued. "You're full of shit! And you wanna know something else? You're doing me a favor by firing me, 'cause I got sick of your pompous, stuck-up ass months ago."

Lily turned and glared at Sandra. Tears were streaming down her face.

"Poor, lil', insecure Lily," Sandra sang, rocking her head from side to side. "I've never seen this side of you before. It's refreshing," she said, laughing. "And I can think of a lot of women at the agency who'd get a kick out of this, including Marilyn." She reached into her pocketbook and pulled out her cell phone. "Let me get a picture of you to send—"

Lily slapped Sandra.

Sandra gasped and staggered back. The phone fell out of her hand and slid across the floor over to where the grungy man stood watching them.

Lily wiped her eyes, straightened her back, turned, and walked back inside the chapel.

Chapter 14

Labor

Violet

"I want to thank all of you for coming out tonight," Mama said, smiling from the podium. "I appreciate the love and support you've shown me and my family. In Philippians 1:21 we find comfort in these words of the apostle, *For to me to live is Christ, and to die is gain.* My sista has gone on from labor to reward. There may be crying and weeping down here, but there will be no tears in glory! Hallelujah!"

"Yes! Yes!" several folks shouted.

"Reverend Cherry, would you please come up and make a few closing remarks, and sing 'No Tears in Heaven' for us? It was one of my sista's favorite songs."

"Be glad to," Reverend Cherry said, rising to his feet.

From where she sat on the second row behind us, Niecee started sniffling.

"Help her, Lord," I heard Miss Emma say.

"Please, Lord," I prayed. "Help us all."

"It is appointed unto men once to die," Reverend Cherry said, after making his way to the podium, "but after this the judgment."

"Say so, preacha!" Deacon Humphrey said.

"We are gathered this evening," Reverend Cherry said, smiling, "to remember before God our dear sister Caroline. To give thanks for her life."

"Oh, God! God, why did you have to take her? Why, Lord, why?" Niecee cried. Her outburst caused Jasmine to start crying again.

"Blessed are they who mourn," Reverend Cherry said somberly. "Sister Peony, Violet, Lily, Ivy, Jasmine, it's always too soon to lose someone you love, but be assured that you will see Sister Caroline again," he said, smiling at us.

"Yes, Lord!" Mama cried. "Thank you, thank you, Lord!" she shouted, waving her hands.

"It would be impossible to describe"—Reverend Cherry clapped his hands—"seventy-nine years of living in two hours."

"Amen," Lily said.

"We can look around and see by the number gathered," Reverend Cherry said, looking around, "that Sister Caroline meant a great deal to a great number. She loved the Lord, and she loved to serve others."

"Yes, she did!" Miss Odessa shouted.

"We find in Psalm 116:15 the following words: 'Precious in the sight of the Lord is the death of his saints.'"

"Amen! Amen!" several people shouted.

"There will be no tears in hea-ven," Reverend Cherry sang, clapping his hands. "No cry-ing in glo-ry. All God's child-ren will be happy, won't you seeee!"

Mama, my sisters, and I stood and sang the spiritual along with Reverend Cherry while Niecee wailed in the background.

I was standing in the vestibule after the wake, holding the red rose Willie, my homeless friend, gave me, and my breath. Willie was reeking as usual. When Warren walked up to us, Willie said, "Good-bye" and abruptly left. I exhaled and teased Warren about scaring off my boyfriend. He didn't find my joke funny and warned me for the umpteenth time about being overfriendly with Willie. He said Willie gave him "the willies."

Up until a month ago, without fail, Willie came into the library where I worked *every* day and hung out for hours. He always brought me a red rose or a bouquet of wildflowers. After repeated patron complaints of him smelling so badly, his visits tapered off. The days he didn't come into the library, he made a point of walking by, looking in, and waving at me.

From where I stood in the vestibule talking to Warren and saying good-bye to folks, I watched Niecee and Jasmine gather at Aunt Caroline's casket. Mama was a few feet away talking to Miss Emma and Miss Odessa. "We need to get the two of them out of there," I said to Ivy when she walked up to Warren and me.

"You're right," she said. "Where's Lily?"

I motioned with my head over in the direction of the mortician's office where Lily was talking, civilly, I hoped, to Mr. Fowler.

"It's probably time we all left," Ivy said, walking off.

I resumed my conversation with Warren and had

turned to thank a member of my book club for coming out, when I heard a scream.

"Niecee!" Ivy screamed, running past me.

I looked back into the sanctuary and saw Niecee down on her knees in front of Aunt Caroline's casket. She was grimacing and holding her stomach. Warren and I took off behind Ivy.

"I think your granddaughter's in labor, Peony," I heard Miss Odessa said.

"Lord, have mercy!" Miss Emma exclaimed.

"What's going on?" Lily asked, running up to us.

"Niecee's in labor," Mama said.

"Lord, have mercy!" Miss Emma exclaimed again.

"Get her up and out to the car!" Lily shouted.

"No!" Jasmine yelled back. "Don't move her!"

"She can't have the baby *here*!" Lily shouted back.

"I'm calling the paramedics," Warren said, flipping open his Nextel.

"Maybe she'll get her tubes tied while she's in the hospital," Ivy said with a chuckle.

"I hope so," Lily said, kicking off her pumps.

Mama, my sisters, and I were back at home seated in the living room. Lily and Russell's twenty-four-year-old daughter, Sabrina, was across the street at Aunt Caroline's house watching the children. Floyd and Floyd Jr. were at the hospital with Niecee.

"Okay. I'll let them know. Bye," Ivy said, ending her call to Floyd Jr. "Niecee hasn't had the baby yet," Ivy said to us. "Her contractions are five minutes apart."

"Whew!" Mama said. "It won't be much longer now."

It was approaching ten thirty. Mama was sitting on the sofa between Ivy and Jasmine. I was seated on the love seat and Lily was sitting across from me in a Queen Anne chair, fuming. "How many more tattoos are you planning to get?" she asked, glaring at Jasmine.

"I don't *know*," Jasmine replied with an eye roll.

Mama looked over at Jasmine. "Baby, please don't get any more."

Jasmine sighed. "I'm not, Mama. I promise."

In addition to the black cross tattooed on the back of Jasmine's neck, "Jazz" and a butterfly were tattooed on her left arm above her elbow, and her latest, a panther—she was a die-hard Carolina Panthers Fan— was tattooed on her right leg.

"That's what you told me the last time," Mama said, "after you got that cross painted on the back of your neck. I don't think nothing of you marking up your body like that, Jasmine."

"I'm not getting any more, Mama. I'm *serious*," Jasmine said, smiling. She had the voice and smile that could melt a block of ice.

"You look ridiculous!" Lily yelled.

"And that's your opinion," Jasmine countered.

"You use that money Lorenzo sends you to pay for stuff like that?" Lily asked.

"And what business is it of yours what I do with the money Lorenzo sends me?"

Lily laughed and folded her arms across her chest. "Maybe *Elroy* paid for that."

Jasmine rolled her eyes at Lily.

"I know you ain't rolling your eyes at me!" Lily yelled, sounding like a fourth grader ready to do battle with a peer.

"Don't start," I said, looking at Lily.

"Mama, why don't you go on to bed?" Ivy suggested.

"I'm gone sit up with y'all a little while longer," Mama said.

"Aren't you tired?" Ivy asked.

Mama shook her head. "I'm all right. Jasmine, what the girls wearing to the service tomorrow?"

"Something decent, I hope," Lily muttered.

"That top and short skirt Shaunda had on won't 'propriate for no wake. And you know that," Mama said.

"She's a growing girl, Mama," Jasmine said. "All them dresses y'all sent her are too little now."

"What about that dress me and Caroline got her for Easter?"

Jasmine sighed. "She said she didn't like it."

Lily scoffed. "I'm sure she didn't. She'd rather walk around looking like a *hoochie*, like her mother."

"She ain't wearing no hoochie mess to the grave-side service!" I said.

"If she doesn't have anything *decent* to wear, let me know," Mama said. "'Cause Wal-Mart is still open and Violet and Ivy can run up there and get something."

Jasmine looked at me. That look told me that Ivy and I would be making a trip to Wal-Mart.

"What kinda work does Elroy do?" Mama asked.

Lily scoffed. "Mama, isn't it obvious?"

"I'm not talking to you, Lily. Now hush! What he do for a living, Jasmine?" Mama asked. "He ain't no street pharmacist, is he?"

"Bingo!" Lily yelled, clapping her hands.

"Lily, stop!" Ivy said.

"Please stop!" I said. "Why don't you go across the street and help Sabrina with the kids?"

"Why don't you go?" Lily retorted in a mocking tone.

Lily was in rare form. And I was more convinced

than ever that grief over Aunt Caroline wasn't the reason for her foul disposition.

Lily stood up. "Lil' sister, you've done some dumb things in your life. But this has got to be the dumbest!"

"Sit down, Lily, and be quiet!" Mama yelled.

"I can't believe you brought a drug dealer to Mama's house!" Lily yelled.

"Mani—Elroy ain't no drug dealer!" Jasmine yelled back. "And why don't you sit down and be quiet like Mama told you!"

"You don't tell me what to do!" Lily yelled.

"Sit down and be quiet, Lily!" Mama yelled.

"I just don't understand you, Jasmine," Lily said, shaking her head. "I just don't understand you."

Here we go! I thought to myself. I knew it would only be a matter of time before Lily lit into Jasmine.

"You irresponsible, foolish, lazy girl!" Lily shouted. "It's not enough that you've made your home in the projects, now you dating a *drug dealer*!"

"You don't know what you're talkin' 'bout!" Jasmine yelled.

"Oh, *really*?" Lily said, smirking. "I know more than you think."

"Lily," Ivy said, "now is not the time."

"Mama, I mean it," Lily said, looking at Mama. "When she calls saying she needs money to turn her phone back on or keep her lights from being turned off, don't send her any money."

I swallowed hard and looked over at Mama. She cut her eyes at me, then looked down.

"And you!" Lily yelled, pointing at Jasmine. "You— you," Lily scoffed, and shook her head, "I have no more words. You're a piece of work!"

Jasmine smiled. "That's what all the fel-las tell me," she said with a wink and a finger snap.

Lily gasped. "I—I got to get out of here!" she said, sticking her feet in her shoes.

"Where're you going?" Mama asked, looking up.

"Up the street. I'll go to Wal-Mart. What size dress does Rashaunda wear?"

"Ten junior," Jasmine replied.

"And get her a bra," Mama said.

Lily stormed out of the house and within minutes we heard her Mercedes squeal out the driveway and speed down the street.

"What's wrong with her?" Jasmine asked, turning up her nose.

Ivy and I just looked at each other.

"Mama, you all right?" I asked. Mama was lying on her bed. Her eyes were closed, but I could tell she wasn't asleep.

"I'm fine. I sho' hope it don't rain tomorrow," she said, sighing.

"Me too," I said. "Reverend Cherry called to see how we were. He said he was going over to the hospital to check on Niecee." Floyd Jr. had called a few minutes before midnight to tell us Mama had another great-grandson.

"That's so nice of him," Mama said, smiling.

"Yeah," I said, smiling back.

"Violet."

"Yes."

"I'm worried about Ivy."

"Why?"

"She's popping pills."

"It's just a muscle relaxer for the back pain she has sometimes, Mama."

Mama moaned. "She ain't addicted to that, is she?"

"No, ma'am."

"You know that can happen to folks."

"That's not the case with Ivy, Mama."

"She said much to you about that McWilliams girl?"

"Not a whole lot."

"I hope she don't let it get the best of her."

"I don't think it will."

"And what's wrong with Lily? She's wound up about something. Is she back?"

"No, ma'am."

Lily had called thirty minutes ago to say she was driving back to Raleigh, to Sabrina's apartment to get Rashaunda something out of Sabrina's closet.

"What possessed her to drive all the way back to Raleigh?" Mama asked, sighing.

"Beats me, Mama."

"Rashaunda could have worn something outta Wal-Mart."

"You right."

"Are she and Russell having problems?"

"Not that I know of."

Mama looked over at the clock, sighed, and closed her eyes.

"Who were you talking to?"

"Nobody," I heard Russell clearly say from the next room.

My eyes popped open. I looked over at the clock; it was 1:41. I nudged Ivy. "Wake up! Lily's back!"

"Don't lie to me! You were talking to somebody!" I heard Lily scream from the next bedroom.

"Lily, go to bed," Russell said.

I then heard a loud smacking sound, followed by a bump against the wall. Ivy and I gasped and grabbed each other.

"Oh, so you gone talk to that lil' ho' in my mama's house!"

"Oh, my goodness!" Ivy shrieked.

"Be quiet," I whispered, "before they hear us!"

Ivy and I heard another smacking sound from next door and then Lily growl, "Give me that cell phone!"

"Go to bed, Lily!" Russell said.

"And she had the nerve to come to my aunt's wake!"

Ivy jumped out of bed and sprinted over to the adjoining wall so she wouldn't miss hearing anything, I guessed. I didn't see how she thought she would; Lily was talking so loud, I feared she would wake up Mama.

"Here! Take the phone and see for yourself. I was calling you to see where you were," Russell said.

For a few seconds, no one next door said anything.

"You need to get a hold of yourself," Russell finally said. "Like I told you yesterday, there is nothing, nor has there *ever* been, anything between Sandra and me."

"Awwwww!" I screamed into my pillow. Ivy turned and ran back to the bed.

"Don't lie to me!" Lily screamed.

"Lily, go to bed before you wake everybody up!"

"Tell me, Russell. She came on to you, didn't she?"

"Honey, please!"

"Did you call her honey too?"

"I'm going to bed. And I suggest you do the same and get any notion out of your head that Sandra and I are having an affair."

"Sandra Harris is my least worry now. I don't plan to *ever* lay eyes on her again."

That was the last thing Ivy and I heard Lily say until five hours later, when she woke us up ordering us downstairs to help fix breakfast.

Chapter 15

Kicking and Screaming

Violet

"I overheard Miss Emma and Miss Odessa talking about us at the funeral home last night," Jasmine said.

Everybody in the kitchen froze. We all stopped what we were doing and looked at Jasmine.

"What they say?" Lily asked, scowling.

Jasmine placed a second pan of biscuits in the oven and looked back at the door. Mama was in the dining room setting the table for breakfast.

"Miss Odessa said it was a shame," Jasmine said softly, "*all* that money was spent on something going in the ground. Then Miss Emma asked, 'How much you think that casket cost?' Miss Odessa said, 'Emma, I don't know, but I'm sure it won't cheap! You know Peony and her daughters love to throw 'way money.'"

"I wish I had heard them!" Lily muttered.

"That won't all," Jasmine said.

"What else they say?" Ivy asked.

"Miss Emma said, 'You'd think, listening to the way folks carryin' on about Ca'line, she was the good Lord's mother!'"

"No, she *didn't*?" Ivy growled.

Jasmine smacked her lips. "Yes, she *did*. Then somebody walked up and they started talking about something else."

Lily grunted and shook her head.

"Y'all see her and Miss Odessa sitting across from us looking self-righteous?" Ivy asked.

"Uh-huh," I said.

"I saw Miss Emma dabbing at her eyes one time," Jasmine said. "Old phony!"

"Truth be told," Lily said, "none of the Harrises have ever cared for us. Y'all know how Evangeline and them acted toward us when we were in school."

"They felt then, and I guess they still do," Ivy said, adding butter to a pot of grits boiling on the stove, "that we think we're better than them."

"And we are!" Lily said, walking over to the stainless steel refrigerator. She opened it, took out a dozen eggs, and slammed the door shut.

"Lord, please help Lily," I prayed softly. So far this morning, she hadn't said one cross thing to anyone. Ivy and I had promised each other that we wouldn't say a word to anyone about what we had heard earlier this morning. I still didn't want to believe Russell was cheating on her, and with, of all people, one of them infamous Harris women.

"So, how're things going between you and the *detective*?" Jasmine asked, grinning at me. "He's cute!"

I laughed. "Yes, he is!"

Lily and Ivy laughed.

"We're not officially dating," I said. "Warren's still *married*. His divorce won't be final until next month."

"Is his wife contesting the divorce?" Ivy asked.

I shook my head. "No."

"That's good," Lily said. "You don't need to be looking over your shoulders for some bitter ex-wife."

"Ain't that the truth!" Jasmine said.

"But we do spend *some* time together," I said, smiling. "Y'all got to keep that hush-hush, because Mama would be upset if she knew."

"Girl, we ain't gone say nothing!" Jasmine said.

"The less Mama knows about *some* things, the better off she is," Ivy said.

"Amen!" Jasmine said.

"Shhhhh!" Mama yelled, hurrying into the kitchen. She ran over to the radio and turned up the volume.

"Today at one p.m., the body of Miss Caroline Rosetta Johnson will be laid to rest," the female radio personality said. "Graveside services will take place at Serenity Estates, Reverend Nehemiah Cherry will be officiating the service. Sister Caroline was a faithful supporter and listener of Geraldine's Gospel Hour. In honor of her, I will play a favorite of hers, 'He's Calling Me' by Dorothy Love Coates. Because one day, my dear friends, God's gonna call those of us who have professed Jesus Christ as our Lord and Savior from labor to life eternally."

"Yes! Yes!" Mama shouted as tears streamed down her face. This set off a tearful chain reaction in the kitchen.

* * *

"Any more cheese eggs?" Floyd asked.

Lily got up from the dining room table, went into the kitchen, and returned with a bowl of cheese eggs.

"Lily," Floyd said, smacking, "I don't know when I last had a big breakfast like this. Everything," he said, looking around the table, "was just delicious. Jasmine, girl, I didn't know you knew how to cook biscuits like this!"

Jasmine looked at Mama and smiled.

One thing Mama made sure we all learned how to do, and do well, was cook. We grew up with a fondness for cooking, and having been named after plants and flowers, with a fondness for gardening also.

"Everything is just delicious!" Floyd said, reaching for another one of Jasmine's homemade biscuits.

"Niecee still crying and carrying on?" Mama asked.

Floyd nodded.

"I thought the doctor had given her something," Mama said.

"They can't give her much, Mama," Jasmine said, "on account of her hypertension."

"She needs to get her tubes tied while she's in the hospital," Lily said.

Jasmine gave Lily a disapproving look.

"Floyd, you need to talk to her about that," Lily said.

"She and the baby could be discharged from the hospital tomorrow," Floyd announced. "So I was wondering," he said, looking around the table at us, "if she could stay here until the end of the week. I'll come back and get her and the boys this weekend."

"That'll be fine," Mama said, smiling.

Floyd exhaled. "Thank you! Thank you, Miss Peony! Me and Daisy sho' 'preciate this."

"Does she know who this child's father is?" Mama asked, leaning forward in her seat, looking at Floyd.

Floyd nodded.

"Whew!" Mama exclaimed, throwing up her hands. "So we don't have to worry about her being on TV making a fool out of herself again?"

"Nooo, ma'am!" Floyd said, shaking his head.

"Praise the Lord!" Mama shouted.

Two years ago, Niecee had appeared on *Maury* in an effort to prove the paternity of her oldest child. Needless to say, everyone in the family, everyone except Jasmine of course, was horrified.

"Rashaunda wants to go with me to the hospital, Jasmine," Floyd said.

"Rashaunda ain't going nowhere, but in that kitchen to help Sabrina wash those dishes," Lily said.

"I can't go, Mama?" Rashaunda asked, looking at Jasmine.

Jasmine shook her head. "You gotta help Sabrina clean the kitchen. Then I need to do your hair. We'll go to the hospital later. After church, okay?"

Rashaunda smiled and nodded.

Mama stood up and pushed her chair under the table. "Jasmine, you tell your friend to go on back to Charlotte, you and the girls gone stay here."

"Huh?" Rashaunda whined.

"What?" Jasmine asked, wide-eyed.

"Uh-huh," Mama said.

"Mama, we can't stay! The girls have three more days of school!" Jasmine cried.

"Calm down, daughter!" Mama said. "Violet and Ivy will take y'all back tomorrow."

Jasmine gasped. "Tomorrow?"

"Yes," Mama replied. "Tomorrow. Tomorrow's Memorial Day. Do Kenya and Rashaunda have school tomorrow?"

"Noooo," Jasmine said, pouting.

"Okay, then," Mama said, exiting the dining room.

"But we're invited to a cookout!" Jasmine called out after Mama.

Mama didn't bother to turn around or comment.

Rashaunda stuck out her bottom lip and stomped out of the dining room.

"Stop that stomping!" Lily yelled.

"Warren! My niece is missing!" I yelled into the phone. "The police won't help us. They say she has to be missing for twenty-four hours before they issue a missing person's report!"

"Honey, calm down. How long has she been missing?"

"About an hour! I think she's run away!"

"What?"

"Yes!" I screamed. "She's mad because she's not going back to Charlotte today! Please help us, Warren."

"Give me a description of her, and what she's wearing," Warren asked calmly.

"She's five five, about 105 pounds. Brown-skinned, with a headful of dark brown and burgundy weave. She has on blue jeans, and is wearing a white T-shirt that has a picture of Beyoncé on the front."

"You last saw her an hour ago?"

"Yes!"

"You think she's hitchhiking her way back to Charlotte?"

"Yes! Allen, Russell, and Floyd Jr. are combing the highways. So far, no sign of her."

"Where's Jasmine's boyfriend?"

"On his way back to Charlotte."

"How long has he been gone?"

"Over an hour now. But she's not with him. Jasmine saw him off and she's called him since he's left. He hasn't seen Rashaunda."

"What kind of car does he drive?"

"She's not in his car, Warren!"

"What kind of car is it, honey?"

"A black Chevy Impala, with tinted windows, big tires, and shiny expensive-looking rims."

"What next, sweet Jesus, what next?" I heard Lily cry out from the front porch.

"Warren, the limos will be here to pick us up at twelve thirty!" I cried.

"We'll find her," Warren assured me.

I hung up the phone and went outside. It was 11:23.

"How could you not know she was missing?" Ivy yelled at Jasmine.

"I thought she was across the street with the other kids!" Jasmine yelled back.

Kenya, already dressed for the graveside service, had her arms around Jasmine's waist. She was sobbing and praying that we find her big sister.

We were all so thankful that Maniac hadn't gotten far. He was sixty-five miles outside McKinley when the highway patrol pulled him over. Unbeknownst to him, Rashaunda was in the trunk of the car, fast asleep. When Warren drove up in front of Mama's house, we were all outside in the yard. So were Mr. Fowler's limo drivers. It was 12:50. Rashaunda was slumped down in the backseat of the Denali. Jasmine ran out of the yard up to the SUV. "Girl, get your butt outta there!" she yelled.

Rashaunda didn't budge.

"C'mon, Rashaunda!" Jasmine yelled, reaching into the SUV for her weeping, pouting daughter. "I'm not playing with you!"

"No!" Rashaunda yelled, kicking at Jasmine.

"You'd better not kick me!" Jasmine yelled, grabbing Rashaunda by her feet.

Miss Sadie and several of the neighbors were out in their yards. I heard someone say, "My Lord."

Unable to get twitching, kicking, crying Rashaunda out of the Denali, Ivy ran out of the yard to help. "Come on, Rashaunda," she pleaded.

Rashaunda didn't budge.

I heard Miss Sadie say, "Lord! Have mercy."

"She won't get out?" Mama asked from where she and I stood on the porch. "A disobedient child with a heart full of foolishness! Let her sit there, leave her 'lone! I got sump'n that'll get her out." Mama turned to go into the house.

If anyone standing in the yard had blinked, they would have missed what happened next. With the speed of Jackie Joyner Kersee, Rashaunda jumped out of the Denali and beat Mama into the house.

Chapter 16

Ellis Coltrane

"Rashaunda, go on back and finish eating. I'm all right."

"You sure, Aunt Ivy?"

Ivy smiled and nodded. When Rashaunda exited the bathroom, Ivy finished cleaning her face. She wasn't hungry, despite the church hospitality committee outdoing themselves making sure she and her family and the large number in attendance had plenty to eat. There was plenty of food at the repast, and from what Ivy heard, it was good.

Ivy felt herself grow sad at the thought that her aunt Caroline would never, ever walk into Charity Chapel again. She took a deep breath to steel herself and ward off the tears threatening to fill her eyes. A jolt of pain ripped through her back. Ivy groaned out loud and fell up against the bathroom counter. When the pain subsided, she reached into her black Chanel purse and pulled out her leather pill case. The victim of a rear-end collision three years ago, she relied on muscle relaxers and Percocet to rid her of the excruciating back pain that would bring her to tears.

"Dreadful teenager!" Ivy spat out as she flipped open her pill case. A pimple-faced teen text-messaging her boyfriend was the cause of her pain, pain that she would likely endure for the rest of her life.

Next to the muscle relaxer in the pill case were two Percocets. Ivy reached in, grabbed one, popped it in her mouth, and turned her thoughts elsewhere. Ellis Coltrane, her college sweetheart, still looked just as good as he did when she first laid eyes on him twenty-four years ago at Fayetteville State University. She was a popular, pretty cheerleader and the freshman class queen; he was the tall, handsome junior class president, and one of the radio personalities at WFSS 91.9 FM, the university radio station. Ivy had loved Ellis madly then, and even now still harbored feelings for him.

The bathroom door opened and two of the church mothers walked in: Odessa Humphrey and Edna Yancey. "Oh, look at you! Just look at you!" Miss Odessa cried, throwing her arms around Ivy. "Still just as pretty as you can be."

"Hello, Miss Odessa, Miss Edna," Ivy said, forcing herself to smile as painful spasms ripped up and down her back.

"How you holdin' up, baby?" Miss Odessa asked with creased brows.

"It's still a shock," Ivy said.

"Yes, it is," Miss Edna said, shaking her head.

"Time is a healer," Miss Odessa said, patting Ivy on the back. "You just keep trustin' and believin', the good Lord gone help you and your family get through this."

"Yes, ma'am."

"It was a beautiful service," Miss Edna said. "Just beautiful."

"Yes, it was," Miss Odessa said. "It was real nice, sump'n dif'rent." Her brows creased again. "I'd never been to a graveside service before."

"Me either," Miss Edna said. "Is that what Peony want too, Ivy? A graveside service instead of a church funeral?"

I just buried my aunt; does she really think I want to discuss burial plans for my mother? Ivy thought to herself.

"Huh, does she?" Miss Edna asked again.

No, she wants to be cremated and her ashes sprinkled around Charity Chapel, Ivy thought. She laughed to herself, thinking of the women's horrified reaction if she verbalized her thought.

"Ladies, I really need to get back and—"

"Sure, sure. You go right ahead, baby," Miss Odessa said, nodding. "You had any of my corn puddin'? I made it special just for y'all."

"No, ma'am, I haven't," Ivy said, making her way to the door.

"Make sure you get some, now, you hear?" Miss Odessa said.

Ivy nodded and exited the bathroom.

"Hel-lo," the big-bellied grinning man said, hurrying up to Ivy as she exited the bathroom.

Ivy nodded hello and shook the man's outstretched hand.

"I'm so sorry for your loss," the man said somberly.

"Thank you."

"My name is O-tis Reid," he said, smiling broadly. "I trust you and your family found the burial services to your satisfaction?"

"We did, thank you."

"Ivy?"

Ivy felt herself grow warm. It wasn't because the Percocet pill had kicked in; the euphoria coursing through her body was because of someone, not something. It was because of Ellis Coltrane. Surprisingly, in all these years, he still had the same effect on her. He could literally make her go weak in the knees. She turned and smiled. Ellis was looking past her at the big-bellied man. "Otis, how are you?" he said.

"Fine," Otis said, reaching out to shake Ellis's hand.

Ellis smiled and shook Otis's hand. "So, I see you've met my lovely ex."

Otis's eyes grew large and round.

"Ivy, you stay away from this man," Ellis said, laughing.

"Now, now, why you gone go and say something like that?" Otis said, laughing.

"You want me to answer that?" Ellis asked, laughing.

"Don't pay him any attention," Otis said to Ivy, with a wave of his hand.

Ivy smiled and wondered about the well-dressed man sporting a Jeri Curl, a *shag* at that.

"So, you were married to this beautiful woman?" Otis asked Ellis, while giving Ivy the once-over.

Ellis shook his head. "Regrettably, no. She's an ex-girlfriend. We were college sweethearts."

"Man, now, why did you let something this gorgeous get away from you?" Otis asked, shaking his head.

"I've asked myself that a million times," Ellis said, staring down into Ivy's face.

Ivy blushed and dabbed at her face with the tissue in her hand. Ellis was still, second to her father, the handsomest man she'd ever laid eyes on. Broad-shouldered, standing six three, the color of cocoa, he was gracious and soft-spoken with a mesmerizing smile. Time had been good to him—no bulging midsection and only a few springs of gray around the hairline.

"Mr. Reid! Mr. Reid! May I have a word?" an elderly woman yelled, hurrying over to where Otis, Ivy, and Ellis stood.

"Yes, ma'am, you may," Otis said to the lady. He looked back at Ivy and said, "It was a pleasure meeting you, and again, my condolences to you and your family."

Ivy smiled and nodded. "Thank you." When Otis walked off, she turned to Ellis. "Who was that?"

"An enterprising, *shrewd* businessman," Ellis replied with a chuckle.

Ivy popped her fingers. "Is that the man buying out many of the smaller morticians around here?"

Ellis nodded. "And I meant what I said, stay away from him. His track record with women is not good."

Ivy smiled. "I'm a big girl, I can take care of myself."

Ellis laughed. "That, I don't doubt."

"Aunt Ivy!" Rashaunda yelled, running over. "Grandma sent me to find out where you were."

"Tell her I'm talking to an old friend."

"Okay," Rashaunda said, smiling.

When Rashaunda walked off, Ellis threw his arms around Ivy and kissed her on the forehead. "Sorry about Miss Caroline," he said warmly.

"Thank you," Ivy said, relaxing in Ellis's arms. When Miss Odessa and Miss Edna exited the bathroom, Ivy pulled away and stood back. "So," she said, smiling up at Ellis, "you came for Aunt Caroline's service?"

"Yes," Ellis said.

"That was real nice of you. Thank you."

"It's good to see you, Ivy. How are you?"

Ivy sighed. "I'm taking one day at a time."

"I followed your death row case in the local paper and on the Internet. I admire your convictions and hard work."

"Thanks, Ellis. So, how've you been?"

"Good."

Ivy had last seen Ellis five years ago at the alumni ball of their alma mater. "The wife and kids okay?" she asked.

Ellis smiled. "The kids are fine."

"And Mrs. Coltrane?" Ivy asked, smiling. She remembered how Ellis's wife gave her the evil eye at the ball and stuck to him like glue.

Ellis sighed. "I'm divorced."

"Oh?"

Ellis nodded.

"Sorry to hear that."

"I've been a single man for three years now."

"Aunt Ivy!"

Ivy turned and looked back. Rashaunda was rushing out of the fellowship hall into the hallway over to where she and Ellis stood.

"What is it, Rashaunda?" she asked.

"Grandma wants you to come and eat something."

"Okay. Tell her I'm on my way."

Rashaunda took off back into the fellowship hall.

"You were saying?" Ivy said, gazing up at Ellis.

"My wife and I separated six months after I last saw you."

"Oh no!" Ivy moaned.

Ellis nodded. "We knew two years before the divorce that we were heading in that direction. We only stayed together for the sake of our youngest, who by the way"—Ellis smiled—"starts college in the fall."

"Sorry to hear things didn't work out for the two of you."

"Thanks," Ellis said, smiling. "But life goes on."

"Was it a contentious, bitter divorce?" Ivy asked.

Ellis pursed his lips together and sighed.

"Sorry," Ivy said.

"I'm hoping and praying," Ellis said with a sigh, "that my ex will one day be able to have a civil conversation with me."

Ivy nodded and smiled. "So, you've been single for three years now. Are you dating?"

Ellis shook his head.

"Seriously?"

Ellis nodded and smiled. "And who, may I ask, is the lucky guy?"

Ivy's brows creased together. "Huh? Oh!" She looked down at her sparkling engagement ring, then back up at Ellis. "His name is Allen."

"I hear he's a judge?"

Ivy nodded.

"And when is the wedding?" Ellis asked.

"Next Saturday."

"Wow!" Ellis exclaimed, opening his eyes wide. "Ivy Shaw is *finally* getting married."

"Yeah," Ivy said, smiling weakly and swallowing with some difficulty.

Ellis leaned forward and hugged Ivy again. "I wish you the best, sweetheart."

"Thank you," Ivy mumbled.

Ellis pulled back, smiled, and stared into Ivy's eyes. "How long will you be home?"

"A week, maybe longer."

"I'm moving here."

Ivy's eyes grew large and round. "To *McKinley*?" she asked, not believing she had heard Ellis correctly.

Ellis nodded. "Yeah."

"You're not!" Ivy laughed and shook her head.

Ellis smiled. "I am."

"Ellis?"

"Yes?"

"Are you pulling my leg?"

Ellis laughed and shook his head.

Ivy laughed. "When?"

Ellis laughed. "Soon."

Ivy's brows creased together.

"Do you not recall how often I said when we dated that when I retired, I wanted to move back home?"

"Yeah, but you're from Hayesfield, not McKinley! And you're still working, right?"

Ellis shook his head. "The software company that I've worked at for the last twenty-three years has been purchased by Microsoft. As a senior manager, I have the option of staying on and relocating from Boston to Seattle, or leaving with a fairly nice severance package. I've decided to do the latter—retire early. The severance package the company's giving me, along with the profits I've made and continue to make from several investments, will allow me to live quite comfortably here."

"Wow!" Ivy exclaimed.

Ellis smiled. "And yes, McKinley is not *my* home, but Hayesfield is only twenty minutes away."

"I—I don't know what to say," Ivy said.

Ellis smiled. "Say, I wish you the best."

"Huh?"

"I'm leasing some retail space in that strip mall under construction in town."

Ivy's eye grew large and round again. "Really?"

"For McKinley's first Subway and its second dry cleaners."

Ivy smiled and shook her head. "You sound like an enterprising businessman, Mr. Coltrane."

Ellis smiled. "Only thing."

"What?"

"The plan was that *we*, Ivy and Ellis Coltrane, would move here and settle down as husband and wife."

"I remember," Ivy said, looking away.

Ellis traced his right index finger slowly down the side of Ivy's face. "You are still the prettiest girl I know, and after all these years, I'm still in love with you."

Ivy looked back at Ellis and smiled. Ellis was *single*, moving to McKinley, and still carrying a torch for her!

"I'm having a house built just outside town. It should be finished by Labor Day."

"Wow!" Ivy exclaimed for the second time.

"Ivy!"

Ivy flinched and looked back. "Allen! Honey, come meet an old friend of mine from college."

Allen walked up to Ivy and placed his arm around her waist.

"Allen, this is Ellis Coltrane," Ivy said, making introductions. "And, Ellis, this is my fiancé, Allen Hayes."

"Pleased to meet you," Ellis said, smiling and extending his hand.

Allen returned the smile and shook Ellis's hand.

"Ivy tells me you're a judge," Ellis said to Allen.

"Yes, I am," Allen said with a nod.

"And she told me you two are getting married next Saturday."

Allen nodded again, smiled broadly, and kissed Ivy on the top of her head.

"Congratulations to you," Ellis said to Allen. "You are marrying a *wonderful* woman."

"Yes, I am," Allen said, smiling down at Ivy.

"Well"—Ellis clasped his hands together—"I just wanted to say hi and let you know my prayers are with you and your family, Ivy. You take care." He leaned forward and gave Ivy a parting embrace.

Ivy smiled. "Thanks again for coming, Ellis."

Ellis nodded, smiled at Ivy and Allen, then walked off.

"I sense that you and Mr. Coltrane were more than college friends," Allen said, watching Ellis walk off.

"We were," Ivy replied.

"So, what happened?"

"Our professional ambitions got in the way."

Chapter 17

Bad News

Violet

After seeing Allen, Lily's family, and Daisy's husband and son off, Mama told my sisters and me that there were a number of things she wanted to tackle first thing Monday. For starters, she wanted to go through Aunt Caroline's closet and pull out some things to give Aunt Louise, Miss Sadie, and some of the women at the church. I was glad to hear Ivy and Lily say they would be home for as long as Mama needed them to be.

Per Aunt Caroline's will, her house along with all of its possessions was Mama's to do with as she pleased. Daisy was given the house, and to Jasmine's and her girls' delight, Mama gave Jasmine, with my consent, Aunt Caroline's car: a silver PT Cruiser. I had bought the car for Aunt Caroline three years ago. I was dating

a man during that time who was part owner of a
Chrysler dealership in Charlotte. "Now you have a way
home, and a way to get around and look for a job,"
Mama said to Jasmine.

After Mama finished laying out plans for the week,
we hit the sack. An hour later, I got up to lower the
bedroom window and overhead Lily and Mama talking next door. Ivy had finally fallen off to sleep and
was no longer, thank goodness, passing gas. She'd
been flatulent all evening. Mama said it was on account of all that corn pudding of Miss Odessa's she
ate at the repast. I leaned up against the adjoining
wall and listened in on Mama and Lily's conversation.

"Russell and I are okay, Mama," Lily said, chuckling.
"So stop worrying."

"You sure?" Mama asked.

Lily laughed again. "Yesss, Mama."

"Russell, he—"

"Russell say something to you?" Lily asked loudly,
interrupting Mama.

"Noooo," Mama said slowly. "You just seem a little
uptight, and he wasn't his usual jolly self."

Lily sighed heavily and laughed again. "Russell and
I are *fine*."

"Are the kids okay?" Mama asked.

"Yes," Lily replied.

"If there was something wrong, you'd tell me,
right?"

"Yes, Mama, I would. Now go to bed. It's almost one
o'clock, and we got a busy day ahead of us."

"Okay," Mama said, sighing heavily. "Good night."

"Good night, Mama."

I listened as Mama made her way down the hallway

and then the stairs. Seconds later, I heard Lily crying softly next door.

I tiptoed to the bed, stumbling in the darkness. When I reached it, I knelt down and prayed for Lily.

Jasmine was backing out Aunt Caroline's driveway in the PT Cruiser with Rashaunda. They were heading to the hospital to pick up Niecee and her newborn: TreShawn. Niecee named her baby after his daddy, who according to Floyd Jr. was currently in jail on an attempted robbery charge. Kenya and Niecee's other sons were in the den watching TV with Mama. When Jasmine returned, she was packing up her new car, which she'd named "Caroline," and hitting the road for Charlotte.

I was in the backyard talking to Ivy about the bombshell she had dropped on me this morning before we went downstairs to breakfast. She was having second thoughts about marrying Allen.

"Ivy, explain to me why," I said.

Ivy sighed. "Professional differences."

"'Professional differences'?"

"Allen believes in capital punishment."

"Okay. So he believes in capital punishment. Is that enough to make you call off your *wedding*?" I asked.

Ivy didn't answer.

"Ivy?"

Ivy sighed and rolled her eyes.

"If I recall," I said, eyeing her sharply, "wasn't it *your* professional aspirations that kept you from marrying someone else, twenty years ago?"

Ivy exhaled and mumbled, "Yeah."

"Are you going to make that same mistake *again*?" I asked.

"I honestly don't think I can be married to a man who is a staunch supporter of something I'm against," Ivy asserted.

"Have you talked to Allen about this?"

"Yes! And we *always* end up arguing! I fought for Mia's life, Violet! With everything I had in me. Allen gave me *no* support, none whatsoever. I need my man, any man I marry, to support what I do."

"What would you have had him do, Ivy, if he supports the death penalty?"

Ivy sighed and shook her head.

"You can't *manipulate* him like you do jurors in a courtroom into seeing things your way."

"I know," Ivy said softly.

"This"—I shook my head and smiled—"doesn't warrant you calling off your wedding."

"I hear you," Ivy said, smiling weakly.

"So, no more talk about calling off this wedding, okay?"

The smile left Ivy's face and tears filled her eyes.

"Ivy, what is it?"

Ivy pressed her lips together and inhaled sharply.

"Ivy, what's going on?" I asked, placing a hand on her shoulder.

"Oh, Violet!" she cried. "I don't know what to do! I don't know what to do!"

Is she experiencing a case of premarital jitters? I wondered. I was taken aback by Ivy's display of emotion. And if this was a case of the jitters, it appeared to be a serious one.

"It's Beatrice!" Ivy spat out. "I don't think she likes me."

"Oh, come now, Ivy!"

"It's true, Violet! I don't think she feels I'm good enough for Allen. I can see it in her eyes and hear it in her voice."

"Other than the snide comment she made that you were "lucky" to get Allen, what else has she said?"

"One Saturday afternoon while at the Hayes's *mansion*, I walked up on her having a conversation with one of her snooty friends. Their backs were to me and I overheard Beatrice say, 'Our children don't always marry who we think is best.' When they looked back and saw me, they flinched and Beatrice covered her mouth with her hand."

"Oh my," I said.

"Her derisive comments not only *hurt*, Violet! They infuriate me!"

"Have you talked to Allen about this?" I asked.

"I've tried," Ivy said tearfully. "And both times he's made light of the situation. He tells me I'm making much ado about nothing."

"Are you?" I asked. "Maybe Beatrice is like most mothers when it comes to their sons," I said, laughing. "They don't believe *any* woman is good enough for them."

Ivy rolled her eyes.

"I don't mean to make light of the situation either," I said. "Maybe you should have a talk with Beatrice."

"No!" Ivy cried.

"Well, talk to Allen again."

"He *loves* his mother, Violet."

"And he loves you *too*. Please don't call off your wedding before talking to him."

"The closer the wedding comes, the more I see I can't go through with it. I just can't."

"You need to talk to Allen, Ivy."

Ivy shook her head.

"Yes, you, do! Talk to him!"

"It won't do any good."

"You don't know that!"

Ivy sighed heavily and nodded. "It's too late now anyway."

"What do you mean?"

"I've accepted a position with the Justice Project."

"What's that?"

"It's a legal group committed to fair sentencing and the abolishment of the death penalty."

"You giving up your practice?"

"No. I'll sit on the southeast regional board of J P as a consultant."

I reached over and hugged Ivy. "Congratulations!" I pulled back and looked at Ivy. "So how does your accepting this position have any bearing on whether you marry Allen or not?"

"Allen and I were planning to start a family right after we got married. I'd agreed to cut back on my hours at the office. Now that I've accepted this position, I won't be able to do that. There are thirty-three cases in my office awaiting my attention."

"Ivy!"

Ivy lowered her eyes.

"Does Allen know about this new job?"

Ivy looked up at me and shook her head.

I shook my head at her. "Why would you accept this position without at least talking to him?"

"This is an opportunity of a lifetime, Violet!"

"But you did this without talking it over with a man you're scheduled to marry in less than two weeks!" I shrieked. "How selfish is that?"

Ivy looked off.

"That wasn't right, Ivy," I said. "And you know that."

"Okay, so it wasn't right!" she muttered.

"You need to talk to Allen. Talk to him, before calling things off. You owe him that much."

Ivy sighed and tears filled her eyes again.

"If he *really* knew how his mother was upsetting you, I believe he would have a talk with her."

"Then she'll hate me and make my life miserable. I don't want to be married to Allen and be miserable, Ivy."

"I know you don't," I said. "I had no idea all this was going on."

"I wanted to say something to you months ago, but then the fire happened—you lost your house, Jasmine got in trouble and Mia's execution date was approaching. So I didn't bother. Now here I stand"—Ivy threw up her hands—"twelve days away from getting married and I—" Ivy closed her eyes and moaned, "Oh God! What am I going to do?"

"Please don't make a hasty decision," I pleaded. "Allen's a *great* catch."

"Yeah, for somebody else maybe," Ivy said sadly.

"You haven't stopped loving him, have you?"

"No! He's the only other man I've loved since Ellis."

"Talk to him, then. Tell him how unhappy and miserable his mother makes you feel."

"Violet?" she said, looking at me through watery eyes.

"Yes."

"If I end up calling off this wedding, I'm going to need some support, *big time*."

"You know I'm here for you, sister."

"And while I figure out what to do, please don't say anything to anyone."

I placed an index finger up to my mouth. "Mum's the word."

Ivy and I had made our way around to the front of the house and were sitting on the front porch steps when a white Ford Taurus pulled into Mama's driveway. A young black lady got out and walked up to us. "Good morning," she said with a nod and a smile. "My name is Alisha Hughes." She flashed an official-looking badge, then asked, "Is Jasmine Shaw here?"

Ivy and I looked at each other, then back at the woman.

"I'm a social worker with the county's Child Protective Services unit," she said.

"Okay," I said, confused, wondering why a social worker wanted to see Jasmine, especially one from Child Protective Services.

"How can we help you, Miss Hughes?" Ivy asked.

"I'm looking for Jasmine Shaw. Are either of you ladies Jasmine Shaw?"

Ivy and I looked at each other again. "No," I finally said. "She's our sister. If I may ask, why do you need to see her?"

"Is Jasmine Shaw here?" Miss Hughes asked.

"Yes, but *why* do you need to see her?" I asked, again.

Miss Hughes cleared her throat. "I need to discuss that with her."

"Miss Hughes, I'm an attorney, the family attorney," Ivy said, standing up. "Please feel free to share the reason for your visit with me."

Miss Hughes sighed and pursed her lips together. "Well, you should know more than anyone that state law gives me the right to speak to your sister without having to explain why to anyone."

"I know, but—"

"I'm not at liberty," Miss Hughes said, interrupting Ivy, "to discuss with you why I need to talk to your sister."

Why is a CPS worker here to see Jasmine? I kept wondering. Then it dawned on me. "Are you here because of what happened yesterday?" I blurted out.

Miss Hughes's failure to answer me was my answer.

"Jasmine's not here right at the moment," Ivy said. "Is there a number? I could have her call you when she returns."

Miss Hughes smiled. "I can come back."

"No!" I yelled, standing up.

Miss Hughes flinched and looked at me questioningly.

"This is our mother's home," I said. "She just buried her sister. I—we don't want her to be upset any more than she already is. Rashaunda's attempt to run away surprised and upset all of us."

"I'm sorry for you and your family's loss," Miss Hughes said. "However, I have to speak to your sis—"

"I can bring Jasmine to your office," Ivy said hurriedly. "Please allow me to do that, please!"

Miss Hughes cleared her throat and then said, "The agency is closed for the holiday. However, I'm on call and working from the police station."

"We can meet you there, that's not a problem," Ivy said.

"I need to see Rashaunda as well," Miss Hughes said.

"I will bring her," Ivy said, bobbing her head.

"I should be back at the police station by three

o'clock. Just let the sergeant at the desk know that I'm expecting you."

"Okay," Ivy said, bobbing her head again.

"If you fail to show," Miss Hughes said, raising her eyebrows, "I will be back."

"We will be there," Ivy said. "I promise you."

Miss Hughes was backing out the driveway when Mama stuck her head out the front door and asked us who she was. Ivy told Mama she was somebody selling life insurance.

Ivy, Lily, and I were in Aunt Caroline's bedroom with Mama. Jasmine was across the street at Mama's with Niecee and the kids. They were having lunch. While Mama sat on Aunt Caroline's bed, Lily pulled dresses, suits, shoes, hats, and pocketbooks out of the closet. Mama was deciding on who she wanted to give Aunt Caroline's pink silk suit to when the doorbell rang.

"Coming in!" the neighborhood news reporter yelled.

"Come on in, Sadie. We're in the back!" Mama yelled.

"Peony, this is a sin-sick world we live in!" Miss Sadie exclaimed when she entered the bedroom. "So much *wickedness*, I've never seen in all my days!"

"Sadie, what's wrong?"

"Sin-sick world, I tell you!" Miss Sadie muttered, shaking her head.

"You can sit here, Miss Sadie," I said, offering Miss Sadie my seat.

"I guess y'all ain't heard?" Miss Sadie said, sitting down and looking around the room at us.

"Heard what?" Mama asked.

"They found one of Emma Harris's granddaughters

yesterday, beat half to death, over near where they building that Golden Corral," Miss Sadie stated.

"What?" Mama shrieked.

"Beat half to death!" Miss Sadie said, shaking her head. "They don't 'spect her to make it."

"What?" Mama shrieked again.

"Odessa said Emma called her late last night and told her. Told her it looked like somebody was tryin' to kill the girl."

"Lord, have mercy!" Mama cried.

"Say she's un-un-rec-reco-nizable." Miss Sadie struggled to get out the words.

"Lord, have mercy!" Mama cried again.

"I was wondering where they were yesterday," Miss Sadie said.

"Huh?" Mama asked, looking dazed.

"None of 'em was at the graveside service or repast," Miss Sadie said.

"It was so many folks at the cemetery and church, I can't say I missed seeing any of them," Mama said.

I don't see how Mama missed seeing, or hearing for that matter, Colette. She was president of the church's hospitality committee, and no feeding took place at the church unless she was there to supervise and bark out orders.

"They got the call, 'cording to Odessa, just before one o'clock yesterday afternoon," Miss Sadie said.

"Lord, have mercy!" Mama cried. "How's Emma doing?"

"She tore all to pieces. She, Colette, and Evangeline spent the night at the hospital."

We heard the front door open and close. Seconds later, Jasmine walked into the room.

"Sadie was just telling us the police found one of

Emma Harris's granddaughters badly beaten," Mama said to her.

"Oh my goodness!" Jasmine shrieked, plopping down on the bed.

"Poochie just can't keep going round town running her mouth, and—"

"It won't Poochie they found," Miss Sadie said, interrupting Mama. "It was the girl that live in Raleigh, that work with your daughter." Miss Sadie looked over at Lily and said, "Sandra."

I gasped out loud. I couldn't believe what I had just heard, and I don't think Ivy could either. Her mouth was ajar and her eyes were large and round. And what was most disturbing, Lily seemed not the least bit fazed by the dreadful news. She was steadily removing clothes from Aunt Caroline's closet, folding them and placing them on the bed next to Mama.

"That girl was some kinda pretty," Miss Sadie said, shaking her head. "The police thinkin'," she said, sighing, "it happened late Saturday night or early Sunday morning."

"Who could do such a thing?" Mama said, shaking her head. *"Who?"*

Chapter 18

The Harrises

Violet

I was trying to keep it together; it wasn't easy. Too much had happened in less than a week and I was coming unglued. Aunt Caroline's sudden death, Lily's personal dilemmas, the untimely arrival of Niecee's third child, Rashaunda's stunt prompting a visit from a CPS worker, Ivy contemplating calling off her platinum wedding, and now this. Per Miss Sadie, Sandra was lying on the third floor of McKinley General in intensive care, footsteps away from death's door. I was so distraught; if I were a drinking woman, I would have been sloppy drunk. My call to Warren went straight to his voice mailbox. "Warren, call me!" was the message I left him.

"Where is he?" Ivy asked, pacing the kitchen floor.

"Maybe he's at the crime scene!" I replied loudly.

"Will you lower your voice?" she yelled at me.

I took a deep breath. "Surely, Lily didn't, no! I'm not going to even think that!"

"You already have!" Ivy said.

"Ivy, you're a lawyer. You know better than anyone, nothing is always what it seems. This is all circumstantial! Right?" I asked, hoping Ivy would say yes.

Instead she said, "I've defended many women—professional, educated women like Lily—who lost it when they found out their husbands were cheating on them."

"I can't imagine her doing something like this," I said.

"I can't either!" Ivy cried.

"What if she *did*? What're we going to doooo?" I couldn't bear Jasmine being in jail a few hours; I surely didn't want Lily in prison for what could be the remainder of her life.

"We would do what we had to do to keep her from going," Ivy said earnestly.

My head started hurting and my heart started racing. "We could end up in prison too, if we knew she was guilty of this and didn't report it!"

"Violet, hush! Before we jump to any conclusions, we need to find out some things."

"Like what?" I asked.

"What time this—this crime occurred. Be sure to ask Warren that when you talk to him. You find out all you can from him," Ivy said, snatching up her keys off the kitchen counter. It was 2:43. She had to leave and take Jasmine and Rashaunda to the police station to see the Child Protective Services social worker.

"Where y'all going?" I heard Mama ask Ivy, Jasmine, and Rashaunda when they walked past her bedroom.

"To Wal-Mart," Ivy said, "to get some things for Niecee and the boys."

"Jasmine, you and the girls gone leave for Charlotte soon as you get back?"

"Yesss, ma'am!" Jasmine replied cheerfully.

"Where's Violet?" Mama asked.

"I'm here, Mama," I said, hurrying to her bedroom.

"I want you to take me to Emma's," she said when I stepped into her room.

Ivy gave me a frightful look as she ushered Jasmine and Rashaunda out of the house.

I broke out in a cold sweat. "To Miss Emma's? Sh-she's probably still at the hospital, Mama," I said.

Mama shook her head. "She's back home," she said, rummaging through her closet. "I'll be ready in ten minutes, soon as I change."

"Okay," I said, running a hand across my queasy stomach.

"I thought Lily would want to go, since Sandra worked for her, but"—Mama sighed heavily—"I guess she's too upset over it."

The house then became dreadfully quiet. Kenya went across the street to Aunt Caroline's to stay with Niecee and her boys, and Lily remained upstairs behind closed doors, where she'd been since we'd come back from Aunt Caroline's after hearing the news about Sandra. I went back to the kitchen and stared out the window.

My cell phone rang, startling me. Fumbling, I pulled it out of my pocket before it stopped ringing. It was Ivy calling.

"What?" I whispered into the phone.

"Keep your ears open while at Miss Emma's."

"Okay!" I said.

"Warren still hasn't called?"

"No!"

"I hope that girl pulls through," Ivy said, sighing.

"Even if she *lives*, someone's looking at attempted murder charges!" I shrieked.

"Will you calm down?" Ivy muttered.

I heard a beep and glanced at the display. My heart started racing again. "Ivy, it's Warren! I'll call you back." I took several deep breaths before connecting with him.

"Hey, Warren!"

"Hey, honey. What's up?"

"I just heard some *awful* news," I said.

"What?" he asked.

"That a woman by the name of Sandra Harris was found badly beaten outside town."

Warren sighed. "You know her?"

"No, not really. Is that true?" I asked, hoping he would say it wasn't.

Warren sighed again and cleared his throat. "Yes, it's true."

"Was someone trying to *kill* her?"

"It looks that way."

"Oh my goodness!" I moaned.

"She was brutally beaten."

I cringed. "Was she robbed?"

"We have no reason to believe it was a robbery attempt. Her purse and wallet were in the car, and there was money and credit cards inside the wallet. And she had on a very expensive watch. That wasn't taken either."

I heard a beep and glanced at the display; Ivy was calling. I placed the phone back to my ear.

"Was she *raped*?" I asked.

"No. No signs of a sexual assault. We do believe she may have been assaulted in town, and that her assailant drove her car outside town in an effort to conceal the crime."

My stomach muscles tightened. "Really?"

"Yep. Now, baby, you got to keep all this to yourself, this is strictly confidential information."

"I will, Warren. Any reason why someone would want her dead?"

Warren sighed. "So far, no."

My phone beeped again. I glanced back at the display screen. Ivy was still on the line. "Warren, could you hold on a sec?"

"Yes."

"What, Ivy?" I said when I clicked over.

"What Warren say?" she asked quickly.

I briefly filled Ivy in and reconnected with Warren. "Any fingerprints?" I asked.

"We're sending the car to Raleigh, to the state crime lab. All the forensic work will be done there."

A lump formed in my throat. I felt faint and slid down the kitchen wall to the floor.

"Baby," Warren sighed, "it's one of the worst crime scenes I've responded to in quite some time. Makes me wonder if there's some lunatic on the loose. You be careful when you go out."

"I will. I heard it happened Saturday night or early Sunday morning."

"Family members say they last saw her around eleven o'clock, so it was some time after that. She was heading back to Raleigh."

"I also heard she's unconscious."

"The doctors don't expect her to make it."

When Mama came into the kitchen to say she was

ready to go, I was sitting at the table in the breakfast nook with my head in my hands.

Miss Emma, five of her eleven children, and a countless number of grand- and great-grandchildren all lived in a single-wide, three-bedroom trailer a mile outside town, where Christmas lights hung around the trailer three hundred sixty-five days a year. Along with the broken-down, rusty vehicles in the front and back yards were cars, vans, and SUVs in running condition and an assortment of children toys. A sofa, two recliners, and several dinette chairs were outside on the makeshift front porch. Adults and teens were standing and sitting on the porch, while puppies and children of all ages ran around in the yard.

"Is that Warren's truck?" Mama asked.

My heart started racing. "Where?"

Mama pointed. "There."

I looked in the direction Mama was pointing and got sick to my stomach. "Yeah. Looks like it."

"You haven't started messing around with him, have you?"

"Mama, didn't you tell me not to date Warren until he was divorced?"

"I'm just checking, that's all. Besides, I shouldn't have had to tell you that. You know right from wrong."

I didn't say anything.

"Looks like Colette's home too," Mama said. "You behave."

"I don't bother Colette," I said, eyeing Colette's Chrysler Pacifica parked along the right side of the trailer.

"It's no secret you two aren't particularly fond of each other."

"I'm cordial to her."

"I've seen you walk right past Colette at church and not open your mouth."

"I've tried to be friendly to her, Mama. I've spoken to her many times, and she's looked me straight in my face and not opened her mouth."

"Two wrongs don't make a right."

"Why should I keep speaking to her when I know she's not going to speak back?"

Mama didn't respond.

"And I can't help it that Warren likes *me*, not her," I said, smiling.

"No, you can't," Mama agreed.

Despite the vehicles, people, and animals in Miss Emma's yard and driveway, I managed to find a parking spot.

"Hey, Miss Peony!" one of Miss Emma's snotty-nosed great-grandsons yelled, running over to my car.

"Hey, baby," Mama said, opening the car door. "Where your grandma?"

"In the house," he said, pointing and looking back.

I got out of the car and fell in behind Mama, while searching the yard for Warren. I didn't spot him. I assumed then that he was in the house talking to Miss Emma.

The inside of Miss Emma's trailer was just as junky as the outside. I'd been by her home many times; this was my first time ever inside it. Despite the clutter it didn't look unclean, nor did it smell bad inside, which was good to know, since she and her daughters cooked a lot of food for church functions.

"Hey, how—how y'all do-doin'?" Miss Emma's

stuttering son, Eddie Ray, nicknamed Nub on account of his having lost two fingers on his right hand in a lawn mower accident, asked when we walked in.

"We holdin' on," Mama said.

"Mu-Muma sho' ha-hated she had to mi-miss Miss Ca'line's fu'nul yesterday," Nub said.

"That's all right," Mama said, patting Nub on the back. "How's your mama holdin' up?"

Nub shook his head and sighed. "Sh-she ain't do-doin' too good, Miss Peony. None—none of us are."

"I'm so sorry," I said.

"Hey, Miss Peony. Hey, Violet," Perry, another one of Emma's sons, said walking into the living room.

Mama and I said, "Hello."

"We're so sorry to hear about what happened to your niece," Mama said to Perry.

"Thank you," he said, bobbing his head.

"Whoever done this better hope I don't get my hands on him!" Nub managed to say without stuttering.

Instinctively, I looked down at Nub's hand: the hand with the missing two fingers. "So y'all think it was a man?" I asked, looking back up at him.

"We don't really know who," Perry said. "We do know a married man was stalkin' her."

"Lord, have mercy!" Mama exclaimed.

"You—you know who?" I asked, swallowing with difficulty.

"Naw, Sandra never told us who he was," Perry said.

"My, my, my!" Mama said.

"She's the first one in this family to go off to college and make sump'n of herself, and now this happen to her," Perry muttered. "We all thinkin' she'd made it back to Raleigh, and she layin' 'side the road half dead."

"I'm so sorry," I said.

"We're praying for y'all," Mama said.

Perry smiled. "Y'all go on in the back," he said. "Mama's in her room. First room on the left."

I was looking and listening out for Warren as Mama and I navigated our way down the narrow, cluttered hallway to Miss Emma's bedroom.

Miss Odessa and the Reverend Clifford Bobbitt were sitting in the room with Miss Emma. "Y'all come on in," Miss Emma said. She was sitting up in a full-size bed dressed in a blue housedress. Her thin gray hair was rolled in small pink foam rollers. Lying on the bed next to her was a black, tattered Bible.

"Gu'ma!" A small child ran into the room up to Miss Emma's bed. "Can I git a Moon Pie?" he asked.

"Yeah!" Miss Emma snapped. "Now, don't come back in heah, botherin' me! I got company!"

The little boy ran out of the room smiling.

"Emma, I'm so sorry to hear 'bout your granddaughter," Mama said.

"Me too, Miss Emma," I said.

Miss Emma nodded and smiled weakly. "Thank y'all."

Miss Emma pointed to places for Mama and me to sit. Her four-post cherry bed and matching nightstand, dresser, and chest took up most of the space in the room. My eyes rested on a black-and-white eight-by-ten photo of a young, striking couple on the dresser. I could tell the woman was Miss Emma, and she was nothing but stunning. The man was dreamy.

Miss Emma saw me looking at the picture. "That's me and my chil'ren's daddy," she said, smiling.

I nodded and smiled back.

"He's been dead now close to ten years," Miss Emma said, her voice trailing off.

Colette, Evangeline, Nub, and their sisters and brothers couldn't help but be anything but good-looking; their daddy was fine as wine and their mama was a fox. Even at seventy-nine, Miss Emma was still a pretty woman. She looked like Lena Horne.

"And you still are beautiful, Mother Harris," Reverend Bobbitt said, grinning broadly. "Beautiful inside and out."

"Thank you, Reverend Bobbitt," Miss Emma said, smiling.

I was willing to bet money that Reverend Bobbitt hadn't left Miss Emma's side since first hearing of the attack on Sandra. He had been kissing up to the Harrises for eight months now in hopes of becoming the next pastor of the spiritually malnourished flock at Charity Chapel. It had come down to him and Reverend Cherry, and the church would be voting on the matter at our next business meeting. I was hoping and praying, like Mama, that enough of us would be able to vote Reverend Cherry in as our next pastor. We believed he was more qualified than Reverend Bobbitt to serve as our church administrator and spiritual leader.

"And that's Sandra's mother over there," Miss Emma said to me, pointing to a picture on the wall of an attractive, busty, caramel-complexioned woman wearing a low-cut, tight red dress.

"She died while Sandra was away in college," Miss Odessa said.

"Lord!" Miss Emma cried. "Please let my Sandra be aw'right! Don't take her away from me too, Lord!"

Tears filled my eyes.

"Mother, we gone believe God for a miracle," Reverend Bobbitt said, clasping his hands together. "He's still in the miracle-working business."

"Yes, he is!" Mama cried, throwing up her hands.

"Keep the faith, Mother! Keep the faith!" Reverend Bobbitt said.

"Amen!" Mama and Miss Odessa shouted.

I shouted "Amen" too.

"You need anything 'sides our prayers, Emma?" Mama asked.

Miss Emma shook her head: "Lord knows, I'd be 'preciative of anythang anybody offer, Peony. My docta done put me on bed rest. I can't do no cookin' or nothin', and I got a houseful of folks."

"I'll have some food brought over," Mama said. "And here"—Mama reached into her pocketbook and pulled out her wallet—"take this." She handed Miss Emma fifty dollars.

"Thank you, thank you!" Miss Emma cried. "The good Lord gone bless you, Peony."

"Mother Shaw, that's mighty nice of you," Reverend Bobbitt said. "Mighty nice! Charity Chapel got some wonderful members, wonderful members!"

"Odell sent some money over by his grandson," Miss Emma said, wiping her eyes.

"Is that Warren's truck outside?" I asked, knowing full well it was.

Mama cleared her throat and looked at me.

Miss Emma nodded. "Yeah. He down the hall talkin' to Colette. We're so glad he's handlin' the case. We think so much of Warren."

"How—"

Mama cut me off and told me to go call Lily and tell her to bring some food over. We still had plenty of food at the house from the donations people had brought over when Aunt Caroline died.

Upon exiting Miss Emma's cramped bedroom I

heard, "Warren, you gone find the person that tried to kill my niece?"

My blood started boiling. Warren, Colette, and a white female police officer were standing in the doorway of a room a few feet away from Miss Emma's bedroom.

"We're doing all we can," Warren said.

I nodded and told Colette how sorry I was to hear about her niece. She didn't say, "thank you," "cat," "dog" or anything. She dismissed me with a slight eye roll. Warren nodded and said hello to me.

"You will make sure there'll be twenty-fo'-hour police protection for her, won't you?" Colette asked, staring up in Warren's face.

"Yes," Warren said.

"You promise?" Colette asked, placing her head on Warren's chest.

"You have my word on that," Warren said.

"Oh, Warren! Who could do sump'n like this?" Colette cried. "Sandra didn't deserve this! She didn't bother nobody!"

Colette's tears flowed for what seemed forever. Warren patted her on the back and assured her that the police department would do all it could to apprehend the person or persons responsible for the attack on Sandra.

Before I could dial home, my cell phone rang. I looked at the display. It was Lily calling.

"I was about to call you," I said when I answered.

"Violet! You and Mama need to come home, quick!" Lily yelled to me.

Chapter 19

OD

Violet

"I'm so, so sleeee-py and tired," Ivy said groggily. She was lying on Mama's bed. Her eyes were closed.

"What happened?" I screamed at Lily. She was sitting on the bed crying and shaking Ivy.

"I don't know! Jasmine brought her back not long after you and Mama left. She said her back was hurting. I came in here and she was lying on the bed and that empty prescription bottle was lying beside her."

I snatched up the prescription bottle.

"How long has she been taking Percocet?" Jasmine asked, running into the room with a wet towel in her hand.

I shook my head.

"I—I didn't know she was taking Percocet," Lily said.

"Ivy, talk to me," Mama said, pushing Lily aside. "Open your eyes and talk to Mama now! How many pills you take?"

"Mama, I'm tired. I—I'm so tired. Let me sleep."

"Here, Mama!" Jasmine said, handing Mama the wet hand towel.

"Don't let her fall asleep!" Lily screamed. "We gonna have to make her throw up!"

"No!" I yelled.

"Was she upset about something?" Mama asked, placing the towel across Ivy's forehead.

"No!" Lily cried. "She just said her back was hurting and she needed to lie down."

"She still having back problems from that car accident?" Jasmine asked.

"Yes," I said.

"Should she be taking Percocet *and* muscle relaxers?" Mama asked.

"I ain't got no college degree like them, Mama, but I know the answer to that question is no!" Jasmine said.

Ivy's eyes opened slightly. "I love Ellisss," she said. "I love him! I love him! He say he loves me toooo."

"Ooooh!" Jasmine exclaimed, her eyes growing large and round.

"She don't know what she's saying," Mama said quickly.

"I love El-lis," Ivy said again.

"That's nice, baby," Mama said, smiling down at her.

"I love Allen toooo," Ivy said.

"That's your fiancé!" Jasmine shouted down at Ivy. "The man you're marrying next Saturday!"

I nudged Jasmine and told her to be quiet.

"Allen! Allen! Allen! Allen! Allen!" Ivy sang. "Ellis! Ellis! Ellis! Ellis! Ellis!"

"Lord, have mercy!" Mama cried.

"What other medicine is she taking?" Lily asked, looking at me.

"Over-the-counter sleeping pills," I said.

"Oh my goodness!" Lily shrieked.

"I love you too, Mama," Ivy mumbled as her eyelids fluttered. When they closed and she lay motionless, gasps filled the room.

"Ahhhhhh!" Lily screamed.

"Dear Lord!" Mama cried.

"Call 911!" Jasmine yelled.

I snatched up the cordless phone on the nightstand and punched in 911. Seconds later I blurted into the phone that I was calling from 309 East Franklin Street because of a possible drug overdose. Mama groaned out loud. Lily jumped up on the bed, straddled Ivy, and started shaking her.

"A drug overdose?" the 911 operator asked me.

"Yes!" I screamed into the phone. "It's my sister!"

"Is she conscious?" the 911 operator asked.

"Yes, no, I'm not sure!" I cried.

"EMS is on the way, ma'am."

I threw the phone down. "They're on the way!" I yelled at Lily. Within minutes, a siren could be heard wailing in the distance.

"Lord, have mercy! What done happened now?" I heard one of the neighbors say to Miss Sadie when the paramedics wheeled Ivy out of the house. Mama didn't stop to talk to Miss Sadie, who was outside with several other neighbors looking over in the yard. She climbed up in the ambulance behind the paramedics. The front door to Aunt Caroline's house flew open and Niecee and the children ran outside. Jasmine ran over and ushered them back into the house. Lily ran behind me to my car; I sped behind the ambulance to the hospital.

Chapter 20

McKinley General

Violet

"Violet! Are you okay?"

"Oh, Warren! It's Ivy."

"Is she okay?"

"Yeah, the doctor is in with her now."

"What happened?"

"She OD'd on meds."

Warren bent down and kissed me on the forehead.
I flinched and looked back.

"Now, do you think I would have done that if your mother was standing out here?" he asked, laughing.

I exhaled and laughed too. "No."

"I miss you."

"I miss you too, and thanks for coming by."

"When do you think we can spend five, ten minutes together?"

"I don't know. I'll call you."

Warren gave me a quick peck on the lips, then turned and headed for the elevator. Somehow, some way, I had to spend some time with him. I missed our private, although brief, moments together.

Lisa Peyton, hospital social worker and member of my book club, came down the hall towards me. "Hey, girl," she said when she approached.

"Hey," I said, hugging her.

Lisa expressed condolences to me for the death of Aunt Caroline, then quickly addressed the matter at hand. "I'm on my way to your sister's room," she said, her brows creasing together. "Can you tell me what happened?"

"She just took too much medication," I answered.

"What medication would that be?" Lisa asked, peering over her eyeglasses at me.

"A muscle relaxer and Percocet."

"Anything else?"

"Maybe, I don't know. She does take something sometimes to help her sleep," I added.

Lisa sighed and opened her eyes wide. "The Percocet and muscle relaxer taken together can be a lethal cocktail. How long has she been taking them, and what for?"

"I'm just finding out about the Percocet," I said. "Ivy started on the muscle relaxer three years ago to ease back pain stemming from a car accident."

"What about the sleeping pills?" Lisa asked, peering over her eyeglasses again. "How long has she been taking them?"

I shrugged. "I don't know."

"Has she ever tried to hurt herself?"

"No!" I exclaimed.

"Don't get upset, Violet," Lisa said calmly. "These are questions we have to ask when people are brought in under these circumstances."

I nodded. "Do you think she'll have to stay overnight?"

"That's not my call," Lisa said. "Dr. Baker, the psychiatrist on duty, will have to see her before she's discharged."

"It wasn't a *suicide* attempt," I asserted.

"Violet, perhaps it wasn't. Again, these are normal hospital procedures that we have to follow."

The door to Ivy's room opened and the attending physician walked out. He motioned for Lisa to come over. Lisa excused herself and walked over. I watched them chat, trying to figure out what the doctor was telling Lisa. Lily and Mama were down at the chapel praying. When the doctor left, Lisa walked back over to me. "I'm going in now to talk to your sister," she said. "After speaking with her, I would like to talk with all of you."

I nodded and headed down the hall to get Mama and Lily.

"Ivy has shared with me that she's been abusing medication for well over a year now," Lisa said, looking around the hospital room at us.

Mama groaned out loud. She was sitting in the chair next to the hospital bed. She looked so tired. All I could think of at that time was what Miss Emma had told me the afternoon she called after Mama and I had gotten home from the funeral home. "You and yo' sistas be strong for yo' mama," she had said. I looked around the room at my sisters and sadly shook my head.

"I asked her if she was trying to hurt herself," Lisa said.

Mama moaned and muttered, "Sweet Jesus!"

"And what did she say?" Lily asked.

"She said she was not," Lisa replied.

"*Were* you trying to kill yourself?" Mama asked, looking over at Ivy.

"No, Mama!" Ivy cried, sitting up in the bed. "I was just in so much pain. I know I shouldn't have taken any more medication, but I just couldn't stand the pain, Mama. I just couldn't stand the pain!" she said, falling back on the bed. "I wasn't trying to kill myself. Please, please believe me."

"When did you start taking Percocet?" Mama asked.

Ivy moaned and closed her eyes. She looked so weak, the doctor had her stomach pumped; I couldn't begin to imagine how bad she must have been feeling.

Mama reached over and grabbed Ivy's hand. "Percocet is very addictive, honey."

Ivy had never been one to tolerate much pain. The slightest ache, she was reaching for a pain reliever.

"I thought you were going to a chiropractor and some acupuncturist," Lily said.

Ivy sighed. "I only went to a couple of appointments. The Percocet and muscle relaxer were a quick and easy way to deal with the pain."

Mama closed her eyes and moaned again.

"You could have died, Ivy!" Lily yelled.

Ivy started sobbing.

To think that a day after burying Aunt Caroline, Mama, my sisters and I could have been making funeral arrangements for Ivy. That scared me. I started shaking. I wrapped my arms around myself in an effort to stop.

"You can't be so careless!" Lily yelled.

"Lily, please!" Lisa said. "I understand that you're upset, but Ivy is in no condition to be chastised."

"I'm sorry. I'm sorry," Lily said.

"Based on what you all shared with the paramedics and admitting nurse, and what Ivy's shared with me," Lisa said, "the doctor and I are ruling out a suicide attempt. However, the psychiatrist on duty this evening will have to see her and make that call."

"I don't think that's necessary!" Lily shrieked.

"Lily, please," I said. "It's hospital procedures."

"How soon can the psychiatrist see her?" Mama asked.

Lisa sighed. "It's hard to say. Dr. Baker is up on the psych ward."

"She won't be moved to the fifth floor, will she?" I asked. The fifth floor was the psychiatric ward.

Ivy started crying again. "I wasn't trying to kill myself!"

"Will she, Lisa?" I asked again.

"I don't believe so," Lisa said.

I exhaled.

"If she has to stay overnight, can I stay with her?" Mama asked.

"I don't see where that will be a problem," Lisa answered.

"I'll stay with her, Mama," Lily said. "You go home."

Mama shook her head. "If anyone stays, it's gonna be me."

"I wasn't trying to kill myself," Ivy muttered.

"We know you weren't, honey," Mama said.

"Mama, I don't like having to take medicine. But I can't stand the pain!"

Mama stood up and walked over to the bed. She smiled down at Ivy and kissed her on the forehead.

"I hate that stupid girl!" Ivy cried. "I hate her for what she's done to me! Because of her, I'm going to have back pain for the rest of my life!"

"Hush, honey," Mama said soothingly. "Don't hate, child, don't hate."

Chapter 21

Agony and Ecstasy

Physically and emotionally exhausted, Ivy awoke from another fitful nap and to her dismay discovered she was still in the hospital. Peony had finally fallen off to sleep and was snoring softly in the chair beside the hospital bed. Tears filled Ivy's eyes and she bit her bottom lip to keep from crying out. *I could have died!* she thought, as tears streamed down her face. *I could have died!* This was a wake-up call like none other, Ivy realized, and she was left with one sensible choice: She would have to cut back her hours at her practice and perhaps resign from the consultant position with the Justice Project in order to properly take care of herself. After today, Ivy vowed with resolve, she would no longer solely rely on medication to address her back pain. Her health came first, and so did any child she would carry in her womb, should she proceed with the wedding and her plans to get pregnant. She would not be popping pills during her pregnancy and placing the health of any child she bore at risk from the side affects of prescription narcotics. *That would be criminal!* The mere thought made Ivy shudder. And, just as soon as she returned to Durham, she planned to call a chiropractor and schedule an appointment. This time around, she intended to keep each and every appointment.

Ivy sighed and ran a hand gingerly across her abdomen. Every inch of her body was racked with pain. Her throat and stomach were extremely sore from the gastric irrigation performed earlier. "Where is that psychiatrist?" she muttered. The hospital social worker had told her the last time she peeped in on her that there had been several admissions to the psych unit that evening, and she had no idea when the psychiatrist would be coming to see her.

As she wiped the tears from her face, Ivy attempted to turn over onto her right side. "Oh God!" she cried out, rolling back over onto her back. In addition to the pain that filled her slender body, she was thirsty. She looked over at Peony and decided not to wake her. Where was Lily and Violet? she wondered. Had they gone home or were they down the hall somewhere? She looked over at the door and prayed that it would open and her sisters would walk back in. After minutes of staring at the closed door, she sighed and looked up at the TV. What was on didn't interest her. She closed her eyes and had resigned herself to taking another nap, which would be like the naps before, she feared, filled with dreams of Mia, Allen, and now Ellis, when the door to her room opened.

"Ivy?"

Ivy gasped and burst into tears. Her handsome, smart, charismatic fiancé rushed over to the bed.

"I got here as soon I could," he said, his brown eyes filled with worry.

Peony stirred in the chair.

"Lily called me. Honey! How are you?" Allen asked, smiling down at Ivy.

"I'm okay," Ivy said softly. "Just sore, and embarrassed. I can't believe I was that careless!"

"Shhhhh!" Allen said, shaking his head. He smiled, then leaned down and kissed Ivy gently on the lips.

Ivy moaned and longed for another kiss. *Oh God, I love this man! I do, I do!* she cried silently, staring up at Allen through watery eyes. As if reading her thoughts, Allen leaned down and kissed her again. Ivy would have given anything for Allen to have picked her up and held her. Many times she'd fallen asleep in his arms, after he'd patiently and lovingly massaged tension and pain from her body.

The phone in the room rang, arousing Peony from her sleep. When she saw Allen, she smiled broadly and said, "Hello, son."

"Hello, Mrs. Shaw," Allen said, smiling back.

Ivy watched the warm exchange between her mother and Allen, then looked up at the ceiling. *Poor Mama!* she thought to herself. Peony was quite fond of Allen, and had made a point of telling her that from time to time. "I don't think you could have done better, honey," Peony said to her as tears of joy ran down her face when Allen came down from Durham and asked her for Ivy's hand in marriage.

Before the phone could ring a second time, Peony had picked up the receiver. "Daisy!" she said seconds later. "Yeah, we're still here!" she soon said. While

Peony chatted with Daisy, Allen smiled down at Ivy and gently removed strands of hair from her clammy forehead.

"Thank you," Ivy mouthed.

"Honey, I'm so glad you're okay," Allen said softly. "I wish I could pick you up and take you out of here."

"Me too," Ivy said, smiling.

"I'm counting down to the hour, darling," Allen whispered, "when you will become Mrs. Allen Hayes."

Tears filled Ivy's eyes again. Allen reached into his right pants pocket and removed a white silk handkerchief. He wiped Ivy's eyes and her sweaty forehead. Feeling compelled to respond to Allen's last comment, Ivy swallowed with great difficulty and said, "Me too" again.

Allen smiled and tears filled his eyes.

"Oh Lord!" Ivy cried, looking away.

"Allen's here!" Peony said loudly into the phone, interrupting the tender, emotional exchange occurring between Allen and Ivy. "Let me talk to him, okay? I'll call you later, soon as we know something. Okay? Bye, now."

As Peony hung up the phone, she eased up out of the chair. "Thanks for coming, Allen!" she said, walking over to him.

"You don't have to thank me, Mrs. Shaw," Allen replied, embracing Peony. "I would have been here sooner had I known," he said, wiping his eyes. "So tell me, what're the doctors saying? How much longer are they keeping her?"

"They're not discharging her until she sees the psychiatrist," Peony said.

"A psychiatrist?" Allen asked, aghast.

Peony sighed and shook her head.

"Why?" Allen asked.

"It's normal hospital procedure," Ivy said, reaching for Allen's hand. "They want to make sure I wasn't trying to"—Ivy sighed and rolled her eyes—"*kill* myself."

"Oh my goodness!" Allen bellowed. "That's nonsense! We'll see about that!" he said.

"Honey, please!" Ivy said, shaking her head.

Peony patted Allen on the back. "Allen, why don't we just let the folks here do their jobs, okay? No need for you to get yourself all worked up over their rules and regulations, okay?"

Allen sighed heavily and pressed his lips together. "Okay," he finally said, nodding.

Peony returned to her seat and Allen leaned down once more and kissed Ivy on the lips. "I miss you," he moaned. "I've missed you terribly."

Ivy burst into tears. "Oh, Allen, I—"

Allen placed his right index finger on Ivy's quivering lips. "Honey, stop crying. It's going to be okay," he said, wiping the tears spilling from Ivy's eyes. "It's going to be okay, I promise you that."

From where she sat, Peony smiled and folded her arms across her chest.

Chapter 22

Friend and Foe

Violet

"So, they're keeping her overnight?"

"Yeah. She's a mess, Warren. More a physical mess than anything."

"Well," Warren sighed, "I'm glad to hear that she's going to be okay. And"—he smiled and wrapped his arms around me—"grateful for these few minutes I have with you."

I laughed.

Warren and I were standing in the living room kissing when the doorbell rang.

"Violet! Peony! Y'all in there?"

"Miss Sadie!" I yelled, freeing myself from Warren's embrace. I hurried to the front door. Miss Sadie was peering through the storm door into the house.

"How's your sista?" she asked when I opened the door.

"Much better," I replied.

"Praise God!" Miss Sadie shouted. "I thought my heart was gone jump clean outta my chest when that ambulance pulled into Peony's driveway. I thought she had taken ill. She here?" Miss Sadie asked, looking around me into the house.

"No, ma'am. The doctor's keeping Ivy overnight, so Mama's staying at the hospital with her."

"I see." Miss Sadie's brows creased together. "What zackly happened?"

"Ivy lost track of how much medicine she'd taken."

"My Lord!" Miss Sadie exclaimed.

"But she's going to be okay, thank the Lord!" I said, with an uplifted hand.

"Praise God!" Miss Sadie shouted, throwing up both her hands.

I smiled, hoping Miss Sadie would leave so I could rejoin Warren in the living room.

"Odell's grandson in there?" she asked.

"Yes, ma'am. He stopped by to see how Ivy was. I'm actually on my way back to the hospital. I ran home to get some things for Mama. Her Bible and some clothes for overnight."

"I see, I see," Miss Sadie said, nodding. "Well, tell Peony I got y'all in my prayers. And I'll see her when she comes home."

"I'll tell her. And thanks for coming by, Miss Sadie."

Miss Sadie nodded, turned, and left.

I ran back into the living room and jumped into Warren's arms.

* * *

I was heading back to the hospital, waiting at a traffic light, when I heard a knock on the front passenger window. I flinched and looked over. Willie, my homeless friend, was standing next to my car straddling his bicycle. I lowered the window. "Hey, Willie."

"Hey, Violet. How you doing?" he asked, smiling.

"I'm doing good, Willie."

"I miss seeing you at the library," he said, leaning into my car. "When you coming back to work?"

"I'm not sure."

"I miss seeing you."

I glanced up at the light. "So, you doing good, Willie?" I asked, looking back at him.

"Yeah," he said, smiling. "I got someplace to sleep now."

"Oh?" I said.

"Yeah, I got in at the shelter over on Main Street, across from the police station."

"That's good, Willie," I said, forcing myself to smile. Smiling, holding my breath, and making small talk with Willie all at the same time was difficult, because he smelled, like always, *awful.*

"You look good, Violet. And you smell nice too."

"Thanks." I looked back at the light hoping it would turn green.

"So sorry about your aunt."

"Thank you, Willie."

"You put that rose I gave you Saturday night in water?"

I looked at Willie and nodded. "Uh-huh. It's beautiful and so fragrant."

"Just like you," Willie said, flashing a tartared, plaque-toothed smile at me.

Why is this light taking forever to change? I wondered,

looking up at the light for a third time. Willie's halitosis and BO were beginning to make me nauseated.

"I see your boyfriend every day."

My head jerked to the right. "My boyfriend?"

"The detective. Heard he got a big case on his hands now."

A car horn sounded from behind. I looked up at the traffic light; it had changed to green.

"Willie, I gotta go. Take care!" I sped off and lowered all the windows to rid the car of Willie's funk.

I blinked my eyes several times to focus, because I couldn't believe what I was seeing.

"Can I help you?" I asked.

Colette jumped and looked back at me. "Uh, what?" she said, her eyes darting about in their sockets.

"What are you doing?" I didn't give Colette a chance to answer. "Why are you standing outside my sister's room?"

"Yo' sister? Yo' sister in there?" Colette asked, sounding surprised. "Wh-what happened?"

I looked over at the door. The name Ivy Shaw was on the partially closed hospital door. I looked back at Colette, who had by now collected herself, because she was eyeing me like she normally did, with contempt.

"If I didn't know better," I said, "it looked like you were eavesdropping."

"'Eavesdropping'? Puh-lease! Girl, you trippin'!" Colette said, stepping back with a neck roll.

"That's what it looked like to *me*."

"I was looking for somebody, okay?"

I narrowed my eyes at Colette and said, "Who?"

"I ain't got to tell you who!" she replied, with another neck roll.

"Warren is not in there, if that's who you're"—I smiled, broadly—"looking for."

"Whatever!" Colette snapped, throwing her hands up and walking off.

I burst out laughing.

Chapter 23

Frustration

"So when you think you'll be back?"

"I don't know," Jasmine replied wearily, her voice trailing off.

"I'm glad Rashaunda and Ivy are okay," Tina said softly.

"Me too. I could just *strangle* Rashaunda for what she did," Jasmine muttered.

Tina chuckled. "Might not be a good idea," she said, chuckling again, "since Social Services is on yo' case."

Jasmine laughed. "Yeah, you're right."

"The cookout was nice," Tina said. "Several folks asked about you."

"Who was there? No! Don't tell me. I don't want to hear *nothin'* about the cookout and good time y'all had."

"And we had a good time *too*!" Tina said, laughing.

"Hush!" Jasmine yelled. "I said I didn't want to hear about it!"

"Okay, okay," Tina said. "Well, can I *at least* fill you in on what's been goin' on in *da hood* since you've been gone?"

Jasmine stretched out on the sofa in her aunt's den. "Yeah, go 'head," she said, lowering the volume on the TV.

Tina, like Jasmine, was a longtime resident of the Githens Court Housing Project. She had four children and, like Jasmine, was unemployed and her only source of income was child support and occasional money from boyfriends engaged in illegal activities. Jasmine listened intently as Tina brought her up to speed on what had happened in the projects since she'd been away. There had been another shooting— no injuries or fatalities this time, three evictions, two break-ins, and a courtyard fight between two women over a guy who in Jasmine and Tina's opinion "won't shit!"

"Mo'Nay got her ass *kicked*!" Tina said, sighing.

"Damn!" Jasmine muttered. "Poor Mo'Nay."

"She won't listen, Jazz. I done told her I don't know how many times, and so have you, that DeAngelo won't shit!"

"The girl's sprung," Jasmine said. "Sprung."

"Ain't that the truth!" Tina muttered.

"Speaking of stupid bitches, do you know NeShell done started harassin' me again?"

"Jazz, naw!"

"Uh-huh. My phone rings the other night, I answer, and some trick say, 'What's up, bitch?' then hang up."

"Say whaaat? Was it NeShell?" Tina asked.

"Naw!" Jasmine replied. "She ain't *that* stupid to call

me no mo', not since we've been to court. It sounded like it was that cockeyed sister of hers."

Tina grunted.

"I'm gone take care of NeShell Scott when I get back to Charlotte. You can count on *that*! And I bet that's where Maniac is."

"Huh?" Tina replied.

"I ain't heard from him! You seen him around?"

Tina sighed. "Nope."

Jasmine pursed her lips together and sighed. "I bet he's layin' up at NeShell's house."

Tina sighed. "I don't know. You think so?"

"You ain't seen him nowhere, and I ain't heard from him."

Tina scoffed. "Jazz, I doubt he's with that ugly, stinkin' heifer. You know how Maniac is. He's somewhere makin' money."

"Yeah, right!" Jasmine snapped. "He's a dog, that much I *do* know."

"Bow-wow!" Tina said, laughing.

Jasmine sighed.

"You tried callin' him?" Tina asked.

Jasmine smacked her lips and gasped. "Naw! And I ain't gone call him. My auntie has died, and he *know* how much she meant to me! You would think the *least* he would do is call me and see how I was doin'!"

"You right. You right," Tina said, agreeing.

"It's bad enough he let NeShell trick him into sleeping with her while he's goin' with me! Then she ends up pregnant with them ugly twins. Now *this*! No lie, Tina. I'm gone curbside that nigga if he don't start treatin' me better. Then NeShell can have him all to her stankin' self!"

"Maniac don't want NeShell, Jazz. How many times I got to tell you that? You're prettier. You fly."

Jasmine smiled. She took great pleasure in hearing Tina say those things.

"I miss you, girl," Tina said softly.

"I miss you too. Guess what?" Jasmine said excitedly.

"What?" Tina replied.

"I'll be *driving* back when I come."

"'Driving'?"

"I got a car!" Jasmine squealed.

"Naw, you don't!" Tina yelled.

"Yes, I do. Mama and Violet gave me Aunt Caroline's PT Cruiser!"

"Shut up!"

"Now we ain't got to ride on no more of them smelly city buses. We can cruise 'round town in a Cruiser!"

"Jazz, that's all right! That's all right!"

"Oh, and we won't be sittin' around talkin' 'bout how we wish we could go somewhere this summer either."

"Huh?"

"Me and my sisters gone each get *ten thousand dollars* from a life insurance policy my aunt had."

"Girl, you need to stop!" Tina squealed.

"Soooo, after I get some rims for the car, we goin' to a travel agency and book us a cruise to the Bahamas *and* a trip to Las Vegas!"

"Yes, yes, yes!" Tina shouted.

"Yes!" Jasmine squealed, envisioning herself lying on a Caribbean beach in a cute bikini, sipping on a Bahama Mama. D.C. was the farthest she'd ever traveled. And traveling was something she longed to do. She loved to sit and listen to Ivy, Lily, and Violet, who traveled extensively, talk about the exciting places they'd visited and planned to visit. They were always kind enough to send her and her girls pictures and postcards of their vacations and buy them souvenirs. And not a day went by that Jasmine didn't tune in to The Travel Channel. It was one of her favorite channels. "And I'm gone take my babies to Disney World too."

"Ahhhhh," Tina cried, "they gone like that."

Jasmine smiled. "Yeah. We might even stay at one of those *fancy* resorts I've seen on TV!"

"Go on, girl, with yo' bad self!" Tina yelled.

Jasmine laughed.

Tina sighed. "You come from good folk, Jazz," she said softly. "Good folk. Your aunt, in death, is still lookin' out for you."

Tears filled Jasmine's eyes. "Yeah," she muttered, "she is."

"I know yo' mama and sisters get on yo' nerves sometimes, but it's only because they love you and want the best for you and yo' kids."

Jasmine closed her eyes and started praying for her friend. Sometimes she didn't bother to mention to Tina the things her family did for her because she didn't want to make Tina feel bad and start griping about her family.

"How Miss Peony doin'?" Tina asked.

"Mama's a tough old bird," Jasmine said, blinking back the tears in her eyes. "She's doin' good." She laughed. "She's just stressin' me out!"

"You wanna trade?"

Here we go! Jasmine thought.

"Huh? Do you?"

"No," Jasmine replied softly.

Tina grunted. "I didn't think so."

"Yo' mama care 'bout you, girl. Yo' sisters too. Mine, shit! Ain't none of 'em worth a damn! They don't care nothin' 'bout me and my kids!"

Jasmine grunted. She had long since stopped trying to make Tina feel better by saying things like "Your mama and sisters ain't that bad, they care 'bout you," because they fell on deaf ears and only propelled Tina into a lengthy, expletive-laced tirade about her family that made Jasmine cringe and cry sometimes. "You don't know, Jazz. I *know* what I'm talkin' 'bout!" she would reply. "My family don't know nothin' 'bout love. My mama didn't teach us to get along with each other. Hell! That bitch don't get along with her own sisters and brothers, so how she gone teach us how to get along with each other? Huh? Tell me how! You didn't grow up like I did, Jazz. You had it good, real good." And while Tina ranted and raved, oftentimes repeating herself about her "unloving, dysfunctional family," about how much she hated her mother, and the verbal and physical abuse she and her nine siblings endured, she wept some awful.

"I told you how my mama cursed me out when I got pregnant my senior year in high school? You would have thought that was the worst thing in the world, me gettin' pregnant. You remember me tellin' you 'bout that, don't you, Jazz? And how she cursed me out just about every day after that?"

"Yeah, I remember," Jasmine said softly, as tears filled her eyes again.

"I was *so* stressed out, and made to feel bad about myself, I stopped goin' to school."

"Uh-huh," Jasmine whispered.

"Yo' mama didn't treat you like that when you got knocked up!" Tina yelled.

"No, she didn't." Jasmine couldn't fathom being cursed out by her mother *or* her sisters, nor could she relate to a childhood void of a mother's love.

"Okay, then," Tina said. "And them *sisters* of mine. Shit! They ain't no better than that *hateful* bitch that gave birth to us. They wouldn't have even cared, much less bothered to get me out of jail like yours did when you got in trouble. I would still be sittin' in the *pokey*, and Social Services would have my kids. I'm tellin' you, Jazz, you blessed and don't know it."

When Jasmine ended her call to Tina, she went into the living room and turned on the stereo to FOXXY 104, a popular R & B station out of Raleigh. The radio personality was playing slow jams. The love ballads got Jasmine to thinking about Maniac. *Why hasn't he called me?* she wondered. Jasmine flipped open her cell phone and dialed Maniac's cell. Her call went straight to his voice mailbox. She pressed the End button on her phone and dialed Maniac's mother's number; Maniac's oldest brother, Wesley, answered. What he told her made her cringe. Maniac was locked up. He had made a stop in Greensboro on his way back to Charlotte on Sunday. A mile outside the city limits, he was pulled over. The highway patrol found a large quantity of marijuana in the trunk of his car.

"How far are you from Greensboro?" Wesley asked.

"I don't know. A coupla hours, I think," Jasmine replied.

"His bond is five thousand dollars."

Jasmine grunted. "What you tellin' me that for?"

Wesley laughed. "I know you got them rich sistas and all, you think you can finagle some money outta them, like you always doin'?"

Jasmine scoffed. "Nigga, please!"

Wesley sighed. "Well, if Sir Charles don't come through for him, Maniac gone be locked up for a long time. 'Cause we ain't got no money," he said, sighing again.

Jasmine pursed her lips together and sighed too.

Chapter 24

Road Trip

"Don't forget what I told you, Niecee."

"I—I ain't forgot," Niecee said, yawning. "If Grandma and them ask where you at, I'm supposed to say you'd ran up the street."

"And that's *all* you say, okay?"

"I got it, Aunt J."

"I'll handle any questions they got when I get back."

"Okay," Niecee said. "Where're you now?"

"I'm leavin' the library."

"What time you think you'll be back?"

"It looks like it's gone take me two hours to get there and two to get back." Jasmine glanced at the clock on the dash. It was 8:10. "I should be back before two o'clock."

"Okay," Niecee said, yawning again.

Jasmine pressed the End button on her cell phone and threw it down in the passenger seat on top of the directions she'd printed off MapQuest's site at the McKinley Public Library for the Guildford County Jail. As she sped down I-85 in the PT Cruiser en route to Greensboro, she turned up the volume on the radio. She was tuned in to the *Russ Parr Morning Show*.

Maniac swaggered into the county jail visiting room in a bright orange jumpsuit and brown rubber flip-flops. Before sitting down, he flashed a big smile and gang sign at Jasmine.

Jasmine rolled her eyes, then sighed. She was mad *and* happy. She was upset with Maniac for being in trouble, and glad to see that he was okay.

A smile soon formed on Jasmine's lips, and if it wasn't for the Plexiglas that separated her from Maniac, she would have jumped up into his tattooed, muscular arms and wrapped her legs around his waist.

"What's up, baby?" he said into the phone on his side of the window.

Jasmine already had the phone's receiver on her side of the window up to her ear, anxiously waiting to hear Maniac's voice. She stared at him for a few seconds before answering. He looked like the hip-hop artist Nelly. And it was because of that and his reputation of being a good lover that girls were always trying to catch his eye and steal him from Jasmine. And when he got missing, Jasmine always feared he was laid up some-where loving somebody else.

Jasmine wanted to respond with a flippant com-ment, but decided against it and said coolly, "I should be asking you that question."

Maniac laughed and ran his free hand down his goatee. He didn't look the least bit distressed or out of sorts. Being in jail, unfortunately, wasn't something that was new to him. He'd been arrested and jailed two other times since he and Jasmine had "hooked up." Once for disorderly conduct, and the second time for simple assault. And as a teen, he'd spent two years in a juvenile detention center for strong-arm robbery.

"I see you took your sweet time comin' to see 'bout me," Maniac said.

"Nigga, I just found out last night you were locked up!" Jasmine snapped.

"Okay, my bad. Calm down," Maniac said, grinning.

Jasmine sighed and crossed her legs. Maniac lowered his eyes. Jasmine had purposely dressed in a low-cut, snug-fitting top and a short denim skirt she'd gotten from Wal-Mart since she'd been in McKinley. When she saw Maniac eyeing her cleavage, she stuck her chest out a bit. "So, when you gettin' out?" she asked, smiling.

Maniac looked back up into Jasmine's face and smiled. "When you get me out."

Jasmine burst out laughing. "Boy, you trippin'!"

"I got thangs I need to do, baby, you know that. And I can't do them in here."

"And?" Jasmine said, opening her eyes wide. "Where do you think I'm gone get five thousand dollars?"

Maniac sat back and stared at Jasmine. "You come down here just to torture me?" he asked, eyeing her cleavage again. "Or"—he looked back up into Jasmine's face—"are you here to help me?"

Jasmine burst out laughing again.

"Baby, stop playin' with me. Tell whatever lie you need to tell yo' mama and sistas, and get me outta here. Okay?"

"I ain't never asked my mama and sisters for that much money."

"First time for everythang, girl," Maniac said with a wink.

"Why don't you ask your *ugly* babies' mama for help?" Jasmine spat out.

Mania laughed. "Now you trippin'. And stop callin' my babies ugly."

"For their sake, I hope them lil' bug-eyed, egghead-shaped thangs don't grow up lookin' like NeShell."

Maniac's nostrils flared. "Stop it, Jazz! You ain't supposed to talk about children like that."

Jasmine sighed and rolled her eyes.

Maniac stood up.

"Hey! Wait a minute!" Jasmine yelled, standing up.

"Get the money and get me outta here, okay?" Maniac said. He placed the receiver on his side of the window on the switch hook, blew Jasmine a kiss, and headed for his exit.

"Maniac!" Jasmine yelled, pounding on the window.

Maniac pimped out of the room without bothering to look back at Jasmine.

Jasmine flopped down into the metal chair she'd been sitting in. Embarrassment kept her glued to the chair for several seconds. *Naw, he didn't just diss me like that!* she thought angrily to herself.

The deputy sheriff in the room with Jasmine cleared his throat. "Ma'am, you have to leave now," he said.

"He didn't even have the decency to ask me how I was doin'," Jasmine cried, looking up at the young black male officer.

"Excuse me?" the deputy said.

"My auntie just died, and he didn't even ask me how I was doin'," Jasmine said, shaking her head. "Selfish bastard!" she muttered as tears spilled from her eyes. "Selfish bastard!"

Chapter 25

Say It Ain't So!

Violet

"Peony, now, I ain't one to go round spreadin' gossip," Miss Sadie said, walking into the kitchen.

Ivy and I started snickering. She had been discharged from the hospital, and we were in the kitchen with Lily and Mama cooking dinner. Jasmine was MIA, and her return trip to Charlotte had been delayed once more; she and Rashaunda had to meet with the CPS worker again. Lily was sitting at the table in the breakfast nook humming along to the radio and peeling white potatoes with Mama. Ivy and I were standing at the oven. She was basting a roast and I was frying chicken.

"But I had to come over and tell you what I just heard 'bout your children," Miss Sadie said, scowling.

Everyone in the kitchen stopped what they were

doing and looked at Miss Sadie. Mama motioned for Miss Sadie to sit down. I walked over to the radio and lowered the volume.

"I think the world of your girls, Peony. You know that," Miss Sadie said, shaking her head.

Mama nodded.

"They're some fine young women. You and Augustus did a fine job raising these girls."

"Thank you, Sadie. So what you hear 'bout my children?" Mama asked.

"Odessa told me," Miss Sadie said, sighing heavily, "that she heard Ivy was tryin' to kill herself."

"Oh my goodness!" Ivy shrieked.

Mama sighed heavily and sat back in her chair.

"I told Odessa that was a lie straight from the pit of hell, and she ought to have been ashamed of herself for repeatin' it."

Mama pursed her lips together and looked out the window.

"*And* she said," Miss Sadie continued, "she heard too that Jasmine spends a lot of time at the Mini Mart, buyin' lottery tickets. Say she won two hundred dollars yesterday and turned right round and spent one hundred of it on mo' lottery tickets."

Ivy, Lily, and I cut our eyes at each other.

Mama sighed again. "Who Odessa hear that from?"

"She said Emma told her. You know Emma's granddaughter, Kiera, works at the Mini Mart."

Mama shook her head. "Well, Sadie, Ivy takes medicine for back pain. She took more than she should have the other day, that's all. She won't trying"—Mama shook her head—"thank you, Jesus!" she cried, throwing up her hands. "She won't trying to kill herself. She was just trying to find some relief from her pain."

Miss Sadie threw up her hands and cried, "Thank you, Jesus!" too. She looked over at Ivy and said, "How you doin', baby?"

Ivy smiled. "I'm doing good, Miss Sadie."

"And as far as Jasmine go," Mama said, "I don't know if she buying lottery tickets or not. I sho' hope she's not. Augustus and I taught our children that gambling is a sin."

"That Emma Harris always running off at the mouth, talkin' bad 'bout other folks' children, when she ought to talk about them grown rusty-tailed children of hers!" Miss Sadie grumbled. "They and their children packed in that tiny run-down trailer with Emma. Don't make no sense!"

"It was a mess of folks over there yesterday!" Mama said, shaking her head. "Violet and I could hardly get inside for all them folks."

"Was it clean in there?" Miss Sadie asked.

Mama nodded. "Just junky."

"Why won't Colette, Evangeline, and the rest of 'em get a place of their own? Or if they want to keep living with Emma, buy sump'n big enough for 'em all to live in!" Miss Sadie said. "They sittin' on *all* that land Emma got from that white man she used to work for."

"They could do that," Mama said.

"They all work, 'sides Nub. And he gets a big disability check, so Emma claims," Miss Sadie said.

Mama nodded.

"I don't understand why they won't do it!" Miss Sadie said, scowling. "Why you think they won't do that, Peony?"

Mama shook her head and started peeling potatoes again. "I don't know why they won't, Sadie."

"Mama, I forgot to tell you," I said, walking over, "Miss Emma called last Wednesday after we'd gotten home from viewing Aunt Caroline's body. She asked me what you were going to do with Aunt Caroline's house. She said something about Nub and his wife getting back together and being interested in renting it."

Miss Sadie grunted. "And Caroline's house and yard would be looking just like Emma's raggedy trailer and junky yard soon after they move in. Besides, this has always been a quiet street. Now, Peony, I ain't tryin' to tell you how to handle your business. But I've known you a long time, and the good Lord knows I don't, and I don't think you do either, want somebody like that woman Nub's married to livin' across from you."

"I ain't renting Caroline's house to none of Emma Harris's folk, you can believe that," Mama said. "Daisy and Floyd plan to move in it when Floyd retires."

"Mama, Daisy and Floyd have been talking about moving back home for five years now," Lily said. "I don't think Floyd's going to retire any time soon. So you should consider renting it out for a while."

"It won't be to none of Emma Harris's folks!" Mama said again.

"I *know* that," Lily said. "You would rent it to someone you believe will take care of it."

"You wouldn't want to sell it?" Miss Sadie asked.

"No!" Mama said. "That house like this house, it's gonna stay in the family."

We heard a car horn blow and looked out the window. Jasmine was pulling into Aunt Caroline's driveway. Niecee's boys and Kenya were in the driveway doing cartwheels. "Go tell Jasmine to come here," Mama said.

Nobody moved.

"Lily."

"Ma'am?" Lily replied.

"Go tell Jasmine I need to see her," Mama said.

Lily stood up and exited the kitchen.

"Well, I'm gonna head home," Miss Sadie said, standing.

"Thanks for stopping by, Sadie," Mama said.

"Miss Sadie, you cooked dinner?" I asked.

Miss Sadie shook her head.

"I'll bring you a plate over later if you'd like."

"Thank you, Violet! That's mighty sweet."

"Mama, you're not going to ask Jasmine about what Miss Sadie told you, are you?" Ivy asked, chuckling, when Miss Sadie left.

Mama didn't answer Ivy. She kept peeling the potato in her hand. "Y'all know anything about what Sadie just told me?" she finally said.

"No. There's no truth to any of that," I said flatly.

Mama looked at Ivy.

Ivy shook her head. "It's not true," she said.

We heard the front door open, then close. Lily entered the kitchen first; Jasmine walked in slowly behind her. Mama motioned for Jasmine to sit down.

Jasmine cut her eyes at me and Ivy, then plopped down in a chair across from Mama.

"Your daddy and I taught y'all that gambling was a sin. Are you gambling?" Mama asked, leaning across the table.

"Gambling?" Jasmine replied, scowling. "Mama, who told you *that?*"

Mama opened her eyes wide. "Are you?"

Jasmine shook her head. "No."

"Emma Harris has a granddaughter that works at the Mini Mart. She say you in there quite a bit buying lottery tickets and you even won some money yesterday, and turned around and spent some of it on more lottery tickets."

Jasmine nodded. "That's true."

Mama dropped her head and sighed heavily.

"Mama, that's not gambling," Jasmine said.

Mama looked up at her.

"Okay, maybe you think it is," Jasmine said.

"How serious of a problem do you have?" Mama asked softly.

Jasmine burst out laughing. "I don't have a *problem*, Mama!"

"You traveling down a dangerous road that leads nowhere but to destruction!" Mama warned.

"Mama," Jasmine said softly, leaning forward, "I don't have a gambling problem."

"You sure?" Mama asked, as her eyes filled with tears.

Jasmine nodded. "Yeah! I'm sure!"

Mama sighed, looking relieved. *If only she knew*, I thought to myself. Her oldest daughter was the one with a gambling problem. Daisy couldn't wait to get her hands on the ten thousand dollars coming her way from Aunt Caroline's life insurance policy. She told Ivy she was planning to use the money to pay off two high-interest loans. She wanted to put an end to the harassing phone calls from the creditors threatening legal action each time she missed a monthly payment. And after she paid off the "loan sharks," she was going to start repaying the money she'd borrowed from Ivy and me.

"So where've you been?" Mama asked.

"Just ridin' around, tryin' to clear my head."

Mama's brows creased together. "What's wrong?"

Jasmine sighed. "Nothing I really want to talk about." She jumped up from the table. "Y'all need any help in here?"

"Yeah," Lily said. "Help Mama with the potatoes. I'm going upstairs to lie down. I have a headache."

Chapter 26

Cry Me a River

Never once had she thought she would feel the pangs of betrayal from her husband. From where she lay on the bed, Lily replayed in her mind the conversation she had overhead on the fourth floor last Friday afternoon. "What did I do to deserve this?" she cried, pounding the mattress. "The good Lord won't put no more on you than you can bear," her mother and Aunt Caroline often said. Lily turned onto her stomach and started weeping. "I can't bear this," she cried. "Oh, God, please help me!"

Russell had called every day since leaving on Sunday. Not once had Lily spoken to him. *What can he say to me?* she wondered, as three questions ran through her fevered mind: Should I leave Russell? Should I stay? And how will I ever be able to face my colleagues again? She feared that by now, everyone at the agency knew. If they didn't, it would only be a matter of time before the rumor made its way off the fourth floor.

Lily had called her supervisor—the agency director—last night and informed her of her aunt's death and plans to be out for the remainder of the week. When the agency reopened this morning, Lily knew her boss would send out an e-mail informing everyone of her loss, and that Marilyn would probably be the first person to call. Sure enough, shortly after nine o'clock Lily's cell phone rang. It was Marilyn. Lily didn't bother to answer her phone. By noon, Marilyn had called two other times, to express condolences, to see how Lily was doing, and to ask if there was anything she needed. Lily hadn't bothered to return Marilyn's calls or the other four calls she'd received from people at the agency. She was embarrassed, and believed Marilyn and her other colleagues were gloating like Charlene about her marital misfortune.

"When did he stop loving me? What did I do to push him into the arms of another woman?" Lily muttered.

Lily rolled over onto her back and stared up at the ceiling. *Once a woman's man steps out on her, the trust in their relationship is gone. Gone! The woman needs to walk out of the relationship with her dignity intact. Too, too many women have such low self-esteem. They'd rather stay with their unfaithful spouses . . .*

Lily sighed and shook her head, as she recalled those words she'd shared with Sandra. "Russell would *never* do that!" she had said, in response to Sandra's "What would you do if Russell stepped out on you?" comment. Sandra scoffed, laughed, and said, "Any man will cheat, if given the opportunity." Lily shuddered at how naive and foolish she must have sounded and how Sandra must have laughed at her afterward.

Could she leave Russell, and find love again at her age? Lily wondered.

"Look at what you've done to me, Russell!" Lily muttered.

The house phone rang. Lily wiped her eyes and looked over at the phone on the nightstand. It wasn't a number she knew. She fell back on the bed and curled up into the fetal position. She'd resigned herself to taking a nap before dinner.

"Lily!" Peony yelled. "You got company!"

Lily's eyes popped open. She sat up on the bed and before she could get herself together, the bedroom door opened. Lily burst into tears. "Wh-what are you two doing here?" she asked.

"We came to check on you, Mom," Sabrina said, running over to the bed.

"Mom, are you okay?" Russell Jr. asked, closing the door behind him.

Lily embraced Sabrina and said, "I'm fine."

Sabrina pulled back. "Are you, Mom?"

Lily nodded. "Yes, yes, I am," she said, smiling weakly at her daughter.

Russell Jr. walked over and hugged Lily. "Mom, tell us, what's going on?"

Lily sighed and ran a hand through her tousled hair. Her children's visit was unexpected. "Did your father send you two here?"

"No, we came on our own," Sabrina said. "Dad doesn't know we're here."

"Have either of you talked to Augustus since he's been back to New Orleans?" Lily asked, wiping her nose and eyes.

"Yeah," Russell Jr. replied.

Augustus, Lily and Russell's oldest child, was a grad

student in the College of Pharmacy at Xavier University. Since the destruction in the city caused by Hurricane Katrina, he and members of his fraternity, Omega Psi Phi, had spent many hours helping rebuild homes.

"Augustus is fine. We're concerned about you and Dad," Sabrina said.

"I think I heard him crying last night," Russell Jr. said, his brown eyes filling with tears. "Are you two getting a divorce?" he asked softly.

"Oh, honey," Lily said, embracing her son.

"Are you, Mom?" he asked, pulling back. "Dad says you haven't talked to him since we left Sunday."

"I love your father, honey. We—we're having some problems right now."

"What kind of problems?" Sabrina asked, as tears ran down her cheeks.

"Nothing that you and your brother should be concerned about."

"Why don't you call Dad and talk to him?" Russell Jr. asked.

Lily sighed. "I will."

"Today?" Russell Jr. asked, his eyes large and round.

Lily sighed. "I can't say when, honey. It will be soon, okay?"

Russell Jr. sighed heavily and placed his head in his hands.

Sabrina hugged Lily again. "I love you, Mom."

"You and your brother look after your dad for me," Lily said, "until I get back."

Russell Jr. looked up. "When will that be?"

Lily shook her head. "I don't know, honey. There's a lot going on around here."

"Grandma was just telling us that Aunt Ivy had been in the hospital?" Sabrina asked, wide-eyed.

Lily nodded.

"Is she okay?" Sabrina asked.

Lily nodded again. "She's fine."

Lily stood up and smiled at her children. "Now let's go downstairs. Dinner should be ready shortly, and I want you two to eat something and hit the road before it gets dark."

Sabrina stood up. "Mom, you and Dad are going to work through this, right?"

Lily smiled. "Of course we are, honey."

"Yes!" Russell Jr. yelled, smiling.

"Now, enough about me and your father, how was your day?"

Sabrina smiled. "Not bad."

Sabrina was a first-year kindergarten teacher.

"Mine was good too," Russell Jr. said, smiling and nodding.

Lily tried to return her children's smiles, but instead burst into tears. Russell Jr. jumped up from the bed. He and Sabrina threw their arms around Lily's shoulders and tried to console her.

Chapter 27

Detective Jackson

Violet

We'd finished dinner, Sabrina and Russell Jr. had left, I had helped Jasmine and Niecee get the kids ready for bed, and was making my way back across the street when Warren came down the street and turned into Mama's driveway. When he got out of his SUV he had a legal-size portfolio tucked under his arm. Mama was in the yard pruning her rosebushes.

"Good evening," Warren said, slowly making his way up to the porch.

"Good evening," Mama said.

When I caught up with Warren, he looked down at me and whispered, "I've been trying to call you."

I tapped my right pants pocket; it was empty. I didn't have my cell phone with me.

"Is Lily here?" Warren asked, looking at Mama, then me.

Mama nodded. "Yes, she's in the house."

"I need to speak with her, well, all of you for that matter," Warren said.

My stomach knotted. I ran up the steps into the house looking for Ivy. Lily was in the den watching TV. I found Ivy upstairs in the bathroom taking a shower. I snatched back the shower curtain. "Warren is here to talk to Lily, and *us*!" I screamed.

"What?" Ivy screamed back.

Ivy turned off the water, stepped out of the bathtub, and grabbed a towel. "Okay, I'm coming!"

When I got back downstairs, Warren, Lily, and Mama were in the dining room, sitting at the table. Mama motioned for me to come in and take a seat. "Where's Ivy?" she asked.

"She's on her way," I said.

The front door opened, then closed and Jasmine sauntered into the dining room. Mama motioned for her to sit down.

I studied Warren's face for some sign of why he wanted to see us. The deadpan expression on his face told me nothing. I looked over at Lily. She appeared to be cool as a cucumber.

"Hey!" Ivy said, walking in with a big smile on her face.

Mama motioned for Ivy to sit down. "Warren needs to talk to us about sump'n."

"Okay," Ivy said, with another big smile.

"I'm here," Warren said, clearing his throat, "to talk with all of you about the assault on Sandra Harris."

Mama frowned. "Whaaaat?"

"What would we know about that?" Jasmine asked, frowning too.

"Yeah, what?" I asked.

"Let me explain," Warren said, holding up his hands. "Dominique Davis, a friend of Sandra's, told Lieutenant Roane—he's assisting me on this case—that she received a call from Sandra Saturday night shortly after eleven o'clock. Sandra was upset. She told Miss Davis that"—Warren looked over at Lily, then around the table at the rest of us—"Lily had made a nasty accusation against her."

"Whaaaat?" Mama said, looking at Lily.

My stomach knotted again.

"She told Miss Davis that Lily assaulted her," Warren said.

"What?" Jasmine yelled.

Mama's forehead wrinkled, and her mouth fell open.

Warren cleared his throat. "According to Miss Davis, Sandra said Lily accused her of sleeping with her husband."

"Oh, snap!" Jasmine shrieked.

"Lily?" Mama said. "Is that true?"

"Um, we"—Lily cleared her throat—"had words."

"This occurred in the vestibule of Fowler's Funeral Home?" Warren asked.

"Yes," Lily replied.

Jasmine gasped and covered her mouth with her hands.

"Did you *hit* her?" Mama asked.

Lily sighed and closed her eyes. "Yeah, Mama, I think I did."

"Dang!" Jasmine exclaimed. She was bouncing up and down in her seat now, clearly amused by what she was hearing.

"Miss Harris also told Miss Davis," Warren said, eyeing Lily, "that you told her you were firing her, and if she didn't stay away from your husband, she was going to be sorry."

"Oh no!" Ivy muttered.

I was floored by the words that left Warren's mouth. And from the expressions on Mama's and my sisters' faces—with the exception of Lily—they were too.

"Is any of that true?" Warren asked.

Before Lily could answer Ivy said, "What is the police department doing, Warren? Interrogating every woman who may have had a run-in with Sandra about her husband? My goodness, you might end up with a long list of women to question."

"Colette and Evangeline believe Lily attacked their niece."

"Oh my Lord!" Mama cried, throwing up her hands.

"They also think all of you," Warren said, looking around the table at us, "know that she's responsible."

Gasps filled the room.

Lily scoffed. "I wouldn't dirty my hands on that bitch!"

"Lily!" Mama screamed, hitting the table with her fist. "You watch your mouth!"

"Look at her hands, Warren!" Ivy said, reaching for Lily's hands. "If she attacked Sandra, there would be bruises!"

"Hold out your hands so Warren can see them!" Mama yelled at Lily.

Lily sighed and did as instructed. "See, Detective," she said, smirking, "no bruises. Satisfied now?"

"If you didn't assault her, you could have paid someone else to," Warren said.

"Warren please!" I shouted.

"I don't believe this!" Ivy cried. "What about DNA evidence, Warren?" Ivy asked. "Did Sandra fight back?"

"Our preliminary investigation did not find any skin under her fingernails. Her car and the clothing she was wearing have been sent to the state crime lab."

Jasmine looked at Lily. "Have you ever been in her car?" she asked, opening her eyes wide.

Lily smacked her lips. "Of course I have."

Jasmine's eyes grew larger and rounder. "Uh-oh! I watch enough of *CSI* to know—"

"Hush, Jasmine!" Ivy said.

"We believe Miss Harris was completely caught off-guard, or she knew her assailant," Warren said.

Jasmine and Mama looked at Lily.

Warren looked briefly at me before opening his portfolio and removing a pen from his shirt pocket. "Did you," he said, looking Lily squarely in the face, "accuse Sandra Harris of having an affair with your husband?"

"Yes, I did," Lily replied.

"Oh my!" Mama cried.

"Did you threaten her?" Warren asked.

I wouldn't look at Lily. I was afraid of what she was going to say.

"Did you tell Sandra Harris to leave your husband alone, and if she didn't, she would be sorry?" Warren asked.

"Dang!" Jasmine yelled.

"Lord, no!" Mama cried.

"Did you?" Warren asked.

"Yes!" Lily screamed. "Yes, I did!"

"Where were you between the hours of . . ." Warren paused before continuing. "Eleven o'clock on the night of May twenty-sixth and two a.m. on the morning of May twenty-seventh?"

Chapter 28

One Hot Mess!

Violet

"Why did you call him, Mama?" Lily asked loudly.

"'Cause I wanted to! That's why!" Mama yelled.

Lily scoffed. "You think he was going to tell you he was messing around with Sandra?"

Mama and Lily were in the kitchen cleaning up after breakfast. Even though the radio in the kitchen was blaring, from where Jasmine, Ivy, and I sat in the dining room, we could hear the conversation quite well.

"I believe him! He won't foolin' 'round with that girl!" Mama yelled.

Lily scoffed again. "'Any man will cheat, if given the opportunity.' That's what the lil' *whore* once told me."

"You watch your mouth!" Mama shouted. "Calling

Sandra names is not helping things, and it ain't right. And Russell is not *any* man!"

"So why he meet her for lunch?" Lily cried. "Huh? Why, Mama?"

"She asked Russell to help her get a job. And from what Russell told me, nothing was said or done out of the way," Mama said.

"Yeah, right!" Lily retorted.

When Warren told us last night that Russell told him he wasn't having an affair with Sandra, Lily scoffed and rolled her eyes.

"Why can't you believe him?" Mama asked. "Russell's old enough to be Sandra's father. She probably looks up to him like a father figure."

"Mama, please!" Lily retorted. "You ever heard of a midlife crisis?"

"So you think that's what Russell's having, and he's gone cheat on you with somebody his daughter's age?"

"He wouldn't be the first middle-aged man to do it!" Lily shrieked.

"She got an answer for everything," Jasmine said, rolling her eyes.

"What about the flowers, Mama?" Lily asked. "What he tell you about the flowers?"

"Russell said he was surprised she sent him flowers. Now, how can he or anybody control what another person does? Besides, the card only said 'Thanks'!"

"Don't forget the rest of it!" Lily said. "'Much *love*, Sandra.'"

"You're overreacting, daughter."

Lily burst into tears. "If—if it's so innocent like you're saying, why didn't Russell tell me she sent him flowers? Huh? Explain that, Mama!"

"And what would you have done if he had, daughter? Fly off the handle like you've done, believe what you heard them women on your job say, and fire Sandra like you're planning to do?"

Lily said nothing.

"Honey, you got to ask him why he didn't tell you. Maybe he just forgot!"

"Yeah, uh-huh! It slipped his mind all right!"

"Now pull yourself together," Mama said, "and go call your husband."

"I don't wanna talk to him!"

"Do you *honestly* believe Russell was messing around with Sandra?" Mama asked.

"Mama, I don't know what to believe!" Lily cried.

"Do you think she would be crazy enough to try to kill somebody?" Jasmine asked, looking around the dining room table at Ivy and me.

"No!" I said. "And how could you ask something like that?"

Jasmine smacked her lips. "You ever seen that show on the Oxygen Channel called *Snapped*?"

I narrowed my eyes at Jasmine.

"It's about women—"

"I've seen the show," I said, interrupting Jasmine.

"What you think?" Jasmine asked, looking at Ivy.

Ivy sighed and pursed her lips together.

Whoever assaulted Sandra, according to Warren, would be facing some serious charges—attempted murder, conspiracy to commit murder, abduction, and felonious kidnapping—and a lengthy prison sentence. And if Sandra died, that person could be facing the death penalty.

"If he's been unfaithful," Lily cried out, "I—I don't think I can stay with him!"

"I hope she don't mess up her good thang," Jasmine

muttered. "She needs to swallow her pride and come down off that high horse of hers."

I nodded. Baby sister was right. I hoped the humiliation Lily was feeling wouldn't cause her to make a rash decision about her marriage.

Jasmine reached into her pocket and pulled out her vibrating cell phone. She flipped it open. "This is Jasmine. Hello. Hello!" She sighed and looked around the table at us. "See," she said, closing the phone, "this is why I have to keep changing my number."

"What're you talking about?" Ivy asked.

"NeShell Scott. She done started messin' with me again."

"That was her?" Ivy asked, frowning.

"Uh-huh!" Jasmine replied.

"She's not supposed to be calling you, nor you her. That was stipulated in the court papers."

"I told you she was stupid!" Jasmine said.

Ivy sighed and shook her head. "What did she say?" she asked.

"She didn't say nothin'! Nobody said anything!"

A puzzled expression covered Ivy's face. "Soooo, how do you know it was NeShell?" she asked slowly.

"I just know!" Jasmine replied, quite agitated.

"Jasmine, please!" Ivy exclaimed, rolling her eyes. "Did NeShell's name and number show up on the display?"

Jasmine frowned. "Naw! The number was private! But it was her!" she asserted, pounding her fist on the table.

"Oh my goodness!" Ivy said, rolling her eyes again.

"It was her," Jasmine said, nodding.

"You don't know that!" Ivy said.

"Oh yes, I *do*!" Jasmine argued.

Sensing Ivy would not be able to convince Jasmine otherwise, no matter what she said, I asked, "And pray tell, how does your boyfriend's babies' mama keep getting your number?"

Jasmine made a face and shrugged.

"From Maniac, you think?" I said.

Jasmine smacked her lips. "Maniac ain't givin' her my number."

I shook my head in disbelief. "He's still seeing her, right?"

"Naw!" Jasmine yelled.

"Yeah, right!" Ivy said.

I burst out laughing.

"Laugh, ha, ha," Jasmine replied angrily. "Maniac's told me he don't want NeShell. He only go over to her house every now and then to give her money and stuff for the kids, so she won't take him to court for child support."

"Do you realize how silly you sound?" Ivy asked.

I burst out laughing again.

Mama came into the dining room and told me she needed butter, pineapple, coconut, and a dozen eggs. She wanted to bake a pineapple coconut cake and take it to Miss Emma's. This was Miss Emma's favorite cake, and she'd always been particularly fond of Mama's.

"I don't think that's a good idea," I said. "Miss Emma wouldn't even talk to you last night when you called her. You think she's gonna want a pineapple coconut cake from you?"

"Mama, I agree with Violet," Ivy said.

"Like Warren said, they're a little wary of us right now. When the fog clears, they'll see that Lily had nothing to do with what happened to Sandra," I said.

Mama sighed heavily. "I hope the fog clears soon, 'cause this about to get the best of me."

"Whatcha think this is doing to me?" Lily asked, sobbing from the doorway. "I'm the *suspect*!"

"Lily, calm down," I said.

"And how am I supposed to do that, Violet? Huh? Tell me that!"

"You haven't been arrested," I said softly.

"That's right, Lily," Ivy added. "Nor have you been brought in for questioning."

"But the damage has been done!" Lily screamed. "I can just hear those folks at the agency now! They're having a *field* day with this. And I know they know. They know by now. I bet that's why Marilyn hasn't called me anymore."

"Why don't you call Marilyn?" I suggested.

Lily shook her head. "No!"

Ivy went over to Lily and hugged her.

"They're probably burning me in effigy now!" Lily muttered.

"'Effigy'?" Jasmine asked, grinning. "They hate you *that* bad?" she asked, opening her eyes wide.

"Yeah!" Lily cried.

"Lily, you're sounding a little paranoid," I said.

"I won't be able to go back there to work! Uh-uh! My career is over!"

"Oh, brother!" Jasmine exclaimed, rolling her eyes.

"It is!" Lily shrieked.

"Lily, I'm not going to believe your coworkers dislike you that much," Mama said.

"I can believe it," Jasmine said.

"Hush, Jasmine!" Mama said.

"But I can," Jasmine said. "Mama, c'mon now. Lily's *conceited* and—"

"I am not!" Lily yelled.

Jasmine opened her eyes wide. "Oh yes, you are!"

Mama sighed and shook her head. "I ain't gone believe it. I ain't. Not everybody that work with you dislikes you."

"Marilyn's your friend," I said, smiling.

Lily scoffed. "That's one person out of . . ." Lily pursed her lips together and squinted. Her eyes darted from side to side. "Two hundred people," she finally said.

"That's mighty sad," Mama said.

"I can't help it that people are jealous of me!"

"Give me a break!" Jasmine muttered, standing up. "I'm going to watch TV," she said, exiting the room.

"You think that's what it is?" Ivy asked. "You think that's why people don't like you?"

"Yeah! What else could it be?" Lily asked, looking clueless.

"Did you hear what Jasmine said?" I asked.

"What?" Lily asked, still seemingly oblivious of why her colleagues didn't like her.

"Your attitude sucks!" Jasmine yelled from the den.

Mama threw up her hands. "You need to mend your ways, daughter. And if you don't come through this a changed person, I don't know what it will take."

"Mama, what time you want to go to the cemetery?" I asked.

It had been a week now since Aunt Caroline's death. The second thing on Mama's list of things to do while my sisters were home was place flowers at Aunt Caroline's grave site.

"I don't feel up to going now," Mama said. "I think I'll just stay round the house today."

Tears filled my eyes. Mama sounded and looked worn out.

"And instead of getting me pineapple and coconut," she said, "get me some cocoa. I'll bake a chocolate cake for the children."

Mama exited the house and slowly made her way across the street to Aunt Caroline's.

When we saw them, I insisted that we leave. Lily and Jasmine objected. They both took off ahead of Ivy and me down the aisle pretending to look for cocoa.

"Well, well, well, if it ain't the Shaw sisters," Evangeline Harris said, with a crooked smile.

"Hello," Ivy said pleasantly.

Walking alongside Evangeline carrying a shopping basket filled with various condiments and paper products was Colette.

"We're so sorry to hear about what happened to Sandra," Ivy said.

Neither Colette nor Evangeline responded.

"Surely, y'all can't believe Lily had anything to do with that," Ivy said.

"You save all that for the courtroom!" Colette snapped.

"Sista," Evangeline said softly, turning to look at Colette, "don't start."

Colette inhaled deeply and pressed her lips together.

"I like y'all's mama and everythang," Evangeline said, with another crooked smile, "but she don't need to be callin' my mama's house."

"Not a problem," Ivy said.

Evangeline's twenty-three-year-old daughter, Poochie,

who had a reputation for being a bully and a brawler, walked up and stood next to her mother.

"And how is Miss Emma?" Ivy asked.

"How you think she doin'?" Colette snapped.

"Lily didn't have anything to do with what happened to Sandra," Ivy said.

"We think differently," Colette said. "And it's just a matter of time before Warren slaps handcuffs on her, and charges the rest of y'all with hindering prosecution."

Ivy gasped and chuckled.

"Did I say sump'n funny?" Colette asked, bucking her eyes.

"Yeah," Jasmine said laughing, "you did!"

I nudged Jasmine and told her to shut up.

"The reason why Warren hasn't arrested *anyone*," Ivy said, "is because he doesn't have evidence to make an arrest."

"Keep thinkin' that, Miss Lawyer!" Poochie said, giving Ivy a cutting look.

Jasmine burst out laughing and said, "Y'all *ridiculous*."

Poochie gasped. "What? What she say, Mama?" she asked, looking at Evangeline. "Did she say we was *ridiculous*?"

"Warren is gonna get to the bottom of this!" Colette yelled. "He told me *that*"—she looked at me—"last night."

"He told me the same thing," I said, "*last* night."

Colette narrowed her eyes at me, then rolled them.

"Listen," Ivy said, with outstretched hands, "we're sorry about what happened to Sandra, but Lily had *nothing* to do with that."

"God knows," Evangeline said, eyeing Lily sharply, "God knows."

"Nub told Mama and me that there was a married man stalking San—"

"He's been cleared!" Colette snapped, interrupting me.

"All we ask," Ivy said, "is that you all not let your emotions cloud your judgment."

"You don't tell us what and how to feel!" Colette yelled, her eyes burning with hatred.

I picked up a can of Hershey's cocoa and said to Ivy, Lily, and Jasmine, "Let's go."

"Again, Lily had *nothing* to do with what happened to Sandra," Ivy said.

"You keep saying that, but Miss Prim and Proper here," Colette said, glaring at Lily, "ain't said nothin'."

Lily scoffed. "I don't have anything to say."

"You one cold, stuck-up heifer," Poochie said. "I don't see how Sandra put up with you."

"Who you callin' a 'heifer,' heifer?" Jasmine yelled.

A small group of people had gathered in the aisle. They were whispering to each other and watching us. I was now not only embarrassed, I was scared. This had the making for one ugly, hot mess if we didn't leave.

"Let's go!" I said.

Nobody moved. Jasmine and Poochie looked like they had squared off to wage war with each other. If blows were thrown, my sisters and I would naturally jump in the fray to defend Jasmine, and Evangeline and Colette would undoubtedly jump in to Poochie's defense. The outcome: all of our names listed in the Crime Beat section of tomorrow's edition of the *McKinley Messenger.* The headline would read: DISTURBANCE AT PIGGLY WIGGLY.

"I tried to help Sandra. I didn't want her to turn out like—"

"Lily, hush! Let's go!" I said, nudging her.

"What?" Evangeline and Colette hollered.

"Let's goooo!" I said again. Lily didn't budge. I felt like hitting her upside her head with the cocoa can in my hand.

"You didn't want her to turn out like *what?*" Colette asked.

"Don't you say another word!" Ivy said to Lily.

"Like us? Is that what you were going to say?" Colette asked. "Just 'cause we don't have fancy jobs, expensive cars, and big houses like y'all don't make y'all no better than us!"

"I didn't say it did," Lily said.

"But y'all *always* thought y'all were better than us!" Colette said, sneering.

The aisle was full of spectators now.

"I'm not going to apologize to you or anyone for having a college degree, excuse me, for having *two* college degrees," Lily said. "Or for having a good-paying job, a nice car, and a home."

"Ain't nobody askin' you to!" Colette yelled.

Evangeline threw up her hands. "Don't go there with her," she said to Colette. "Because the God *we* serve owns the cattle on a thousand hills! Hallelujah! Hallelujah! Anything we want or need, all we got to do is ask him!"

Lily chuckled and rolled her eyes.

"You better be glad I ain't like I used to be," Evangeline said, glaring at Lily. "'Cause if I was, I'd knock yo' teeth down your throat."

This was typical Evangeline. I'd seen her do this many times at church. Whenever someone was getting the best of her in an argument, she always got religious on them and then made reference to her "past" life as a brawler.

"I could have a Mercedes, a Lexus, and—and—"

"BMW," Colette said, finishing the sentence for Evangeline.

"Right, thank you, sista. Like y'all. But I don't want one," Evangeline said. "They don't drive no better than my Chevy Impala outside."

Lily and Jasmine burst out laughing.

"That's funny?" Poochie asked, glaring at them.

"Yeah, heifer," Jasmine said, "it is."

"You got one mo' time to call out my name," Poochie said, throwing up her hands and inching toward Jasmine.

"And what, what?" Jasmine asked, stepping forward, wringing her neck.

I grabbed Jasmine by her arm and pulled her back.

"Material thangs aren't important to me," Evangeline asserted. "I'm tryin' to win souls for Christ."

"Amen, sista!" Colette said.

Lily narrowed her eyes at Evangeline. "On your back?"

"What?" Evangeline hollered.

"You're such a damn hypocrite," Lily said. "According to what I heard, from your niece, you haven't mended *all* your ways."

Evangeline threw up her hands. "I'm not gone stand here and listen to lies."

"Mama, let's go before I whup this bitch's ass! I ain't saved like you," Poochie said.

"There's probably a long list of women with an ax to grind with Sandra," Lily said. "She confided in me about a lot of things. Things that she wasn't proud of.

I know who paid her college tuition. Y'all sho' as hell
didn't! And I know who put the deposit down on her
town house and who cosigned for that car she drives.
I didn't have *anything* to do with what happened to
Sandra, okay?"

"Let's go, Mama!" Poochie said. "Before I go off up
in here!"

"Heifer, I will wipe the floor with your ass!" Jasmine
said, lunging forward.

I don't know who threw the first punch; it happened so fast. I do know I was hit upside the head with
a bottle of ketchup. Ivy fell up against me after a
punch Poochie intended for Jasmine landed upside
her head. The carton of eggs she was holding slipped
from her hand and fell to the floor along with the can
of cocoa in my hand.

"Ladies! Break it up! This is a place of business! Take
it outside!" the store manager said, hurrying down the
aisle, huffing and puffing. The store's pudgy security
guard was with him saying into a walkie-talkie that there
was a disturbance at the Piggly Wiggly.

"Let's go!" I yelled, scrambling to my feet. Ivy and
I grabbed Jasmine and started dragging her down
the aisle.

As she was being dragged away by Colette and
Poochie, Evangeline yelled, "If yo' sista had anythang
to do with my niece being in the hospital, after we
make sure she spends the rest of her life in prison, we
gone sue the rest of y'all for everythang you got! And
you," she said, pointing to Ivy, "Miss Fancy-Dressin'
Lawyer! You won't be able to do a damn thang about
it! We saw you on TV. Yeah, uh-huh! And just like you
couldn't stop them from executin' that woman, you

won't be able to stop the state from executin' yo' sista if my niece dies!"

"We are praying that Sandra pulls through," Ivy said tearfully.

"Ivy! Let's go," I said.

"You better hope she does," Evangeline yelled. "'Cause if she doesn't, you gone be on TV again, tryin' to get another death sentence overturned."

Chapter 29

Exposed

Violet

We finally made it back home with the ingredients Mama needed for her chocolate cake. I ended up having to get them from a supermarket across town. Mama, thank goodness, was still across the street at Aunt Caroline's when we returned home.

"I hope Mama don't hear about what happened," Ivy said, sighing.

"You can forget that," I said. I could see Miss Sadie now, coming up the walkway frowning and shaking her head, coming to tell Mama what she'd heard from Miss Odessa. "Y'all better hope the store manager doesn't press charges!" I cried.

"He said he wouldn't!" Ivy said.

"We're going to make Mama sick!" I muttered, shaking my head.

"I truly don't understand you," Ivy said, glaring at Jasmine. "The judge, your probation officer both said to you in *English* that your probation would be revoked if you were involved in misbehavior of any kind. Have you forgotten that, or do you think they were joking?"

Jasmine sighed, rolled her eyes, and strutted into the kitchen.

"And, Lily! You weren't helping matters!" Ivy yelled.

Lily threw up a hand at Ivy and followed Jasmine into the kitchen. Ivy and I were right behind them.

"Jasmine, I have something for you to read," Ivy said, glaring at Jasmine with her hands on her hips.

"And what's *that?*" Jasmine asked, scowling.

"Mia's diary," Ivy replied.

Jasmine scoffed. "Why would I want to read her diary?"

"Mia doesn't want you to end up in prison," Ivy said.

"And I ain't, okay?" Jasmine snapped. "And I don't appreciate you talking to that convict about me in the first place."

"And it's because of that *funky* attitude of yours that you're on probation!" Ivy yelled.

"Y'all chill out! Please!" Lily said, walking over to the refrigerator. She pulled open the door and removed a bottle of water. "Nobody's getting in trouble."

"I wish they would shut up!" Jasmine mumbled.

Ivy gasped and looked at me. "You hear them?" she asked.

I sighed and shook my head in disbelief.

Ivy looked at Lily. "Need I remind you that you are *unofficially* a person of interest in an attempted murder case! And Colette and Evangeline Harris should be the last two people you'd want to pick a fight with!"

"Amen!" I said, clapping my hands.

"And why don't you"—Ivy smiled and narrowed her eyes at Jasmine—"bring Lily up to speed? Tell her about your visit with the social worker on Monday."

"What?" Lily shrieked.

Jasmine smacked her lips. "It won't nothing," she said rather nonchalantly.

"Earth to Jasmine!" I yelled. "I wouldn't call a visit with a CPS worker 'nothing.'"

Lily walked over to Jasmine. "What's going on?" she asked, looking quite concerned.

Jasmine sighed again. "Alisha Hughes, she's a social worker with the county, she thinks Rashaunda needs some counseling."

"For what?" Lily asked.

"Duh!" I yelled. "You forgot about what happened on Sunday? Running away . . . hiding out in a car's trunk!"

"She's out of control," Ivy said. "Defiant! And she's going to end up in trouble, with a record like her mammy here, if something isn't done. She's meeting with a therapist today at one o'clock who will assess her need for counseling."

Lily sighed and shook her head.

"And if this lady says she needs counseling," Jasmine said, rolling her eyes, "she's gone refer us to an agency in Charlotte."

"I hope you follow through with any recommendation she gives you," Lily said.

Jasmine nodded. "I will."

"She won't have a choice," Ivy said. "Miss Hughes said she was going to transfer the case to Charlotte

Social Services and it wouldn't be closed until the therapist's recommendations were followed."

"This could all have been avoided," Lily said, looking at Jasmine. "We've been telling you for years that you needed to get a handle on Rashaunda."

"I know," Jasmine said softly.

"But you did *nothing*," Lily said. "Now you got CPS breathing down your neck having to intervene on her behalf." She sighed. "I sure hope Mama doesn't hear about this."

"You need to move out of the projects," I said.

"I like living in Githens Court."

"Jasmine, please!" I exclaimed.

"I do!"

We were so busy trying to hammer some sense into Jasmine's empty head, we didn't hear the front door open and close, nor Mama enter the kitchen. "And Sadie was just here yesterday, talking about what fine ladies y'all were," Mama said, startling us. "You on probation?" she screamed, walking up to Jasmine.

Jasmine looked up at the ceiling. Her eyes rolled around in their sockets and filled with tears. When she blinked, the tears streamed down her cheeks.

"For what?" Mama yelled, now standing nose to nose with Jasmine.

"Mama, calm down," I said.

"What . . . are . . . you . . . on . . . pro-bation for?" Mama yelled.

Jasmine's mouth opened, but nothing came out.

"Answer me!" Mama yelled.

"Mama, please!" Ivy said, walking over.

Mama looked back at Ivy; Ivy stopped dead in her tracks. She then returned her intense gaze at Jasmine, who looked like she was convulsing. "I ain't gone ask you again!"

"Fo-for fi-fighting," Jasmine stammered.

"'Fighting'?" Mama asked.

"Yes, ma'am."

"When this happen?" Mama asked, looking around the room at the rest of us.

I looked down at the floor. No one said anything.

"Somebody better answer me!" Mama yelled.

"Three months ago," Lily finally said. "Ivy and Violet went to Charlotte and bailed her out of jail."

"'Jail'!" Mama yelled. Her outburst echoed throughout the room. "My Lord!" she cried. "And no one bothered to tell me!"

"We didn't want to worry you, Mama," Ivy said.

"Is that why you *lied* to me about who that woman was talking to you and Violet in the yard Monday morning," Mama asked, "so I wouldn't 'worry'?"

Ivy's head dropped.

Here we go again! I said to myself.

"I am disappointed in you," Mama said, looking back at Jasmine. "And if Augustus was alive, he would be too."

"I'm sorry," Jasmine cried.

"You gone keep that appointment today. And I'm going with you to make sure you do."

"Mama, that ain't necessary. Ivy's going with us," Jasmine said.

"I'm not stopping Miss Ivy from going," Mama said, rocking her head from side to side. "She can *drive* if she wants to! 'Cause if you can't cool Shaunda's heels, don't worry 'bout taking her back to Charlotte. She's gone stay right here with me."

"But, Mama!" Jasmine cried.

"But, Mama, nothing! She stuck up over there under Niecee, who ain't no kinda role model for anybody, holding TreShawn. Wanna know what I overheard when I went over there this morning?" Mama didn't give whimpering Jasmine time to ask. "Your twelve-year-old daughter asking Niecee what it feel like to be pregnant. What it feel like to have babies."

Jasmine dropped her head.

"Look at me!" Mama yelled.

Jasmine raised her head.

"She said one of her friend's pregnant. Is that true?"

Jasmine nodded.

Mama threw up her hands. "Lord, have mercy!"

For what seemed like forever, no one said anything. Mama finally exhaled. "You gone get help for Shaunda, whether this woman she sees this afternoon say so or not!"

"I am, Mama. Just as soon as I get back home, I promise," Jasmine said.

"You home now," Mama said, walking away.

Jasmine was outside sulking. She, Rashaunda, Ivy, and Mama had gotten back from the therapy appointment. Jasmine's plans to leave for Charlotte after the appointment had been aborted, by Mama. She had other plans in mind for Jasmine.

"I ain't movin' back here!" Jasmine whined, following me down the porch steps. "I don't wanna move back here!"

"I don't think it's a bad idea," I said without looking back.

"Whatever! Where're you going?"

"To the library."

"Yeah, right. You going to see Warren."

I spun around. "Will you hush! Just 'cause Mama's mad at you now, don't try to get her upset with me."

Jasmine rolled her eyes and plopped down on the top porch step.

I jumped in my car and sped out the driveway.

Chapter 30

Busted

Violet

"Honey, stop worrying?"

"Okay."

Warren kissed me on the forehead and embraced me.

We were standing out on his deck, gazing up at the sky. There was a full moon and a sky full of twinkling stars. Warren was a stargazer. Since our acquaintance, I'd developed a fascination for staring off into the galaxy too.

It was late; it was after ten o'clock. I should have been home an hour ago. I just couldn't pull myself away from Warren. It had been more than a week since I'd been to his house. I had called Ivy on her cell at nine o'clock; she told me Mama still wasn't talking that much to anybody. She was in her room reading the Bible and watching *The Word Network*. I prayed Mama would find the consolation she needed from the Good Book and televangelists, because my sisters and I surely weren't giving it to her. And if there was such a thing as people turning over in their graves, Daddy and Aunt Caroline had flipped several times in theirs.

I felt powerless. I wanted to make everything right. I wanted to make Jasmine wiser, take away Mama's grief, Lily's heartache, and Ivy's physical pain and angst. As I gazed up into the night sky, I started crying again over my inability to do any of that.

Warren held me tighter and gently kissed my tears away.

"I don't think I've ever been more scared in my life than Monday afternoon," I said, looking up at him.

"Shhhh," he said.

"I'd never seen anyone OD before. It was *terrifying*!"

"I know, baby."

"Since then, it's been one thing right after another!"

Warren kissed me on my forehead again.

"Warren, do you think a woman could have inflicted those types of injuries on Sandra?"

"An enraged woman, yes," Warren replied.

"Lily has a temper, but I've never known her to physically assault anyone. She didn't do it."

Warren didn't say anything. This was his first major case since joining the McKinley Police Department, and with him as one of its two lead detectives, I imagined the pressure he was under to solve it was overwhelming.

"Are you close to making an arrest?" I asked.

"I hope so. The lab results should be back by the end of the week."

"Is it possible that they could come back sooner?"

Warren sighed. "Anything's possible, but I seriously doubt it."

"I just hope Sandra pulls through."

Warren's Nextel rang. He reached into his pocket and pulled it out. "Jackson," he said into the phone. "The file's on my desk," he said seconds later.

"You got to go?" I asked when he ended the call.

"No."

"What time is it?"

Warren flipped open his cell phone. "Ten oh five. You ready to go?"

"No."

"'No'?"

I shook my head.

I parked on the street in front of the house and crept around to the back. Buddy, a golden retriever in the yard behind us, started barking. I yelled for him to hush. It was now approaching midnight. I slowly and quietly unlocked the back door and entered the house. It was dark and quiet inside. I locked the door behind me, took off my mules, tiptoed through the kitchen, then down the hall toward the stairs. The door to Mama's bedroom was open. It was dark in her room, so I couldn't tell if she was in bed or not. I assumed and hoped she was. I tiptoed past her room and hurried to the stairway, holding my breath.

"Daughter, where're you coming from?"

I jumped and dropped one of my mules. It made a loud bam when it hit the floor.

A light popped on in Mama's room. "Violet, come here," she said.

I swallowed hard, turned around, and eased back down the hall to Mama's bedroom.

"You can't sleep?" I asked, smiling from the doorway.

Mama was lying on her back looking up at the ceiling. She didn't bother to look over at me. "You remember where we were last week this time?" she asked.

I cleared my throat. I couldn't bring myself to answer. Last week this time, Mama and I were at the hospital huddled together crying, outside the hospital room where Aunt Caroline's cold body lay.

Mama looked over at me. "Where you coming from?"

For a few seconds I couldn't and didn't say anything, nor could I avoid Mama's all-knowing gaze. "Warren's," I finally said.

Mama sighed, reached over, and turned out the lamp. I turned and staggered down the hall toward the stairs with my hands over my mouth trying to suppress my hiccupping sobs.

Chapter 31

Mulling

Violet

Mama was up early, rattling pots and pans. Gospel 680 was blaring from the radio. "Touch Me, Lord Jesus," a spiritual by the Angelic Gospel Singers, was playing on the radio.

Ivy was the first to go downstairs. She was going to tell Mama she was having second thoughts about marrying Allen. Given how Mama was so fond of Allen, Ivy assumed Mama wouldn't take the news well.

When Lily and I got downstairs, Mama told us she didn't want any of us leaving the house, for fear we'd run into some of Miss Emma's folks again and end up in trouble. When she called over to Aunt Caroline's and told everyone there to come over for breakfast, she told Jasmine the same thing. I could barely look at Mama. I was still feeling bad about being caught last night.

When the *McKinley Messenger* arrived with a thud on the front porch, we had finished breakfast and were in the den watching *The Price Is Right*. Niecee and the children had gone back over to Aunt Caroline's, and I had by now apologized to Mama, several times, for having gone over to Warren's last night. Mama excused herself and returned with the morning paper and the Bible. She handed Lily the Bible and told her to read and meditate on two scriptures: Proverbs 18:24—*A man that hath friends must shew himself friendly: and there is a friend that sticketh closer than a brother.* And Galatians 5:22–23—*But the fruit of the Spirit is love, joy, peace, longsuffering, gentleness, goodness, faith. Meekness, temperance: against such there is no law.*

Mama opened the newspaper, handed me the supermarket flyers, and turned to the obituary section. She always read that section before any other.

"I hate my babies had to miss their last days of school," Jasmine mumbled from where she was lying on the floor.

"Me too," Mama said.

"They really aren't missing that much, are they?" Ivy asked.

Jasmine sighed and shook her head. "Just end-of-year classroom parties and award assemblies. Kenya's getting two awards this year."

"Two?" I asked, smiling.

Jasmine smiled. "Yeah. For outstanding citizenship and for being on the A honor roll all year long."

"That's great!" Mama said. "What about Shaunda? Did she make any honor rolls?"

Here we go! I said to myself.

Jasmine cleared her throat and looked back at Mama. "Mama, Rashaunda didn't make her grade."

"I know," Mama said coolly. "She told me that yesterday. I only asked to see if you were going to lie to me again about her having done so."

Jasmine sighed and turned her attention back to the TV.

"Oh!" Mama exclaimed. "They're hiring at the Nursing and Convalescent Center. The housekeeping department has *four* openings."

"Wow!" I said. "Cheryl told me they were hiring."

From where she was lying on the floor with her back to Mama, I saw Jasmine roll her eyes. "Oh yeah?" she said.

"They got a big ad in the paper," Mama said excitedly. "I bet your cousin Cheryl can help you get on there. She's worked in that department for years! I'll call her and ask."

"Mama, I'm gonna look for a job just as soon as I get back to Charlotte."

Mama threw the classified section of the paper down on the floor. "Doing *what*, daughter?"

"I don't know," Jasmine muttered, "something."

"What do you want to do?" Mama asked, scowling.

Jasmine sighed and shrugged. "Ain't nobody gone hire me with a record. Don't y'all know that?"

"What I know!" Mama yelled. "Nothing beats a failure but a try!"

"It ain't gone happen, Mama!" Jasmine argued.

"You don't know that!" Mama fired back. "I think Cheryl can get you on at the convalescent center. And I know she'll try if I ask her."

The telephone rang. "If it's Beatrice, tell her I'm resting!" Ivy yelled.

"And how long do you think you're going to be able to avoid this woman's phone calls?" Mama said, reaching for the phone. "The wedding's nine days away!"

Ivy pursed her lips together and sighed heavily. Allen's mother had pissed her off the last time they talked with her comment that Aunt Caroline's death couldn't have come at a worse time. And each time Beatrice Hayes called, she asked when Ivy was returning to Durham. Last night she had called excited because she had received some last-minute RSVPs from some "prominent individuals": a running back with the Carolina Panthers and the mayor of Durham and his wife. Ivy didn't talk to her then or when she called earlier this morning; she had Lily tell her she was resting. Lily did as Ivy told her. Beatrice remarked that there would be plenty of time for Ivy to rest during her honeymoon and to have Ivy return her call as soon as possible.

Beatrice Hayes was pressing Ivy to make some definite plans regarding the rehearsal dinner and bridal party breakfast. Unbeknownst to her, they were the furthest things from Ivy's mind. And if she knew Ivy was thinking about calling off a wedding that was getting more extravagant by the day, she would be mortified. As a surprise to Ivy, she told Lily in confidence that Peabo Bryson and Regina Belle were slated to serenade her and Allen at the reception.

"I will give Ivy the message, Beatrice," Mama said into the phone. "I . . . uh-huh . . . I understand. All right. No, I can't say when she'll be leaving. Uh-huh. I'll give her the message. All right. Bye now."

"What she talking about now?" Ivy asked, when Mama ended the phone call.

"The same thing," Mama said, shaking her head.

To Ivy's surprise and relief, when she told Mama that she might call off the wedding because she wasn't sure if she was ready to settle down, Mama didn't take the news too badly. She hugged Ivy and told her to pray about the matter and ask God to guide her.

"I think you just got a case of premarital jitters," Jasmine said, looking up at Ivy.

Ivy chuckled. "You think that's what it is?"

Jasmine nodded.

All that talk about Ivy's wedding got me to day-dreaming about a platinum wedding of my own. If things continued to go well between Warren and me, and I was praying that they would, I wondered how long it would be before he asked me to marry him. A year? Two years, maybe?

"Who are those people?" Lily asked, looking over at the newspaper in Mama's lap.

I looked over at the paper too. There was a picture of a large group of black folk standing in front of a run-down trailer. Some were crying, others scowling.

I removed the paper from Mama's lap. "It's the Harrises!" I said.

Ivy snatched the paper out of my hands. "*Family Can't Contain Grief Any Longer*," she read.

"*She was the first one in this family to leave home and go to college. She was tryin' to make sump'n of herself,' seventy-nine-year-old Emma Harris said about her granddaughter, twenty-four-year-old Sandra Harris. 'We are all very proud of her.'*

"*The attack on Mrs. Harris's granddaughter has rocked McKinley to its core. Mrs. Harris said she last talked to her granddaughter on the evening of May 26, just before eleven p.m. Miss Harris was heading back to*

Raleigh to prepare for a trip to Atlanta the following morning. Her family reports that she was savagely beaten late Saturday night or early Sunday morning. Some members of her family fear if an arrest isn't made soon, the trail for her assailant will grow cold. Colette Worrell defends what some consider slow going by the police department. She believes Detective Warren Jackson is doing all that can be done to make an arrest. She said Lieutenant Jackson is keeping her abreast of the investigation.

"Sandra Harris remains in a coma at McKinley General. The vicious, brutal assault against her has McKinley residents in arms. There hasn't been a murder in this town in ten years, nor a crime this heinous in more than five years. The family is maintaining a prayer vigil for Miss Harris in shifts at McKinley General, where her condition remains unchanged. This reporter was unable to reach Lieutenant Jackson, who is heading up this investigation, at his office and he has not returned this reporter's phone calls. When asked if they could think of anyone who would want to do such a vile, vicious thing to their niece, Evangeline Harris and her sister Colette said they could, but refused to say who. The family is offering a reward of five hundred dollars for any information leading to an arrest."

"Don't leave this house! Y'all hear me?" Mama said, after Ivy finished reading the story. "I mean it! Don't leave this house!"

Lily ran upstairs crying.

"Mama, Jasmine and Rashaunda are supposed to meet with the social worker again today. Remember?" Ivy said.

"Call her and ask her if she would come here," Mama said.

Ivy reached for the phone.

"Not you!" Mama yelled. "Jasmine! Get up and call that woman!"

"I can't believe Odessa!" Mama said, slamming down the phone. It was almost noon. We were setting the table for lunch. Miss Odessa had called Mama and told her the Mothers' Board had called a meeting and had decided in light of what had happened to get someone else to speak at the upcoming Women's Day Program. Mama told Miss Odessa she and the women were out of order, and that she should have been notified of the meeting. With Mama being president of the Mothers' Board, meetings were not to be held without her knowledge, and if any were to be called, it was Mama's place to do it. Miss Odessa told Mama that since she was vice president of the Mothers' Board, she thought she had the authority to call meetings too. Mama told Miss Odessa she couldn't have been more wrong on the matter, and that she needed to read her copy of the church's bylaws.

When we asked Mama what she was going to do about what had happened, she sighed and said, "Nothing." She didn't feel it was an issue worth fighting in light of all that was going on.

Chapter 32

Unwelcome Advances

Violet

I was standing in the front door about to go outside and over to Aunt Caroline's house to check on Niecee and the kids when the white Buick pulled into Mama's driveway. Seymour Edwards threw open the driver's door and hopped out. He scooted around to the other side of the Lucerne and opened the front and rear passenger doors. I turned and went down the hall to Mama's bedroom. I could hear her moving around in the master bathroom. "Mama!" I called out. "You got company!"

Mama stuck her head out the bathroom. "Is it Mavis and Viola?"

"Yes, ma'am."

"Let 'em in, and tell 'em I'll be right out."

"Okay."

Mavis Edwards and Viola Whitfield were long-standing members of Charity Chapel, church mothers in fact, who tended to side with Mama on church matters. I gathered they were here to talk about the meeting Miss Odessa had earlier denouncing and removing Lily as Women's Day speaker. I had no desire to stick around while they did that, because they had a tendency to badger me about not being married. Although she had long since stopped trying, Miss Mavis at one time tried her best to hook me up with her philandering son, Seymour, who reportedly had a slew of children by a number of women—including Miss Emma's daughter, Colette, all over McKinley.

I hurried back to the front door and stepped outside. "Hello!" I yelled, smiling and waving.

Miss Mavis and Seymour greeted me with big smiles and merry "hellos."

"My, my, my! It's some kinda pretty over there," Miss Viola said. She was leaning on her three-prong cane looking over at Aunt Caroline's yard. "Just look at those flowers!" she exclaimed.

"Look at Peony's roses, Viola!" Miss Mavis said, admiringly.

Miss Viola whirled around and gasped. "Oh my!" she said, placing a hand on her chest. "Mavis, I don't think I've seen prettier roses!"

"Me either," Miss Mavis replied.

"Peony and Caroline were blessed with green thumbs," Miss Viola said.

"Yes, they were," Miss Mavis said, nodding.

From where he was standing in the yard, Seymour gave me the once-over as he chewed on a toothpick in the corner of his mouth.

"Come on in, ladies, and, gentleman," I said.

Seymour and the women slowly made their way up to the porch and into the house. Mama was coming down the hall, smoothing down her dress.

"Afternoon!" she yelled.

The visitors returned Mama's greeting.

"Y'all come on in here," Mama said, stepping into the living room, "and sit down."

Miss Viola danced into the living room behind Miss Mavis singing along with the kitchen radio, "We're gonna be in the great cor'nation that'll be held, in the middle of the air!"

"Yes, Lord! Sing the song!" Mama shouted.

"Gonna be in the great cor'nation that'll be held, in the middle of the air!" Miss Viola sang again.

"Glory! Glory!" Miss Mavis cried out, clapping her hands. "My Redeemer lives! Hallelujah! And I'm goin' up to meet him, oh, thank you, Jesus, one sweet day!"

"Yes, yes," Mama said, dabbing at the corner of her eyes.

I allowed Mama and her peer laborers in Christ to sing, testify, and get their praise on for a few minutes before I asked if anyone wanted anything to drink.

"I'll take a glass of water," Miss Mavis said.

Miss Viola shook her head. "I'm fine, thank you."

I looked over at Seymour, who had yet to go into the living room and sit down. He was standing in the doorway next to me. "Would you care for something?" I asked.

"Yeah," he replied seductively. "You," he mouthed.

I abruptly looked away and took off for the kitchen.

"Need any help?"

I took a deep breath. "I think I can manage, Seymour," I said, without looking back.

"I didn't know you were a scrapper," he said, chuckling.

I looked back. "What?"

"I heard about that"—Seymour started chuckling again—"fight between you and Colette at the Piggly Wiggly."

"Wait a—"

"I had you pegged wrong, girl," Seymour said, interrupting me. "You look like you wouldn't hurt a fly, and you slugging it out with Colette."

"Hold up! Wait a minute!" I exclaimed. "Colette and I were not fighting, okay?"

"Ain't what I heard," Seymour said, shaking his head and grinning. "Heard y'all were calling each other names and after Colette hit you with a ketchup bottle, you really lit into her."

So she did throw that ketchup bottle at me? I thought to myself.

"You—you heard wrong, okay?" I said, hearing anger and embarrassment in my voice. And what wasn't helping matters was the fact that I could clearly see that Seymour was getting a rise out of this. I took a deep breath in an effort to calm myself.

"Uh-huh, if you say so," Seymour replied, with a shrug and a smile. "Pretty as you are, you ain't got to *fight* nobody over no man."

"What? Oh my goodness!" I shrieked. "I don't believe this!"

"I didn't want to believe it either," Seymour said derisively.

"Seymour, listen."

"Hey, baby, calm down," Seymour said softly, walking up on me.

I threw up my hands. "You wanna back it up a little bit?" I said, narrowing my eyes at him.

Seymour smiled and took a few steps back.

"Thank you," I said.

Seymour gave me the once-over again and started chewing on his toothpick.

Minutes later, I was heading back to the living room with Miss Mavis's glass of water and with Seymour trotting behind me.

"Odessa was way outta order!" Mama said.

"Yes, she was," Miss Viola said, wheezing. She leaned forward and started coughing. She sounded like a puttering car engine.

"Get her some water, honey," Mama said to me.

I dashed out of the room and back into the kitchen. When I returned to the living room, Seymour had taken a seat next to his mother. His feet were stretched out in front of him and he was resting his head on the back of the sofa.

"You don't want anything, Seymour?" Mama asked.

Seymour grinned. "I saw that chocolate cake in the kitchen, Miss Peony. I wouldn't mind," he said, clearing his throat, "having a slice of that."

Mama quickly turned to me. "Violet, go get Seymour a slice of cake, and some lemonade."

Seymour broke out into a big grin and started rubbing his stomach. "Thank you, Miss Peony." He looked over at me and winked.

When I returned to the living room with refreshments for Seymour, Miss Viola was asking Mama how Ivy was.

"She's fine," Mama said.

"Praise God!" Miss Viola said.

"Yes, yes!" Mama said.

"Where is she?" Miss Viola asked.

"Upstairs taking a nap," Mama replied.

"She's gone be a beautiful bride," Miss Mavis said, smiling.

Mama smiled and cut her eyes at me. I wondered then if she would tell her friends that Ivy was contemplating calling off her wedding.

"You catch the bouquet okay?" Miss Viola said, looking at me.

"O-tay!" I said, bucking my eyes and grinning broadly like Buckwheat on *The Little Rascals.*

Mama cleared her throat and cut her eyes at me again.

"Don't let Jasmine get it now," Miss Mavis said, somberly. "She still got a lil' time 'fore she need to settle down. You, well, that's a different story."

Oh, Lord, give me strength! I prayed.

"Yeah, don't let your baby sister beat you going down the aisle," Miss Viola said quite sternly. She looked over at Mama and asked, "Does Jasmine have a friend, Peony?"

Mama frowned and grunted. "Some joker brought her here Saturday. She introduced him to me as her friend."

"Uh-huh," Miss Viola said, nodding.

"Violet, baby, what you waitin' on?" Miss Mavis asked.

"She waitin' on me, Mama," Seymour said, laughing, "to pop the question."

Mama, Miss Mavis, and Miss Viola thought what Seymour said was funny too. They broke out into a fit of laughter. Miss Viola laughed so hard she started puttering again.

Mama reached over and patted her on the back.

When Seymour finished off the slice of cake and

the glass of lemonade, he stood up, walked over to me, and handed me the dessert plate, fork, and glass. "Miss Peony," he said, looking back at Mama.

"Yes, Seymour?"

"That was delicious!"

Mama smiled. "Thank you, but I can't take credit for all that. Violet made the lemonade."

"Oh?" Seymour asked, turning to look at me. "Is that a fact?"

Mama nodded.

"It was *sweet*, just like her," he said, winking at me.

"Ooooh! What a kind thing to say," Miss Viola said, smiling.

I tried to refrain from rolling my eyes out of annoyance, but didn't succeed in doing so.

"You aw'right, Violet?" Miss Mavis asked, eyeing me sharply.

"Yes, ma'am. I'm fine."

"You don't look particularly so," she said, creasing her brows.

"She's probably tired," Mama said. "We all are."

"I imagine y'all are," Miss Viola said, shaking her head.

"We ain't gone stay too long, Peony. We just had to come over and talk with you about what Odessa did," Miss Mavis said. "What you think we ought to do? You know we behind you one hundred percent."

I turned and left the room. To my chagrin, Seymour followed me. I didn't know how long it would take Mama, Miss Mavis, and Miss Viola to sort through their dilemma and come up with a plan of action. What I did know, I had no intention of hanging around keeping horny Seymour company.

He tapped me on the shoulder. "You wanna go for a ride?" he asked, tugging at my ponytail.

I looked back at him, smiled, and said, "No."

"What, you scared Warren gone see you?" he asked, laughing. "You ain't got to worry about that. Colette got him tied up for the moment."

"Oh," I said, trying not to sound the least bit bothered.

"Uh-huh. I saw his truck at Miss Emma's house when I passed it on the way here."

I looked at my watch; it was 2:33. Colette was a manager at the Wal-Mart, and she worked the day shift. She didn't get off work until five o'clock. "Warren's probably talking to Miss Emma," I said.

"And Colette," Seymour said quickly. "Her van was in the yard. Since this thing happened to her niece, she's taken leave from work."

I swallowed dryly and wondered at that very moment if Colette was crying in Warren's arms again.

"Warren's been over there quite a bit. Uh-huh," Seymour said slowly, "in the last coupla days."

I sensed Seymour was trying to get a rise out of me again, which he did, but I was determined that I wasn't going to let him know that.

"He's dedicated to his work," I said, smiling.

"You wouldn't give me the time of day, but soon as Warren pop up and ask you out, you go."

"Seymour, I don't know what you're talking about," I replied.

Seymour laughed. "You know what I'm talking about. Everybody know, Warren got a thang for you."

And everybody knows you're one of the biggest male whores in town, I wanted to say. Instead, I smiled and said, "Is that right?"

"I wanna know, do you have a thang for him?"

"Warren and I are friends, okay?"

"So let's go for a ride, then."

"I'm gonna have to pass on that."

Seymour sighed. "Why?"

I didn't have to come up with a fib or think too long and hard for an excuse in order to spare Seymour's feelings. "Mama doesn't want us leaving the house," I said. "She's afraid we might run into some of the Harrises around town and—"

"We can go for a ride out in the country. I'll talk to her," Seymour said, turning to leave.

"No!" I yelled.

Seymour stopped and looked back at me.

"To be honest." I sighed, smiled, then frowned. "I don't feel up to it."

"C'mon, Violet," Seymour whispered, advancing on me.

His cell phone rang.

Saved by the bell! I thought happily to myself.

Seymour reached into his pants pocket and pulled it out. He looked at the display, then at me, and said, "Excuse me" and walked out of the room.

I went back into the living room and told Mama I was going over to Aunt Caroline's.

"Where's Seymour?" she asked.

"He had to take a call. He's outside."

Mama nodded. I said good-bye to the church mothers and went outside.

Seymour was leaning up against his car smiling and chatting away. When he saw me, he stood up and abruptly ended the call. My gut told me he was talking to a woman.

"You change your mind? You ready to go?" he asked, grinning.

"Nice-looking car," I said, smiling.

"Thanks! So c'mon and get in."

Before I could shoot Seymour down once more, his cell phone rang. He glanced down at the phone, then stuffed it back in his pocket.

"Aren't you going to answer that?" I asked.

"No, they can leave a message," Seymour said, looking up at me.

"You mean *she* can leave a message," I said, laughing.

"Aww, c'mon now," Seymour said, smiling.

"Playa, playa," I sang, hurrying out of the yard, clutching my cell phone. While at Aunt Caroline's, I was going to give Warren a call.

Chapter 33

Recollections

Violet

"Fix me two hot dogs!" I heard Niecee yell out to Rashaunda, who was in the kitchen.

"Okay!" Rashaunda yelled back.

I slowly made my way down the hall to the guest bedroom. Niecee was lying in bed with the cordless phone up to her ear. We'd all just had lunch less than two hours ago, and she was getting ready to eat *again*!

"I told that motherfu—"

"Niecee!" I yelled.

"Oh!" Niecee shrieked. "Aunt Vi! Hey!" she yelled, sitting up in the bed. Her newborn was lying on the bed beside her, wide-awake staring up at the ceiling. "Listen, I gotta go," Niecee whispered hurriedly into the phone.

I groaned softly. I felt a migraine coming on, my first

in days. The TV was on, the volume was up too loudly, I felt, and on the screen were scantily clad young women dancing to rap music.

When Niecee ended her call, she rolled off the bed and picked up her baby. "It's time for your bottle, ain't it?" she said, smiling down at TreShawn.

"Could you turn that down?" I asked.

"Yeah, sure, Aunt Vi," Niecee replied, picking up the TV remote from the floor. She clicked off the TV.

"Who were you talking to just now?" I asked.

"One of my friends."

"Your friend call you?"

"Nooo," Niecee replied, looking at me out the corner of her eye.

"I hope you're not over here making a ton of long-distance calls to your friends in D.C.," I said.

"I'm not," Niecee replied quickly.

"The phone company sends a bill every month, so I'll see when it comes," I said with raised eyebrows.

Niecee sighed and looked away.

"I thought you were going to breast-feed TreShawn."

"I was, but I changed my mind."

"That's one quick way to lose weight," I said.

"Yeah," Niecee said slowly, "that's what Mama told me."

Where did my sister go wrong? I wondered, eyeing my twenty-five-year-old, overweight, hypertensive, border-line diabetic niece. Floyd Jr., Daisy's eldest son, was a cop; Cedric, her second child, was a sergeant in the army; and her youngest son, Kevin, was a grad student studying psychology at Howard University. I was so proud of my nephews and, like Mama and my sisters—with the exception of Jasmine—sorely disappointed with my niece. I'd prayed and wished so many times, like I was doing as I stared at her then, that she would get her life together and become a woman the family could be proud of. Here she stood before me, holding her third child, whose father in her parents' and siblings' estimation was a "bum" like her other boys' fathers. She was unemployed, and like Jasmine—whom she adored—had no marketable job skills. And like Jasmine, didn't have a problem calling me asking for money when in a bind. Her last call to me for money was less than a year ago.

Niecee had allowed her newborn's father to move into the Section Eight house with her and her sons. During the two months that he lived with Niecee—according to Daisy—they were constantly at each other's throats. Their verbal and physical spats often spilled out of the tiny house into the yard and street. The mother of all brawls occurred when Niecee came home and caught him making out in the kitchen with one of her neighbors while Rakeem and Brandon were watching cartoons down the hall. The melee resulted in extensive damage not only to the house Niecee lived in, but to the house of the "trick" messing around with Niecee's "boo" also. Niecee chased the girl down the street to her home—a subsidized house as well—and broke out several windows. To keep her from facing criminal charges from the D.C. Housing Authority for destruction of property, I went to D.C. and hand-delivered a cashier's check totaling one thousand dollars to Daisy, who was at her wits' end, to pay for the damages. Niecee's behavior, unfortunately, squashed any chance of her ever receiving public housing again. And up until her recent return to Daisy and Floyd's, she'd been a modern-day nomad, bunking up at various friends' homes with Rakeem and Brandon in tow.

"She's driving me crazy!" Daisy cried, that day I was in D.C. Floyd was lying in his recliner, passed out from having "one too many," Rakeem and Brandon were running around all over the place, and Niecee was in her parents' bedroom, lying on the bed watching TV.

I took several deep breaths and looked up at the ceiling. I could hear Kenya, Rakeem, and Brandon laughing and playing outside. Their laughter was carefree, and it instantly transformed me from a place of frustration to one of happiness. Memories from my childhood surfaced and I smiled.

My aunt Caroline's home was one of my favorite places to visit, especially in the summertime. There was a swing for my sisters and me to play on in the backyard, and over under the elm tree was a picnic table where we sat creating shades of nail polish by mixing several colors together. When we weren't taking turns on the swing or playing hopscotch, jacks, or painting our finger- and toenails, we were stuffing ourselves with an assortment of fruit. In addition to the vegetables she grew, Aunt Caroline had a pear tree, an apple tree, and a grapevine in her backyard. And she always planted watermelons. Many summer afternoons, my sisters and I left her house complaining of bellyaches for having eaten so much. The memories brought tears to my eyes.

"You okay, Aunt Vi?" Niecee asked, staring at me.

I straightened my back, smiled, and nodded. "Yeah, I was just thinking about old times."

Niecee smiled.

"You know," I said, nodding, "maybe I could move over here and stay until your daddy retires."

"Yeah, you and Mr. Warren could," Niecee said, grinning.

I flinched, and looked back to see if anyone was behind me and overheard Niecee's comment.

Niecee laughed.

"What do you know about me and *Mr. Warren*?" I asked, staring at her.

Niecee grinned. "Aunt J told me y'all go together."

"Listen," I said, inching close to my grinning niece, "if Mama heard that, she would be upset. 'Mr. Warren' is still a married man, and she'd rather I not date him until he's divorced."

"I know that," Niecee said, bobbing her head. "You ain't got to worry," she said, smiling. "I ain't gone say nothin'. Aunt J told me it was a secret."

I exhaled.

"Aunt Vi," Niecee said, her tone serious, "you do want to have babies and get married, right?"

"Yes, I do," I replied.

"You think you'll marry Mr. Warren and have babies by him?"

I shrugged.

"Now, if things don't work out between you two"— Niecee grinned and her eyes twinkled—"Mr. Charles is still available."

I burst out laughing.

"Mr. Charles" was one of Floyd's coworkers. When I debuted as an *Ebony* bachelorette, Floyd took a copy of the magazine to work and passed it around, trying to help me find love. I received fifteen e-mails from his coworkers. Eight were *married*; three—Mr. Charles being one of the three—were old enough to be my father; and the four that I did go out with were full of jive.

"You want chili and onions!" Rashaunda yelled from the kitchen.

"Yeah, just a little!" Niecee yelled back. Her outburst caused TreShawn to start whimpering. Niece shushed and rocked him in her arms. "Well, Aunt Vi," she said, looking up at me, "I hope things work out between you and Mr. Warren. 'Cause I heard old men can give you worms."

I burst out laughing.

Niecee opened her eyes wide. "Why are you laughing? I know you've heard that too."

"Yeah," I said laughing, "I've heard that, but I don't believe it's *true*."

Niecee's eyes widened again. "You hook up with Mr. Charles, you'll find out," she said as if warning me.

"Let me assure you," I said, holding up my hands, "me and Mr. Charles hooking up, that ain't gone happen."

"Good!" Niecee exclaimed.

"Now go feed my nephew," I ordered, smiling.

Niecee smiled back and headed for the door. As she passed me she stopped, looked up at me, and said, "Stop worrying, Aunt Vi. I'm gone get it together. I promise."

"I pray so," I said.

I followed Niecee down the hall to the kitchen. After conversing with Rashaunda, I went outside and sat down on the back porch step. Being out back got me feeling melancholy again. I flipped open my cell phone and dialed Warren's Nextel, wondering the entire time if he was still at Miss Emma's.

"Hey, sweetie," he said, after two rings.

"Hi, handsome," I said.

"How are *you*?" he asked.

"Okay. And you?"

Warren sighed. "Busy as usual."

"Where are you?"

"At the station."

"You been there all day?"

Warren sighed again. "No."

I wanted to, but couldn't bring myself to ask him if he had been to Miss Emma's.

"How's everybody else?" he asked.

"Ivy's still sorting through her dilemma, Mama caught me sneaking back in the house last night, Li—"

Warren gasped. "Oh, honey! I'm sorry," he said.

"Everything's fine," I said.

"I'm sorry," Warren said again.

"I enjoyed myself last night."

"Me too."

"So, how's the Harris case com—"

"Violet, hold on a second," Warren said, interrupting me.

I listened as he chatted with a man speaking in a loud, hurried voice. I heard the man say, "I think we have a break in the case." Seconds later, Warren said to me, "Honey, I have to go. I'll call you later."

"All right. Bye."

"Bye."

I stared at my phone, wondering what that was all about. *Could Warren and the man have been referring to the Harris case? And why didn't Warren mention to me that he'd been by the Harrises?* I eased up from the porch step and walked out into the backyard.

"Aunt Vi!"

I turned around.

Standing a few feet away with her hands on her hips was Kenya. "Wanna play dodge ball with us?" she asked, smiling.

I smiled back. "Sure," I said.

Chapter 34

Dread

Ivy paced the bedroom floor wringing her hands, wishing she could make time stand still. And just as sure as she was black and female, she knew Beatrice Hayes wouldn't stop calling until she spoke to her.

"Dear God! What am I going to do?" Ivy whispered, stopping to look at herself in the full-length mirror. What she saw made her lower her eyes, eyes ringed with dark circles, from her image in the mirror. She looked awful and she'd lost *more* weight. The circles and weight loss were from worry, stress, and a lack of sleep. The week leading up to Mia's execution, she'd dropped one dress size. Allen had jokingly said to her one night, "Honey, you're fading away."

Ambivalence over whether to marry Allen, Ivy's aunt's sudden and unexpected passing, and her trip to the hospital for abusing meds had also taken a drastic toll on Ivy. "I *am* fading away!" she cried, looking back up at herself in the mirror.

Ivy covered her face with her hands and burst into tears. She turned away from the mirror and, through her quivering fingers, read the time on the digital clock on the nightstand; it was 8:33. She dropped her hands and sighed. Allen would be calling soon; he always called just before *Larry King Live* came on.

Why does life have to be so complicated? How do I tell a man I love that I can't marry him? Ivy wondered, staring down at her sparkling, three-carat diamond engagement ring. As tears filled her eyes again and began rolling down her cheeks, she recalled the day she first met Allen. It was five years ago, and she bumped into him, literally, at the courthouse in Durham one morning. They were both hurrying to catch the same crowded elevator. He was a district court judge at the time, and as fate would have it, she ended up arguing her cases that same day in his courtroom. A week later they ran into each other again at the Lawyers' Ball. They spent the entire evening dancing and talking to each other.

Before Allen called, Ivy shuffled to the dresser and picked up her BlackBerry. She couldn't bear another conversation with him, pretending everything was okay. It wasn't fair to him, or her.

"Ivy! Phone!" Jasmine yelled.

Ivy ran out of the bedroom to the stairway. "Who is it?" she whispered down at Jasmine.

"Who you think?" Jasmine whispered back. "It's Beatrice!"

Ivy sighed and went back into the bedroom. She plopped down on the bed and stared at the phone on the nightstand. "She got the phone?" she heard Peony ask Jasmine.

"You got the phone, Ivy?" Jasmine yelled.

"Yeah, I got it!" Ivy yelled, picking up the receiver.

"Hello! Ivy! Ivy! You there?"

"Yes, Beatrice. I'm here," Ivy replied, smiling.

Beatrice exhaled. "How're you feeling, dear?"

"Okay."

"Wonderful!"

You don't mean that! Ivy said to herself. *I'm sure you've called me "foolish" and a host of other things, and cried yourself to sleep at night, wondering why your son still wants to marry a prescription junkie.*

Beatrice emitted a long, exasperating sigh. "Now, I wish I could say the same for myself," she said tartly.

"Beatrice, what's wrong?" Ivy asked, alarmed.

"I think I'm going to *lose* my mind!" Beatrice exclaimed. "I don't believe I worked this hard planning my girls' weddings, or my own! Do you have *any* idea when you will be home to help *me*?"

Ivy closed her eyes and fell back on the bed.

"Ivy?"

"No, Beatrice, I don't," Ivy finally said.

Beatrice sighed. "I've been trying to reach you *all* day! Did Lily and Mrs. Shaw tell you I called?" she asked sternly.

"Yes, they did. I apologize for not getting back to you."

"Well," Beatrice snapped. "I—hold on one second, dear."

"Sure."

"Rosa! Rosa!" Beatrice yelled.

"Yes, Ms. Haze!" Ivy heard Beatrice's housekeeper answer.

"Mr. Hayes and I would like some more pie and brandy before we retire tonight."

"Yes, ma'am," Rosa said.

"And," Beatrice said, with a long exasperated sigh, "don't forget to vacuum the chaise in the sunroom. I'm having guests tomorrow, and we will be having lunch out there."

"Yes, ma'am, Ms. Haze."

Ivy chuckled to herself and wondered how much longer Rosa Gonzales would work for pretentious, bossy Beatrice Hayes. Beatrice's track record with housekeepers was like Lily's; it wasn't good.

"Ivy?" Beatrice soon said into the phone.

"I'm here," Ivy answered cheerfully.

"I don't want to make *all* the decisions about the menus for the rehearsal dinner or the bridal party breakfast. Can you give me *some* idea of what you'd like for entrees? The caterers need to know. They should have known a month ago!"

Ivy sighed.

"And I still want to have a bridal shower for you before the wedding," Beatrice whined.

Poor Beatrice! Ivy thought with dismay. She was bound and determined to make sure her only son's wedding would be something that people would talk about for quite some time. Ivy's wedding planner, a sorority sister, had quit out of frustration a month into planning her wedding. She'd grown weary of Beatrice's intrusiveness, and Beatrice had talked Ivy out of hiring another wedding planner. She told Ivy she would rather handle things.

"I'm not getting married," Ivy blurted out.

"I was thinking lamb would be a good choice for— honey, what did you say?"

"I'm not getting married," Ivy said again.

Beatrice gasped. Seconds later Ivy heard a loud crashing noise followed by Rosa hollering, "Ms. Haze! Ms. Haze!"

Ivy pressed the switch hook and dialed Allen's mobile. Her call went straight to his voice mailbox.

"This is Allen Hayes. I can't take your call at this time, please leave a message and I will get back to you."

Beep.

"Allen . . ." Ivy paused and cleared her throat. "Call your mother."

Chapter 35

Sprung

"Hey, girl!"

"Hey."

"You still in McKinley, I see," Tina said.

"Still here."

"How's Rashaunda and Ivy?"

"They're good."

"You don't sound *good*."

Jasmine sighed. "Girl, my mama and sisters are trippin' *big* time."

"What *now*?"

"They tryin' to make me stay here!"

"Shut up!" Tina yelled.

"Girl, yeah! I ain't stayin' in McKinley!"

Tina burst out laughing. "I heard that! So when you comin' back?"

Jasmine muttered, "I don't know."

"What's going on, Jazz?"

"You ain't gone believe what I'm about to tell you," Jasmine said, chuckling.

"Do I need to sit down?" Tina asked, laughing.

"Yep!"

"Okay, wait a minute!"

Jasmine heard Tina yell out, "Don't come in here botherin' me, I'm on the phone with Jazz," then a door slam shut.

"Okay, I'm back," Tina said quickly into the phone.

"My sister Lily is a suspect in an attempted murder case," Jasmine said matter-of-factly.

Tina didn't respond.

"Ti-na? Hel-lo! You there?" Jasmine yelled loudly into her phone.

"Jazz, wh-what did you just *say*?" Tina asked softly.

Jasmine could hear disbelief in Tina's voice. "You heard me," she replied, chuckling.

"Girl, naw!" Tina shrieked.

"Uh-huh," Jasmine grunted. She was sitting on the living room floor in her aunt's house in her night-gown; the stereo was playing softly in the background. "Mo' drama poppin' off here at 309 East Franklin Street," she said, sighing.

Jasmine quickly filled Tina in on the details surrounding Sandra Harris's assault and how the Harris family thought Lily was guilty. Tina listened intently, interrupting from time to time to ask questions.

"And her aunties and niece tried to run up on me and my sisters at the supermarket."

"No, they didn't!" Tina exclaimed.

"Yes, they did," Jasmine asserted. "And I was gone beat them bitches down, if *Violet* and *Ivy* hadn't pulled me back."

Tina burst out laughing.

"Especially that niece. I wanted to clock that heifer like I did NeShell."

"I know that's right!" Tina yelled.

When Jasmine finished filling Tina in on what had happened since they last talked, Tina chuckled and said, "So, Ivy's not gettin' married and Lily could be on her way to prison?"

"You got it," Jasmine said, sighing wearily. "Drama, drama, drama!"

Kenya ran into the living room and threw her arms around Jasmine's neck. "Good night, Mommy."

"Night-night, baby."

Kenya kissed Jasmine on the cheek and darted back out of the room.

"I talked to Maniac," Jasmine said with a heavy sigh.

"He called?" Tina asked excitedly.

Jasmine grunted. "Hell, naw! Guess where he at?"

"Where?" Tina asked.

"Jail!"

"Jail? Where?"

"In Greensboro."

Tina grunted.

"Tell me what I should do, Tina. He needs five thousand dollars in order to make bail."

"Whew!" Tina exclaimed.

"Should I use part of the money I'm gettin' to get him outta jail?"

Tina sighed. "Jazz, I—I don't know."

"I don't want him locked up," Jasmine cried.

"I know," Tina said softly.

Jasmine started crying and telling Tina how much she loved Maniac and how she was hoping that they would be together forever. But like so many things in life, Jasmine had come to know that there were no guarantees she and Maniac would be together forever. She'd hoped the same thing with Rashaunda's dad and every other guy she had dated after he broke her heart. All of her past relationships ended bitterly and with her deeply depressed and foolishly forging ahead into another relationship. She would feel like the biggest fool in the world if she bailed Maniac out of jail and he ended up leaving her too.

"You make poor choices in men!" her aunt Caroline once told her, when Jasmine called her, depressed and crying over a breakup.

"He's the best thing that's happened to me in a long time, Tina," Jasmine cried.

Tina sighed.

"I could use that money for me and my kids, you know?"

"Yeah, I know," Tina replied.

"I love him, but sometimes I wonder if he really loves me."

Tina said nothing.

"I drove *two* hours to see him the other day and he didn't even ask me how I was doin'. I deserve better that this." Jasmine heard Tina sigh. "Do you have any idea how that made me feel?" Jasmine asked. "I cried all the way back from Greensboro. I had to pull over a few times to get myself together."

"Oh, Jazz, I'm sorry," Tina said.

"I want him to be with me because he *loves* me."

"I know," Tina said.

"He always singing 'Forever My Lady' to me," Jasmine muttered.

"Well, you know—"

"Uh-uh!" Jasmine yelled, interrupting Tina. "Don't try to make excuses for him. If he really *loved* me like he's told me he do, he would have asked me how I was doin'!" she said, breathing loudly. "And asked about my family too!"

"Maybe he grew up in a home like me, Jazz. Where he wasn't shown no affection and therefore he don't really know how to show it to nobody else."

Jasmine wiped her eyes. "You think that's what wrong with him?"

"I ain't no psychiatrist or nothin'," Tina said, "but what else could it be?"

Jasmine shook her head. "I don't know. But what you just said makes sense."

Chapter 36

Lie Low

Violet

For the second day in a row, we were on house arrest. I was sitting at the table in the breakfast nook rereading the latest story, STILL NO ARREST MADE, in the newspaper about the Harris case. Warren was photographed standing in front of the police station talking to a reporter. Colette, Evangeline, Poochie, and several other Harris family members were standing nearby. Also standing in the midst was Reverend Cherry, Reverend Bobbitt, Miss Odessa, Deacon Humphrey, Deacon Robinson, and my homeless friend, Willie.

Lieutenant Warren Jackson, lead detective with the McKinley Police Department on the Sandra Harris assault case, says the police department is doing all it can to apprehend the person or persons responsible for the heinous crime perpetrated against twenty-four-year-old Miss Harris. In a show of support for the police department, several Harris family members came down to the police station yesterday afternoon. Surrounded by the relatives of Sandra Harris, Lieutenant Jackson said that an arrest would be made, but not before the police department had sufficient evidence to do so.

In a case that's getting colder by the day, Lieutenant Jackson contends the police department is doing all it can to bring justice to Miss Harris and her family. He would not comment on specifics of the case, nor deny or confirm rumors that there was a person of interest. He would only say that no charges have been filed or warrants issued.

News of no arrest in the case is troubling to 83-year-old Ruby Drum, longtime McKinley resident. She fears, like many in town, that a depraved man is roaming the streets and liable to strike again without warning. "I'm sleeping with my dead husband's shotgun next to my bed," Mrs. Drum said. "And it's loaded!"

Ruby Drum is not alone. Residents all over McKinley are arming themselves against the madman they fear is wandering the streets. Which is all the more reason why Mayor Skip Braswell hopes this crime is soon solved. When questioned about the town residents' fear, Lieutenant Jackson said, "We believe this is an isolated incident. We have no reason to believe a madman is wandering the streets of McKinley."

Before the crowd dispersed, Evangeline Harris led those gathered in prayer. The family is planning a prayer vigil tonight at the site where Miss Harris's bloody, battered body was found six days ago. Her condition remains unchanged at McKinley General. She remains in intensive care.

Ivy staggered into the kitchen and sat down across from me. I slid the paper across the table to her. She hadn't gotten into bed until after three o'clock this morning, after Allen left heading back to Durham. Immediately after his mother told him Ivy had called off the wedding, he hit the road to McKinley.

Ivy and Allen sat in the living room behind closed doors, crying and holding each other. Ivy had told me when she climbed into bed this morning that each time she looked into Allen's tear-streaked face, she found herself unable to tell him the real reason why she'd called off the wedding. Realizing the "differing professional beliefs and aspirations" excuse she'd initially used on me was weak, Ivy told Allen she'd called off the wedding because she was simply "emotionally overwhelmed." Losing Mia's case, along with the sudden and unexpected passing of Aunt Caroline followed by her recent hospitalization, had taken an enormous toll on her not only emotionally, but physically as well, and she needed time to get herself together. Allen bought that excuse and expressed relief that it wasn't because—he'd feared—she'd suddenly fallen out of love with him. I asked Ivy if she told Allen about the consultant position she'd accepted with the Justice Project; she said she did not. Allen's parting words to her were that he would inform his mother and everyone that their wedding had not been called off; it had only been postponed until further notice.

From where I was seated, I looked out the window and watched Jasmine walk across the street from Aunt Caroline's house to Mama's mailbox. The mail carrier had just pulled off. I didn't know who was more anxious to get their share of the insurance money: Daisy or Jasmine. Daisy called every day asking if the check had come. Out West where there was a plethora of casinos in Phoenix and its neighboring cities of Scottsdale and Glendale, Daisy had decided to extend her stay in Arizona by two more weeks. She'd even instructed us to mail her ten thousand dollars to her out there if Mama received the money before she headed back to D.C. Ivy and I never believed for one minute she would make good of her earlier claim to repay us and pay off her high-interest loans. We believed she would squander every penny of her inheritance trying to get rich.

I watched Jasmine shuffle quickly through the mail. Her arms soon fell down to her sides: no insurance check, I surmised.

"Violet?"

I looked across the table at Ivy. "What?"

"You think Warren will tell you if he's seriously looking at Lily as a suspect?" she whispered.

I shook my head. "I don't know, and I'm not going to ask him."

"What's he doing here?" Lily screamed, running into the kitchen. "I ain't going to jail!" she cried.

Before I could figure out what she was talking about, Mama rushed past the kitchen toward the front door. I looked out the window and broke out in a cold sweat. Warren was pulling into the driveway.

"I ain't going to jail!" Lily screamed.

Ivy and I jumped up from the table and ran outside. Warren parked the Denali, removed his sunglasses, and stepped out. My gaze averted to his waist. His handcuffs were glistening in the sunlight. I got dizzy.

"Good morning, Warren," Mama said.

"Good morning, Miss Peony, Violet, Ivy," he said, walking up to the porch.

"No, Warren, please!" I said, bursting into tears. "She didn't do it!"

Warren's eyebrows creased together.

"Are you here to arrest my sister?" Ivy asked.

"No, no," Warren said, shaking his head.

Ivy and I exhaled. I ran back into the house. Lily was sitting on the kitchen floor looking stoned out of her mind. "He's not here to arrest you," I said.

"Thank God!" Lily cried.

I helped Lily get up off the floor and seated in a chair. Warren came into the kitchen behind Mama and Ivy. "I know all of the attention this case has gotten in the paper lately has been somewhat unnerving," he said.

"Yes, it has been," Mama said.

"We want an arrest made soon like the Harrises," Ivy said.

"I know, I know," Warren said, nodding. He sighed, then looked at Lily. "The family still believes you're guilty."

Lily moaned and pressed her chapped lips together.

"What do you think?" Ivy blurted out.

Warren sighed.

"Oh, dear Lord!" Mama cried.

Ivy held up her hands. "Warren, I apologize. I had no right to ask you that. Forgive me."

Warren and I hadn't gotten a chance to talk again yesterday, and I was about to ask if there had been a break in the case when he said, "The investigation surrounding this case is ongoing." He sighed heavily, then said, "The run-in that some of you had with Colette and Evangeline hasn't helped matters."

Mama narrowed her eyes at us and shook her head. If we were children, I think she would have pulled Daddy's black belt from the closet and whipped us the other day, for the incident at the Piggly Wiggly.

"So, I'm asking all of you," Warren said, looking around the room, "to lie low until we wrap things up."

"You think that'll be soon?" I asked.

"I can't say," Warren said, opening his eyes wide. "So in the meantime, no trips to the supermarket, Wal-Mart—"

"They're not going anywhere, Warren," Mama said. "They're not leaving this house!"

Warren nodded. "Good."

"I still can't believe they think I'm capable of something like that!" Lily cried.

"Sandra's coworkers say you two had a great relationship," Warren said.

"You talked to them?" Lily asked, choking on the words.

"No, Lieutenant Roane did."

"What else did they say?" Lily asked.

Warren's brows creased together again.

"What did they have to say about me?" Lily asked as tears filled her eyes.

Warren cleared his throat and said, "Nothing that has any bearing on this case."

Just when I thought the family drama was over for the day, Kenya ran over to set it off again. Lily was upstairs napping. Mama, Ivy, and I were on Jasmine's case about moving out of the projects. Mama was trying to persuade Jasmine to apply for one of the housekeeping positions at the Nursing and Convalescent Center where our cousin Cheryl worked and to move back to McKinley. Mama told Jasmine she had talked to Cheryl, and Cheryl agreed to put in a good word for Jasmine to her supervisor. Jasmine's adamant protests against moving out of the projects and back to McKinley abruptly ended when Kenya ran into the house smiling broadly.

Kenya had called her father. He and his new bride, Yolanda, were back from their honeymoon to the

Bahamas and wanted to spend some time with Kenya. Lorenzo told Kenya to tell Jasmine he was coming to McKinley to get her. Kenya hadn't seen her daddy since his wedding two weeks ago. She was a junior bridesmaid.

Jasmine flew into a rage. "He's supposed to call me! I've told Lorenzo not to send messages to me through you!" she yelled at Kenya.

"Don't yell at her!" Mama said. "Maybe he tried! Does he have your new phone numbers?"

"He doesn't have them, Grandma," Kenya said, her big brown eyes filled with tears.

The fighting between Jasmine and Lorenzo upset Kenya. My sisters and I felt Jasmine still carried a torch for Lorenzo and was bitter because he had moved on. Jasmine had tried unconvincingly many times to make us think otherwise.

"Okay, so maybe he don't have my new numbers, he could have told Kenya to have me call him!" Jasmine said, flipping open her cell phone. "Lorenzo's full of mess, always has been, and Kenya knows that!"

"Don't have Kenya in y'all's *mess*," Mama said.

"I wanna go with Daddy and Miss Yolanda!" Kenya cried.

"You ain't going nowhere, but back across the street!" Jasmine yelled.

Kenya ran into Mama's bedroom crying.

"Jasmine, you're overreacting," I said.

"I am not!"

"Why are you so angry? Lorenzo has a right to see Kenya," Ivy said.

"Like I said, he's supposed to communicate with *me*! He's going to respect me."

"So you're feeling disrespected?" I said.

"Yep!"

"I ain't buying that," I said.

"Me neither," Ivy said.

Jasmine pursed her lips together and angrily punched in numbers in her cell phone.

"That may be a part of it," I said, "but I still think you're a scorned woman with a score to settle and out of spite, you're using Kenya to get back at Lorenzo because he doesn't want to be with you. And that's not right."

"Naw, it ain't right," Mama said.

The call Jasmine had been trying to make to Lorenzo finally went through. Why she thought we wanted to hear her yell at him was beyond me. She pressed the Speaker button on her phone and held it up above her head.

"Your visitation request has been denied!" she yelled when Lorenzo answered the phone.

"Jasmine, I'm not going to argue with you," Lorenzo said calmly. "I'll be there tomorrow to pick up my baby."

"I be damned!" Jasmine yelled.

Mama stood up and slapped Jasmine. Jasmine flinched and staggered back. Tears filled her eyes. If there was such a thing as having the taste slapped out of your mouth, Jasmine just had it slapped out of hers.

"Why wasn't she in school any this week?" Lorenzo asked.

"Because she wasn't!" Jasmine yelled.

We heard Lorenzo sigh.

"I'm sure Kenya told you my aunt Caroline died. We're here comforting my mother. Is that so hard for you to understand?"

"I'm sorry about your aunt."

"Whatever!"

"Yolanda and I would like to keep Kenya for the summer."

"No!" Jasmine yelled.

"And why can't we?"

"Because I said so."

"That's not good enough."

"Well, that's how it's gone be."

"We'll see about that."

"Yeah, whatever!"

"You want to go out like that? Huh? Is that how you want it, Jasmine?"

"Nigga, what you talkin' 'bout?"

Mama swung at Jasmine. Jasmine ducked. Mama picked up the *TV Guide* from the sofa and threw it at her. It hit Jasmine on her left arm below her butterfly tattoo.

"You leave me no choice, Jasmine."

"What you talkin' 'bout, Lorenzo?"

"I'm meeting with a lawyer next week."

Jasmine laughed out loud.

"Monday morning at ten o'clock."

Jasmine stopped laughing.

"I meant what I told you. I don't want Kenya growing up in Githens Court. I heard about the shooting over there last week!"

"And where you stay ain't that much better!" Jasmine fired back.

"I've moved. Kenya didn't tell you?"

"No, she didn't!"

"Yolanda and I bought a town house across town, in Emerald Park."

"And how can you afford to live over *there*, Mr. Garbage Collector? Yolanda ain't making that much money as a customer service rep with Alltel."

"I got a promotion on my job. I'm a supervisor now."

A sheepish expression covered Jasmine's face and

she cut her eyes at us. It wasn't in her to congratulate the man.

"We have a room set up for Kenya."

"Oh, he—"

Mama threw the TV remote at Jasmine before she could say what I believed would have been an expletive.

"Kenya's not happy living in Githens Court. And you know that," Lorenzo asserted.

"Whatever!" Jasmine screamed.

"Calm down, Jasmine," Ivy said.

Jasmine was breathing fast and hard and sweating profusely.

"Why didn't you get counseling for her like the counselor at the school told you?" Lorenzo asked.

"Wh-what?" Jasmine stammered. "Ain't nobody told me nothin'!"

"Jasmine, you're lying. I met with Kenya's counselor yesterday. She told me she had a conference with you back in January and suggested to you then that you get counseling for her."

"Oh Lord!" Mama moaned, sitting down.

"Ke-Kenya's all right. She don't need no counseling," Jasmine argued.

"She's scared to play outside, afraid she's going to get shot! She's having nightmares—"

"'Nightmares'!" Mama hollered.

"Kenya's all right, Lorenzo! Okay?" Jasmine snapped.

"You are so damn irresponsible," Lorenzo muttered.

"Who you calling 'irresponsible'?"

"You! And if you want to keep living in *da hood*, by all means do so. But my baby's days of living in fear are over!"

"Oh, we gone see 'bout that!" Jasmine yelled, looking over at Ivy for support.

Ivy shook her head at Jasmine.

"Come get your baby," Mama said, standing back up.

"Miss Peony, is that you?"

"Yes, Lorenzo, it is," Mama answered, walking over to Jasmine.

"I'm so sorry to hear about your sister," Lorenzo said compassionately.

"Thank you," Mama said. "How's your mother?"

"She's fine."

"Tell her we all said hello."

"I will. And I'll see you tomorrow."

We all heard the click on the other line.

"He's going to see a lawyer about gettin' custody!" Jasmine cried. "I bet that—that wife and mother of his got something to do with this! They don't like me. Yolanda thinks she better than me. Well, we gone see! They ain't gettin' Kenya!" she yelled, stomping her feet.

Mama said nothing.

"Why you not saying sump'n, Mama?" Jasmine cried.

"What you want me to say?" Mama asked. "That Lorenzo don't stand a chance of getting custody of his daughter? I can't say that, because I think he got a real good chance. Kenya is just as much his as she is yours. Don't forget that. And you're making it real easy for a judge to grant him custody."

Jasmine looked over at Ivy.

Ivy threw up her hands. "I agree with Mama."

Mama threw up her right hand. "Psalm 127:3. *Behold, children are a gift from the Lord, the fruit of the womb is a reward.* Your daddy and I raised you in the church, Jasmine. You went to Sunday school *every* Sunday. Vacation Bible school *every* summer. When was the last time you and your children been to church?"

"Kenya goes to church with Lorenzo and his mother," Jasmine replied.

"Let me rephrase my question," Mama said. "When

was the last time you and your children went to church together?"

Jasmine sighed heavily and dropped her head.

"Daughter, look at how you living. You're on probation, the county's on your case over Shaunda, do you really want your children?"

Jasmine gasped. "Yes, Mama!" she cried. "What kinda question is that to ask me?"

"Then why don't you start acting like it?" Mama said, scowling. "'Cause if Lorenzo takes you to court, you might not have a leg to stand on. And another thing! If you keep living like you living, and where you living, Kenya and Shaunda liable to wind up hurt, or worse: dead. You ever thought about that?"

Jasmine started sobbing.

"When the insurance money gets here, I'm giving you your money. It will break my heart if you took that money my sista left you and spent it foolishly. But it's yours to have, and do what you will with. Get more tattoos, buy more jewelry and cell phones for you and Shaunda."

"I'ma get a job, Mama. Soon as I get back. I promise you," Jasmine said, bobbing her head.

"Jasmine, why not move back here," Ivy said, "and use some of that money for school? You don't have to stay here forever."

"And you got somewhere to stay, rent free," I added.

Mama looked over at me. "And where's that?" she asked, placing her hands on her hips.

"In Aunt Caroline's house," I said.

"Uh-uh," Mama said, shaking her head. "If she moves across the street into *that* house, she's paying me rent! Her days of living off me, y'all, and everybody else will be over. It's time, past time, she assumed some grown-up responsibilities! And she gone start by paying me back that five hundred dollars I sent her two weeks ago, with interest!"

"I know I need to do sump'n different, I hear y'all," Jasmine said, sniffling.

"So what's the problem?" I asked.

"I've lived in Charlotte for almost thirteen years now. All my friends are there."

"It's time you made new friends," Mama said.

"Your friends in the violent projects are more important to you than your children's well-being?" Ivy asked.

Jasmine sighed and dropped her head.

"If that's what you're saying," Mama said, "then when Lorenzo comes tomorrow to get Kenya, he needs to keep her, you go on back to Charlotte, and leave Shaunda here."

Jasmine burst into tears.

I looked at Jasmine in amazement and wondered: *How difficult can this be?*

I was lying across my bed talking on my cell phone to Warren, when his phone beeped. He put me on hold, because his incoming call was from the police station. When Warren reconnected with me, what he told me caused the hairs on the back of my neck to rise. Sandra Harris was no longer in a coma.

Chapter 37

R. J. Latimore

Violet

According to reports from Warren and Miss Sadie, the Harris family had flooded the hospital. Even though Sandra was conscious and breathing on her own, her doctor wasn't permitting any visitors and that included law enforcement.

Lily was walking around in the same silk purple pajamas from yesterday looking like a zombie in *Night of the Living Dead*. Since hearing that Sandra had been miraculously snatched from the Grim Reaper's clutches, she believed it would be just a matter of time before Sandra implicated her as her assailant. I feared if this didn't end soon, Lily would lose her mind. Ivy and I were huddled together in the breakfast nook reading the newspaper. The prayer vigil Evangeline and Colette had last night, like the previous stories on Sandra's assault, was front-page news. Evangeline and Colette were photographed along with a large crowd holding candles, with bowed heads. Several church members from Charity Chapel were sprinkled throughout the crowd. Reverend Bobbitt was standing before the crowd with uplifted hands and closed eyes. CHURCH PASTOR LEADS GROUP IN PRAYER were the words under the picture.

"Misprint! Misprint!" I yelled. "He *ain't* the pastor of Charity Chapel."

"Amen!" Mama said, from the kitchen sink.

Ivy looked at me and whispered with raised eyebrows, "Not yet."

I sighed and returned my attention to the newspaper.

"Prayer vigil at crime scene last night drew large crowd," I read out loud. *"Evangeline Harris said her family believes strongly in the power of prayer and believe God will heal Sandra and restore her to health.*

"The police remain tight-lipped about the case, and there is still no arrest. Despite that, the family believes an arrest is imminent. A deeply religious family, some of the members have been fasting since the incident. The victim's grandmother was unable to attend the prayer vigil, and remains at home per doctor's orders in bed. The family received a donation late yesterday afternoon, in the amount of ten thousand dollars."

"Whaaaat?" Jasmine exclaimed, walking over to Ivy and me.

"Who sent them ten thousand dollars?" Ivy asked, looking at me.

"Maybe it was the white man Miss Emma used to work for," I said.

Mama grunted. "Trust me, if he had, his picture would be in the paper, *on* the front page."

Jasmine whistled. "Ten thousand dollars!"

I read on. "*Colette Worrell said that the money was a blessing to the family and part of it would be added to the reward fund they had started, while the majority would go toward retaining a lawyer in the civil case they were sure to bring against the person responsible for the attack against their niece.*"

"Where did they get ten thousand dollars?" Ivy asked.

"The answer's right here," I yelled, tapping the paper. "Listen!"

Mama ran over and stood behind me.

"*Russell Latimore,*" I read, "*an acquaintance of the victim, wired the money to the family late last night. Fifty-four-year-old Latimore is an investor and certified public accountant with the firm Latimore, Crutchfield and Spaulding in Raleigh, North Carolina. When he returned to his home yesterday afternoon after a weeklong overseas business trip, Peyton Fields, Miss Harris's roommate, informed him of what had happened to Miss Harris.*"

"What?" Ivy yelled, snatching the paper out of my hands. "*Mr. Latimore is planning to visit the Harris family today,*" she read. "*The family won't confirm or deny rumors that Mr. Latimore and Miss Harris are romantically involved. Efforts by this reporter to reach Mr. Latimore at his home have been unsuccessful.*"

"Oh my goodness!" Ivy shrieked. "Lily!"

"Whaaat?" Lily grunted, from the doorway. She had even started sounding like a zombie.

"Do you know a man by the name of Russell Latimore?" Ivy asked.

Lily squinted.

"Russell Latimore!" I yelled. "Do you know him?"

Lily shook her head.

"This could be the 'Russell' involved with Sandra!" Ivy said, breathing fast and loud.

"Jesus! Jesus! Jesus!" Mama shouted, waving the dish towel in her hand.

"Oh Lord, I hope it is!" I cried.

"And all this time," Jasmine said, looking back at Lily, "you thinkin' *your* Russell messin' round with that skank!"

Mama hit Jasmine with the dish towel. "Watch your mouth!" she yelled.

Ivy started pacing the kitchen floor and rubbing her forehead. "We got to find out who Russell Latimore is, and if he and Sandra are seeing each other."

"How we gone do that?" Lily asked, her eyes large and round.

"Miss Sadie!" I yelled.

"Yes!" Mama yelled, throwing down the dish towel. "If anybody can find out, Sadie can!"

Ivy and I ran out of the house. Mama and Jasmine were close on our heels.

"Y'all leaving me!" Lily cried from the porch.

Mama looked back and told her to go back into the house.

Like the bloodhound we knew her to be, Miss Sadie was able to track down the information we needed. According to Miss Odessa—Miss Sadie's source—Russell Latimore, a widower and father of five, and Sandra, according to Miss Emma, were romantically involved. Latimore's youngest child was Sandra's age. He and Sandra had started dating two weeks ago. Miss Emma, Colette, and Evangeline objected to Sandra dating him, because of the age difference. Sandra, however, was "goo-goo eyed" over the wealthy man nicknamed "R.J." who lavished her with gifts and money.

When we returned home, Lily was standing at the front door anxiously waiting to hear what we'd found out from Miss Sadie. "What Miss Sadie say? What she say?" she asked, twitching like a drug addict in need of a fix.

Mama was the first person to answer her. "I told you your husband wasn't messing around with Sandra. He told you that too!"

Ivy and I ushered Lily into the den and filled her in on what Miss Sadie had told us.

"Oooooh, what have I done?" she cried. "I've messed up! I've messed up!"

"Go call your husband," Mama said.

"I don't know what to say to him!"

"Humble yourself in the sight of the Lord, and He will lift you up!" Mama said. "Tell Russell you're *sorry*, honey. Ask him for your forgiveness," she said, reaching for the phone.

"You calling him?" Lily asked.

"No, I'm calling Reverend Cherry."

"Why, Mama?" I asked.

"To help me get a prayer through!"

Ivy was drenched in Summer by Eternity and looking fabulous in a Diane von Furstenberg ethnic-print sundress.

"Do you think it's such a good idea for you to see Ellis?" I asked, staring at her. We were sitting outside on the porch.

Ivy sighed. "It's not a date, Violet," she said, turning to look at me.

Ellis Coltrane was in town on business—so he claimed—and had called the house earlier; Mama was listed in the phone book, thus making it real easy for him to get in touch with Ivy, who had told him at Aunt Caroline's repast that she would be home for at least a week.

"So why did you change clothes and put on perfume?" I asked.

Ivy smacked her lips. "Oh, this old dress?"

"Whatever!" I retorted.

Ivy pursed her lips together and looked back out into the yard. "He's only stopping by to say hello."

"I think the phone call would have been sufficient, in light of things," I said, glancing down at Ivy's left hand. She wasn't wearing her engagement ring today.

"I still have feelings for Ellis," she said, catching me eyeing her bare ring finger.

I grunted.

Ivy laughed. "It's been over *twenty* years, and I still can't shake the feelings I have for him."

"What about Allen?" I asked abruptly. "You still have feelings for him?"

Ivy looked at me and smiled. "Yes," she said softly.

"Are they stronger than the feelings you have for Ellis?" I asked.

Ivy nodded.

I exhaled. *There was still hope!* I thought happily to myself. "So, when are you going to tell him the real reason for you calling off the wedding?"

Ivy sighed and looked back out into the yard.

"He deserves to know the truth, Ivy!"

"Yeah, you're right," she said, turning to look at me. "I owe him that."

"Aunt Vi! Aunt Ivy! Look at me!"

Ivy and I looked across the street.

Rakeem was riding one of the neighborhood boys' tricycles on the sidewalk in front of Aunt Caroline's house. Ivy and I smiled and waved.

"You ever wonder if we might end up like Aunt Caroline?" Ivy asked. "Single and childless."

"That thought has crossed my mind," I said. "But only God knows."

"I want so badly to get married and have children," Ivy said softly.

"Ellis might be ready to settle down now since his last child is heading to college. Do you really think he would want to have more children if, let's say, you two were to end up together?"

Ivy squirmed a little in her seat, then said, "I don't know."

"Probably not," I said.

"What about Warren?" Ivy asked, turning to look at me. "Does he want more children?"

"I don't know," I said. Warren and his soon-to-be ex were the parents of a ten-year-old girl.

"You think you'll marry him?" Ivy asked.

"If our relationship deepens, and I hope it will, and if he asks me, yeah," I replied with a big smile.

"You think he wants to get married again?"

I shrugged. "I don't know."

"Has he ever said?"

I shrugged again. "We've never talked about marriage."

Ivy smiled at me. "A bit of advice: Find out, before you make too much of an emotional investment in him."

I nodded. "I will."

Ivy smiled and looked back out into the yard. It was a sunny, warm day. Several of the neighbors, elderly widows like Mama who had lived on Franklin Street for as long as I could remember, were sitting out on their porches, swatting flies and sipping on sweet tea and lemonade. A dark blue Ford Explorer came down the street and pulled into Mama's driveway. The front door at Aunt Caroline's house flew open and Kenya ran across the street smiling and waving her hands. Jasmine stepped out of Mama's front door, scowling.

"Behave, Jasmine, behave!" I said, standing up.

Lorenzo turned off the SUV engine, threw open the driver's door, and jumped out. He scooped Kenya up in his arms; Kenya squealed with laughter.

Jasmine sauntered down the porch steps into the yard. Reverend Cherry was inside talking to Mama and Lily. If Jasmine acted a fool out in the yard, he would be talking to her later.

I walked down off the porch into the yard. Lorenzo's wife, Yolanda, smiled and waved to me from inside the SUV.

"She better not get out!" Jasmine muttered, eyeing Yolanda sharply.

"You ready to go, baby girl?" Lorenzo asked Kenya.

"Yes, Daddy."

"Go give your mama a kiss," he said, putting her down.

Kenya ran over to Jasmine and hugged her.

"You be good, baby. And call me," Jasmine said, hugging Kenya tightly.

"I will, Mommy."

Kenya hugged me, then ran up on the porch and hugged Ivy. She then dashed into the house, hollering, "Grandma, I'm gettin' ready to go!"

The silence out in the yard became unbearable. Fearing that the slightest thing would set off fuming

Jasmine, I didn't see the need to engage in small talk with Lorenzo *or* his wife, and prayed that Ivy would follow my lead.

Mama walked Kenya outside and told Lorenzo to take care of her grandbaby. Lorenzo walked up on the porch and hugged Mama. He told her she didn't have to worry, he would take good care of his "princess."

Rashaunda stood out on the porch across the street looking over into the yard. When Kenya yelled and waved good-bye to her, Rashaunda—without speaking or waving back—turned and reentered Aunt Caroline's house. I returned to my seat on the porch with tears in my eyes and sorrow in my heart for my twelve-year-old niece.

Chapter 38

Angst

Violet

I closed my cell phone and placed it in my pocket. Warren still had not been allowed to interview Sandra, and neither had the state crime lab faxed him a report. I looked out the kitchen window over at Aunt Caroline's house. Floyd's Cadillac was backed into the driveway. He'd come back to pick up Niecee and her children. The insurance check had finally come, much to Daisy's delight. She screamed in my ear and shouted, "Thank you, Jesus!" when I told her. Jasmine, surprisingly, wasn't as jubilant. She'd been sulking all day, more so after Lorenzo's visit. I saw her several times outside in the backyard talking on her cell phone.

Russell Latimore had finally arrived in town, per Miss Sadie. She said Miss Odessa was at Miss Emma's

house when he drove up in a "big black, pretty car."
Miss Odessa described him to Miss Sadie as a tall,
handsome man with wavy salt-and-pepper hair. She
said he looked like a "big shot." Miss Odessa also told
Miss Sadie that she saw him slip some money to Miss
Emma, and heard him tell her if she needed "anything," all she had to do was ask.

I walked slowly past the living room and looked in.
Ivy and Ellis were sitting next to each other on the
sofa. They were smiling and chatting away. Ellis was
dressed in a navy suit and showing Ivy pictures of the
house he was having built in town. I was hoping and
praying Ivy wouldn't tell him she had called off her
wedding, or that he would notice she wasn't wearing
her engagement ring. I felt Ivy was quite vulnerable,
and feared that if Ellis made a move on her, she would
give in to his advances.

I sighed and shook my head. I spent more time worrying about my family members' problems; I rarely
took time to attend to my own. There was a lingering,
burning question I needed to ask myself, and answer:
Was I going to rebuild? I could use the insurance
money I got to finance that if I did, or I could bank
the money and continue staying with Mama. The
thought of building a home with Warren as his wife
excited me. I'd lain in bed many nights fantasizing
about that very thing. But Ivy had touched on an in-
teresting point: Warren might not want to get married again. I'd heard many divorcees say they would
never remarry; I hoped Warren wasn't one of them.
For my emotional well-being, before the infatuation I
had for him became love, I needed to know. And
based on the response I got from him, I would know
whether to rebuild or continue staying with Mama.

While Ivy chatted and laughed it up with Ellis, and Jasmine sulked, and Lily wandered from room to room upstairs fearing she was minutes away from being hauled off to jail, I went into the den to watch the local evening news with Mama. We were watching the news on WRAL TV 5 when Miss Sadie called. "Turn your TV on! To Channel eleven!" she yelled. "They talkin' 'bout Emma's granddaughter!"

I grabbed the remote, changed channels, and yelled out for Ivy.

"What? What?" she yelled, running into the den.

I pointed to the TV.

"It's been a week since the brutal attack on twenty-four-year-old Sandra Harris. Miss Harris, a resident of Raleigh, was here in McKinley visiting relatives when she was abducted and assaulted," the brunette, female reporter said. "Her family"—the reporter, standing in Miss Emma's junky yard, paused, looked back at Miss Emma's trailer, then back at the camera—"living here in this mobile home believe an arrest is only hours away."

The story continued with the reporter interviewing Miss Emma. She was in her cramped bedroom, sitting on her bed holding an eight-by-ten photo of Sandra. Evangeline and Colette were sitting beside her.

"God has blessed us with a miracle," Miss Emma said.

Evangeline and Colette threw up their hands and said, "Hallelujah!"

"However, my grandbaby is not out the woods yet," Miss Emma said tearfully, shaking her head. "She still got a long road ahead of her."

"Is she still in intensive care?" the reporter asked.

"Yes," Evangeline replied.

"And the police department has an officer guardin' her around the clock," Colette interjected.

"Mrs. Harris, do you and your family feel your granddaughter's life is still in danger?" the reporter asked.

"Yes!" Colette and Evangeline replied.

Miss Emma nodded.

"Any reason why anyone would want to *harm* her?" the reporter asked.

"Yes," Colette replied doggedly, looking straight into the camera. "But we've been asked by the detective handlin' the case not to say."

The story then continued with the reporter back outside Miss Emma's trailer promising to report any new developments or arrests in the case.

"I'm going to prison for the rest of my life!"

Ivy, Mama, and I gasped, flinched, and looked back. Lily was standing in the doorway, crying and shaking.

Chapter 39

Apprehension

Violet

"Mama, can I goooo?" Ivy asked, whining. "Please! Please! We won't be gone that long."

Ellis wanted to take Ivy by the house he was having built, and from the pictures Ivy showed Mama and me, it was a McMansion.

"Whew!" Mama exclaimed. "That's a mighty big house," she said, looking at the pictures. "It's beautiful, and almost as big as Lily's."

"Can I go?" Ivy asked, opening her eyes wide.

Still thinking it was best we stayed home to avoid running into any of Miss Emma's folks, Mama handed Ivy back the pictures, shook her head, and said, "No."

Ivy sighed and shuffled back to the living room. I

heard her say to Ellis, "I can't go." I heard him say to her, "Maybe the next time."

Next time? *Hmmmm!* I said to myself. I wondered then if Ivy had told Ellis she'd called off her wedding.

When Ellis finally left—two hours later—Ivy came into the den where Mama and I were seated. Sulking Jasmine was over at Aunt Caroline's, and Lily—who still hadn't bathed or brushed her teeth—was curled up on the sofa, looking scared out of her mind. Ivy plopped down in one of the recliners and called Allen, who wanted to drive down and visit. Ivy told him not to. Mama and I cut our eyes at each other. Allen had called earlier to speak to Ivy. I lied and told him she was "resting." I couldn't tell him the truth, that she was dolled up and sitting in the living room smiling up in her ex-boyfriend's face. Allen asked me to have Ivy call him when she got up. Before saying good-bye, he expressed to me his "undying love" for Ivy and hope that in the very near future she would make his dream come true of becoming his wife. He sounded so pitiful, for a second I thought about telling him the real reason why he and Ivy weren't getting married next Saturday.

When Ivy ended her call with Allen, she picked up the TV remote and started flipping through the channels. When she came across the show *Cops*, Lily started crying. "Please, turn it someplace else?" she mumbled.

We settled on *Sanford and Son* on TV Land and were watching it when my cell phone rang. I started hyperventilating when I saw the name and number on the phone display. "It's Warren!" I said, breathing loud and fast. I flipped open my phone. "Warren?"

"Baby, we've made an arrest, and we have a confession," he said.

I jumped up. "They've made an arrest!" I screamed. "They've made an arrest!"

Cries of joy filled the room. Lily rolled off the sofa onto the floor on her knees. "Thank you, Jesus! Oh, Lord, thank you!" she cried. "Thank *you* for sparing my life!"

Ivy jumped out of the recliner and ran over to Lily. She knelt down beside her and hugged her.

"Oh, dear God, I thank you!" Lily cried.

"Yes! Yes! Thank you, Jesus!" Mama shouted, standing up.

"I need to go call Russell," Lily said, jumping to her feet.

"Yes, you, do," Mama said. She walked over to Lily, took Lily's face in her hands, and said, "You need to mend your ways."

"I am, Mama," Lily cried. "I promise! Starting with my husband. I'm going to *save* my marriage!" she declared, running out of the room.

I pressed the Speaker button on my phone and sat back down. When Warren told us who he had arrested, I went numb. The state crime lab had lifted a thumbprint off a bloody red rose petal found wedged between the driver's seat and the console in Sandra's car. They ran the print through the FBI fingerprint database and got a match. This person's fingerprints were on file because of a previous arrest and conviction seven years ago. This *person* had also confessed to being responsible for the fire that destroyed my home. That person was Willie—my homeless friend.

Warren said Willie told him the fire to my home was an accident. He entered my home that fateful evening—and it wasn't the first time he said he had jimmied the lock on my sliding glass door and entered my

home while I was away—lit some of the scented candles
I had throughout my home, helped himself to food in
the refrigerator, watched TV, and rummaged through
my dresser drawers and closets, touching and smelling
my belongings. I shuddered when Warren told me he
found several of my personal possessions—a five-by-
seven photo of me, several pieces of my lingerie, and
some of my scented candles—things I thought were
long gone, in the brown leather knapsack Willie always
had slug across his shoulder.

Warren said had it not been for the bloody rose petal,
the Harris case would still be open because Willie's
prints weren't found anywhere else in Sandra's car. I
shuddered again thinking, had it not been for that rose
pctal, Willie would have been free, cycling around town
free to inflict harm again without warning.

Despite Willie's dastardly deed, I felt a tremendous amount of sadness for him. While on the other
hand, I was happy and thankful that Lily was no longer
a suspect in the case and relieved to know I wasn't
responsible—like I believed all along—for the fire to
my home.

When the state crime lab faxed its findings to the
police department, Warren and two police officers
walked across the street and apprehended Willie at the
homeless shelter. When Willie saw Warren and the officers, he asked Warren, "What took you so long?"

Without the advice of counsel, Willie gave details of
how he abducted and assaulted Sandra. When asked
"why" he did it, he said he overheard Lily arguing with
Sandra in the vestibule at the funeral home. He followed Sandra outside and confronted her. Sandra
cursed him and commented that Lily and her sisters
were nothing but a bunch of "stuck-up phonies." That

angered Willie. He told Warren I wasn't "stuck-up," that I had always been kind to him, and was one of the nicest people he'd ever met. He also told Warren he loved me. He said Sandra pulled off and almost hit him with her car. He hit the hood of her car, she stopped, lowered the driver's window, and cursed him some more. Later that night, he was riding by the Mini Mart on his bicycle and spotted Sandra's car in the parking lot. From the parking lot, he watched her laugh and talk with a female cashier in the store. He hid his bike behind the store and slipped into the backseat of Sandra's unlocked car. When she exited the store and got back in her car, he held his pocketknife to her throat and made her drive outside the city limits. He said he wouldn't have hurt Sandra if she had apologized. He asked her several times to do that, and each time she refused. A female detective phoned Warren while he was interrogating Willie and reported that Sandra's doctor had given the okay for her to have visitors. Miss Emma, Colette, Evangeline, and Russell Latimore were the first people to visit her. Sandra told them that a smelly black man tried to kill her.

"You think they hold us responsible for what happened to Sandra?" I asked.

"Oh dear!" Mama cried.

Warren sighed and said, "I hope not. I will talk to them."

"Thank you, Warren! Thank you! We'll be much obliged," Mama said.

"Can they sue us?" I asked, looking at Ivy.

"They could file a lawsuit against us. I don't believe it will get far. It would be a frivolous lawsuit at best," Ivy said.

"Warren, how's Sandra?" I asked.

"She's no longer in ICU," Warren said. "She's been moved to a private room, and her doctor believes she's going to make a full recovery."

I shook my head. "Warren, you told me plenty of times not to become overly friendly with Willie. I didn't listen!"

"Violet, please," Warren said, "don't beat yourself up for what's happened."

"Don't, Violet," Ivy said.

"Wille wants to see you," Warren said.

"See me?" I shrieked.

"Yes," Warren replied.

"For what?" Ivy yelled.

"He wants to apologize to her for breaking into her home and accidentally setting it on fire."

"I—I don't know," I said.

"He seems remorseful," Warren said.

"I don't know if I can," I cried.

"It's your decision," Warren said.

"What do y'all think I should do?" I asked, looking at Mama and Ivy.

"He needs help," Mama said sadly. "Pray for him, and accept his apology."

"Poor Willie," I said. "Do you think he'll get the help he needs in prison?"

Ivy looked at me and shook her head.

Warren sighed. "I hope so, because that's exactly where he's going, and for a very long time."

An hour after Lily's tearful telephone call to her husband, which was the first time she'd talked to him since he left after the repast following Aunt Caroline's graveside service, he drove up on the street in front of

Mama's house. Lily had showered and brushed her teeth, thank goodness, and was upstairs on my laptop e-mailing her coworkers.

I went across the street to Aunt Caroline's and returned home just before eleven o'clock. Mama was in her room: asleep. I tiptoed into her room, turned off the TV and light. When I got upstairs, Ivy was sitting on the floor in the room we were sleeping in, with her ear pressed to the adjacent bedroom wall. "Shhhhh!" she whispered to me. I quietly closed the bedroom door and tiptoed over. I got down on my knees and pressed my ear to the wall. I could clearly hear the conversation next door between Lily and Russell.

"Russell, darling!" Lily cried. "Can you *honestly* forgive me?"

"I already have. I told you that," Russell said.

"I can understand if you hate me."

"I don't hate you, honey. My love for you has not changed."

"You told me there wasn't anything going on between you and Sandra, and I refused to believe you. My in-insecurities. Wow!" Lily laughed. "I can hardly say the word. I spoke and reacted out of *fear*. Fear that I had lost you to a another woman, a *younger* woman."

"Hush, honey."

"Poor, poor Sandra!"

"Shhhh!" Russell said.

"I was wrong about her, Russell. So wrong! I pray she forgives me, and God too, for my sin."

"Honey—"

"I feel responsible for what's happened to her!" Lily cried.

Russell sighed. "Me too."

"Why?"

"That day she called and asked me to meet her for lunch. I had a feeling she wanted to talk to me about something more than a position with the school system."

"Really?"

"Yeah."

"I had no idea she was unhappy at Social Services."

"She was afraid to say anything to you for fear you would be upset."

Lily sighed. "Knowing me, like I do, I would have reacted negatively to that news."

"I asked her if there was anything else she wanted to talk to me about, and she said no. She mentioned she'd started dating someone. I asked her how that was going. She smiled and said okay. I wished I had pressed her on the matter. I didn't bother to ask her anything about the man, his name, or nothing."

"Stop, Russell. You are in *no way* responsible for any of this. If I hadn't lashed out at Sandra at Aunt Caroline's wake, that homeless man wouldn't have—have—"

Lily burst into tears.

"Shhh," Russell said.

"Russell. I—I've got to fix this! If it's the last thing I do, I'm going to make this up to Sandra. She didn't deserve what happened to her, and she has a right to hate me. But I hope she finds it in her heart, someday, to forgive me." Lily sighed. "Sandra said something to me last Saturday at the funeral home that hurt, but it was the truth."

"What was that, sweetheart?"

"She said I didn't deserve you."

"Oh, Lily."

"No, no, no. She was right, Russell. The *old* Lily

didn't deserve a man like you. Looking back, I don't know how *I* lived with myself."

"Don't, honey."

Lily laughed. "Like Dr. Phil always says, 'you can't change what you won't acknowledge.' Well, I realize that, and I'm admitting I *was* all those horrible things people at the agency"—Lily chuckled—"my own family too, said I was."

"It's never to late to begin anew," Russell said, laughing.

"No, honey, it's not. Before you got here, I e-mailed Charlene Powell, her supervisor, and the accounting manager about my decision to send her to Chicago to the social work conference in July with the other social workers. I noted in my e-mail that if money couldn't be found to cover her expenses, I would personally take care of them."

"Oh, honey. That was so good of you."

"That was my second step toward starting 'anew.'"

"What was your first?" Russell asked.

"Calling and apologizing to you. I'm changing for the better, baby. So look out! For the new and improved Lily Shaw-Davenport!"

Ivy and I looked at each other as tears filled our eyes. Then it got kinda quiet next door. Ivy and I heard what sounded like kissing, followed by Lily moaning, "Oh, Russell, I miss you! You have no idea how much I've missed you!"

"Oh, baby, I've missed you too!" Russell moaned back.

"Oh, Russell!" Lily moaned louder. "Hold me, honey! Hold me!"

More moaning could be heard from next door.

"Ooooooh!" Ivy whispered, looking at me. "I

know she ain't about to get her freak on up in Mama's house."

I burst out laughing.

"Oh yes! Yesssss!" Lily moaned.

Ivy burst out laughing and jumped up from the floor. I jumped up too. We eased out of the bedroom and tiptoed downstairs to the kitchen. I went straight to the freezer and removed a half gallon of Breyers Snickers Bar ice cream. Ivy and I finished off the entire half gallon before going back upstairs an hour later. To our surprise, Lily and Russell were still going at it.

Chapter 40

Ain't Gone Let the Devil Steal *My* Joy!

Violet

"Y'all have done it again!" Floyd said, grinning and rubbing his stomach.

Lily laughed and shook her head.

We were having breakfast and it was a big, scrumptious spread. With the exception of the biscuits Jasmine made, Lily had cooked everything else.

"Thank you, Lily!" Floyd said, after she placed a second helping of cheese eggs on his plate.

Mama, seated at the other end of the dining room table, was holding and feeding TreShawn. I was walking around taking pictures of everybody. Sunday had rolled around again, and Lily, Jasmine, Rashaunda,

Ivy, and I were heading to Charity Chapel with Mama after breakfast.

Before we sat down for breakfast, we stood around the dining room table holding hands while Mama prayed. She thanked God for seeing us through a trying week. She asked God for his continued guidance in our lives, to look in on the Harris family, and to restore Cedric to good health. Before saying "Amen" she asked each of us to make our prayer requests known to God. Lily prayed for Sandra to have a full and speedy recovery and that Sandra's heart not be hardened against her. I prayed that Willie would get the help he needed and that Colette and her family wouldn't hold us responsible for what had happened to Sandra. Ivy asked God to strengthen her for her continued work within the judicial system and to empower her to do the right thing as far as Allen was concerned. She also prayed for physical wellness. Jasmine asked God not to let Lorenzo try to take Kenya away from her.

"Well, honey," Russell said, after finishing breakfast, "I need to hit the road if I'm to get back in time for Russell Jr. and me to make it to church."

"Okay," Lily said, smiling. "Tell Reverend Jacobs and everyone I'll see them next Sunday."

"Brother-in-law, you need a mug of coffee to take with you?" Ivy asked.

Russell's and Lily's brows creased together.

"To keep you awake," Ivy said, grinning. "Violet and I heard you and Lily moving around kinda *early* this morning."

"Ooooooh!" Lily exclaimed, blushing.

I burst out laughing.

"What y'all talking 'bout?" Mama asked.

Ivy burst out laughing.

"What's so funny?" Mama asked.

Jasmine started giggling. "I'll tell you later, Mama."

Lily and Russell had woken Ivy and me up shortly after four o'clock, moaning and groaning from the next room.

Russell, looking slightly embarrassed, said his good-byes to us and with blushing Lily behind him made his way outside.

"Niecee, pass me the molasses and another of one of Jasmine's delicious biscuits," Floyd said, rubbing his stomach again.

"Daddy, how much *more* are you going to eat?" Niecee asked, looking over at Floyd.

"Leave my granddaddy alone," Brandon mumbled, pouting.

Laughter rang out around the table.

"Yeah, let the man eat," Mama said.

Forty-five minutes later, Floyd, tearful Niecee, and her sons said their good-byes and headed back to D.C. An hour later, Mama, Rashaunda, Jasmine, Lily, Ivy, and I, dressed for church, gathered in the living room. The latest CD by Cheryl and the Gospelettes was playing softly in the stereo CD player. In Mama's lap was the family Bible: a large black leather Bible, where the words *Holy Bible* were written in gold leathers on the front. It was filled with entries of family births, deaths and marriages. Last week while we were on house arrest, Mama made two new entries: Aunt Caroline's sunset and TreShawn's sunrise.

Mama gave each of us an *Our Daily Bread* booklet, and asked that we recite a scripture before leaving for church. My sisters and I hadn't done that since we were little. Growing up, every week we had to learn a scripture and be prepared to recite it to Mama and Daddy on Sunday morning before we left for church. When we got to church, at the conclusion of the children's hour—a ten-minute period of time set aside during the worship service where the youth of the church came up front to receive godly instruction from a church mother or deacon—we, along with our peers, were asked and expected to recite a scripture.

"Who would like to go first?" Mama asked, smiling at us.

"I'll go," Ivy said, raising her hand.

Mama nodded.

"*Trust in the Lord with all your heart, and lean not on your own understanding.* Proverbs 3:5," Ivy said.

"Psalm 71:3," Lily said, "*Be my rock of refuge, to which I can always go. Give the command to save me, for you are my rock and my fortress,*" she said tearfully, as her voice trailed off.

"You keep meditating on that one," Mama said to her.

"I will," Lily said, nodding.

"I have two," I said, holding up two fingers. "Micah 6:8. *He has showed you, O man, what is good. And what does the Lord require of you? To act justly and to love mercy and to walk humbly with your God.* Jeremiah 31:13. *Then maidens will dance and be glad, young men and old as well. I will turn their mourning into gladness. I will give comfort and joy instead of sorrow.*"

"Yes! Yes!" Mama shouted. "'I will turn their mourning into gladness'!"

"Mama?"

"Yes, Jasmine," Mama answered, wiping her eyes.

"I've been meditating on the one you said to me the other day: Psalm 127:3," Jasmine said softly.

Jasmine opened her arms and motioned for Rashaunda, who was sitting beside me, to come to her. Rashaunda got up and walked over to Jasmine. Jasmine pulled Rashaunda down into her lap, and as tears filled her eyes and ran down her face, she said, *"Behold, children are a gift from the Lord, the fruit of the womb is a reward."*

"Oh, Jesus!" Lily cried out.

Ivy and I burst into tears too.

"Oh, thank you, Jesus!" Mama shouted, rocking back and forth.

Jasmine hugged Rashaunda and kissed her on the cheek.

"Oh, Mama!" Rashaunda said, squirming about.

"That's good, daughter," Mama said, nodding. "You keep meditating on that one," she said, flipping through the Bible. "Here's one I want you to read and meditate on too." She handed the Bible to Jasmine. "Ephesians 4:24."

"And that ye put on the new man which after God is created in righteousness and holiness," Jasmine read.

"Read it again," Mama said.

Jasmine did as she was told, then handed the Bible back to Mama.

"I have one," Mama said. *"Praise be to the God and Father of our Lord Jesus Christ. The Father of compassion and the God of comfort, who comforts us in all our troubles, so that we can comfort those in trouble with the comfort we ourselves received from God. Second Corinthians 1:3 and 4."*

"Amen!" my sisters and I said.

"What about me, Grandma?" Rashaunda said.

"I haven't forgotten about you," Mama said, smiling. "Come here."

Rashaunda walked over to Mama.

"Read this," Mama said, pointing.

"Psalm 118:24!" Rashaunda exclaimed with a big smile. "*This is the day which the Lord hath made; we will rejoice and be glad in it.*"

"Amen! Amen!" Mama cried, throwing up both hands.

My sisters and I said, "Amen" too.

"And don't *ever* forget the things Augustus and I taught you," Mama said, looking around the room at my sisters and me. "Keep God first and foremost in your life. Your life will be sweeter, more rewarding when you live in accordance to His Word. And don't ever forget"—she smiled—"that I love you."

I was weaving through the church lot in search of a parking space after dropping Mama and Ivy off at the church entrance, when I saw the Chrysler Pacifica pull up in front of the church. The back doors and front passenger door of the Pacifica opened and several children hopped out. It was 10:50; worship service would start at eleven o'clock sharp, beginning with a thirty-minute devotional period of songs and testimonies. I quickly found a parking space, turned off the car engine, grabbed my purse, opened the driver's door, stepped out, and literally jumped out of my right pump. I don't know how she managed to get from the church entrance to where I was parked so fast. Colette was glaring at me out the driver's window of the Pacifica.

I collected myself, smiled, and said, "Hello."

Colette didn't return my smile or greeting. She continued to glare at me. For a second, I was afraid to move away from my car, fearing if I did she would run over me in the parking lot.

"I hope you and yo' sister Lily don't think y'all off the hook with what happened to my niece."

Thinking it best not to say anything, I didn't respond.

"'Cause y'all ain't!" Colette yelled. "You two are just as guilty as that man who tried to kill her."

Still thinking it best not to say anything, I remained silent and prayed that someone would drive up and that in her heart of hearts, Colette didn't mean what she just said.

I took a deep breath, closed the car door, and started walking toward the church. My heart was beating wildly.

"Violet! I know you hear me talkin' to you!" Colette yelled.

I stopped and looked back at Colette. "I'm truly sorry about what happened to Sandra," I said as compassionately as I could.

"Yeah, you sorry all right!" Colette shouted. "And you and yo' sister Lily gone pay!"

I turned and started walking quickly to the church. Colette gunned the Pacifica. I jumped and fell over onto the hood of a parked car.

"One more thing," she said, pulling up beside me. "I don't intend to sit back and let you *have* Warren. I have every intention of making him mine!" she yelled before speeding away.

Deacons Othello Sharpe and Spencer Peoples—two deacons I liked and respected—along with Miss Odessa, were the devotional leaders for the day. After a song by

Miss Odessa, a prayer and a scripture reading by the deacons, the devotional period was open for testimonies from the congregation. From where she was seated in the Mothers' Corner, Mama stood up.

"I got to praaaay to get along. I got to praaaay to get along," Mama sang, with uplifted hands and closed eyes.

"Sing it, sista! Sing it!" Deacon Peoples said loudly.

My sisters, Rashaunda, and I were seated midway in the middle seating section in the church. When Mama stood up, Lily moaned, "Oh, Mama!" Ivy, seated next to Lily, placed her arm around Lily's shoulders.

"Giving honor to God, my Lord and Savior Jesus Christ," Mama said, "I stand this morning to say thank you!"

"Yessss, thank you, Lord!" Lily cried.

"Praise him! Praise him!" I heard Miss Sadie say.

"I thank the Lord for seeing me and my family through a week of trials and tribulations," Mama said.

"Ahhhhh, thank you, Jesus!" Lily shouted.

"Praise him! Praise him!" Miss Sadie said again.

"I look over there . . ." Mama paused, smiled, and pointed in our direction. "Where my children and granddaughter are seated. The good Lord knows I'm thankful."

"Say so, sista!" Deacon Sharpe said.

Mama continued. "But one person is missing."

That did it. Jasmine and Lily were already crying; Ivy and I started bawling too.

"Help 'em, Lord!" I heard Miss Odessa say.

Two senior ushers hurried over to us with tissue and church fans.

Mama continued. "My sista Caroline ain't with us," she said, her voice cracking at the end. "Sh-she's gone on."

"Yes! Yes!" Deacon Jackson said, sorrowfully, from the Deacons' Corner.

"My sista wouldn't want us to be sad this morning. No! No!" Mama said. "She would want us to rejoice. Rejoice! My grandbaby recited Psalm 118:24 this morning before we left home. 'This is the day which the Lord hath made; we will rejoice and be glad in it.'"

Lily stood up and started stomping her feet. "Hallelujah! Hallelujah!" she shouted.

"Thank you, Jesus! Thank you, Lord!" Mama shouted.

Ivy, Jasmine, and I stood up too and joined Mama and Lily in a rousing chorus of praise to God.

"If God's been good to you," Mama sang, "you ought to tell it! If he brought you through, you ought to tell it!"

And that's what we did, we told it. Miss Emma thought my sisters and I carried on when Daddy died; too bad she didn't witness what we did that Sunday morning. I imagined Miss Odessa would tell her. Little did two-faced Miss Odessa know, I didn't care what she told Miss Emma. Like my sisters and my mother, I was getting my praise on and I wasn't going to let her or hateful Colette steal my joy.

Chapter 41

Unexpected Guests

Violet

"Is that Allen's car?" Mama asked.

"Yeah, I believe it is," I said. It was approaching two o'clock, and we were on our way home from church. Allen's Jaguar was parked on the street in front of Mama's house. From where she was sitting in the backseat of my car, I heard Ivy sigh. I looked back at her from the rearview mirror.

"Did you know he was coming?" Mama asked, looking back at her.

"No, I didn't," Ivy replied.

When I pulled up beside Allen, we all waved and smiled. By the time I'd entered into the driveway and parked, Allen had exited his car and entered the yard. He opened the car doors for Mama and Ivy. When Ivy stepped out of the car, he kissed her on the forehead and said, "Hey, darling." Ivy smiled up at him and mumbled, "Hey" back.

"Allen, how are you?" Mama asked, hugging him.

"I'm okay," he said.

Allen didn't look okay. He looked like he had been through the wringer.

"You gone stay and have dinner with us?" Mama asked, smiling at him.

Allen shrugged and opened his eyes wide.

Poor thing! I thought to myself.

"Stay, won't you?" Mama said, patting him on the cheek.

I cut my eyes over at Ivy. A half smile was plastered on her face. She looked like a mannequin. I cleared my throat. Ivy flinched and looked at me. With my eyes and no spoken words, I told her to tell Allen the truth this time.

"Okay, Mrs. Shaw. I'll stay for dinner. Thank you," Allen replied, smiling and bobbing his head.

Mama headed for the house and I followed. Minutes later, Allen and Ivy entered the house and went into the living room. I went upstairs to change clothes and was heading downstairs to start dinner with Mama when Lily, Jasmine, and Rashaunda walked into the house. They'd swung by the supermarket after church to pick up some things for dinner. After slipping out of their church clothes and changing into casual attire, they joined Mama and me in the kitchen.

"You think she's going to be honest with him this time?" Lily asked me.

Unable to keep Ivy's secret from them any longer, I'd told Lily, Jasmine, and Mama the real reason for her reluctance to go through with the wedding.

"I hope so," I said.

"It'd be a shame if she didn't," Jasmine muttered.

"Yeah, it would be," Mama said. "Maybe I should go in there," she said, throwing up her hands.

"No!" I shouted.

"No, Mama," Lily said, shaking her head. "Ivy needs to handle this on her own."

Mama sighed. "Yeah, you're right."

Forty minutes later, we still hadn't heard a peep from Ivy and curiosity had gotten the best of us. Mama told me to go see if Ivy and Allen wanted something to drink. I scooted out of the kitchen, and before knocking on the living room door pressed my ear to it. I could hear Ivy and Allen talking. Their voices were low and I couldn't make out much of what they were saying. I did hear Ivy say, "She's difficult and condescending" before I knocked on the door.

I entered the living room with a big smile on my face. Ivy and Allen were seated on the love seat. Allen had an arm around Ivy's shoulders. His brows were creased and his lips were pursed. Ivy on the other hand, seemed a bit more relaxed.

"You two want anything to drink?" I asked, trying to get a read from Ivy of what was going on.

Ivy smiled. "Yeah, I'd like some lemonade."

"Allen," I said, "what about you?"

Allen looked up at me, nodded, and said, "I'll take some lemonade too. Thank you."

"Okay! I'll be back in a jiffy," I said.

I was bombarded with questions when I returned to the kitchen: "What're they doing?" "Does Ivy look happy?" "How does Allen look?" "They say anything to you?"

When I returned to the living room, Ivy and Allen

were still sitting close together on the love seat. As I handed them their drinks, I asked if they wanted anything else. Ivy shook her head and said, "No, we're fine."

"Fine." Did that mean what I was hoping it meant? I wondered, leaving the room.

While the pork roast, hen, sweet potato casserole, and macaroni and cheese baked in the oven and the collard greens simmered on the stove, Lily, Jasmine, and Rashaunda ran up the street to Wal-Mart to get a few toiletries for the house. Mama went outside to get some roses off her rosebushes. She wanted to make an arrangement for the dining room table. I headed down the hall to the den. As I passed the living room, I looked over at the door and wondered, *How much longer are they going to be cooped up in there?*

I plopped down in one of the recliners in the den and picked up the TV remote. The light was blinking on the answering machine; I pressed the Play button. The message was from Niecee; they'd made it back to D.C. safely. After the message played, I thought about calling Warren to see how his day was going. He had told me last night, when he called to say good night, that he wouldn't be at church today because he had to wrap up some things on the Harris case. I wondered if that meant him having to go to Miss Emma's house. Before turning on the TV, I went upstairs to get my cell phone. I returned to the den and dialed Warren's mobile. After five rings, my call went to his voice mailbox. "Just calling to say hi," I said, after his greeting. I then called the police department. A gruff-sounding male answered.

"McKinley Police Department."

"Detective Jackson," I said.

"Hold on," the man said.

Seconds later, the gruff-sounding male reconnected with me.

"Ma'am, Detective Jackson has left for the day. He is expected back tomorrow. You can leave a message or call back then."

"No message. I'll try to reach him later," I said.

Where is he? I wondered, pressing the End button on my cell phone. *And why hasn't he called me?*

"Violet!"

I eased out of the recliner and went down the hall. "Yeah, Mama," I said, stepping outside.

Mama was standing between her yellow and pink rosebushes. Standing next to her was Warren. "Hey," he said, smiling at me.

I threw up my hand and waved.

"I'm on my way to Uncle Odell's," he said. "I stopped by to speak to your mother."

"Oh?" I said, looking at Mama.

"I came over to tell her the obvious," Warren said, smiling, "that I'm quite fond of you, Violet. And that it is my intention to see you once my divorce is final."

I could feel a grin forming at my mouth. I placed my hand there to conceal it.

Warren continued. "And in the meantime, I will respect and abide by her wish that we not see each other until then."

I nodded.

"You come from decent folk, Warren," Mama said, smiling. "I've known your relatives for a long time. They're a quiet, hardworking set of folk."

Warren smiled back.

Mama sighed and her brows creased together. "My Violet here," she said, looking over at me, "would like to get married someday. I'd rather she not waste her time with someone who doesn't want the same thing."

"I—I understand," Warren stammered.

"But she's grown. She can do as she please," Mama said, throwing up hands.

"Granted things didn't work out between me and my soon-to-be ex-wife," Warren said. "The experience has not made me bitter. I don't want or intend to grow old alone, Mrs. Shaw," he said, smiling. "I do hope to remarry again."

"I see," Mama said with a nod. She then turned and started snipping away at her rosebushes again.

Warren looked over at me and winked.

I winked back.

"Thank you for your time, Mrs. Shaw, and it was a pleasure talking to you."

"Likewise," Mama said. "You have a good afternoon."

When Warren backed out the driveway and drove off, Mama looked over at me and smiled.

I ran down the porch and planted a big kiss on her cheek.

The front door opened and Ivy and Allen stepped outside.

"You two all right?" Mama asked.

"Couldn't be better," Ivy said, smiling.

Chapter 42

Plans and Promises

Violet

"Well, Caroline, you ain't gone believe all that's happened since you been gone. Then again"—Mama laughed—"you might. Oh, by the way, I gave Sadie that blue suit of yours. She was tickled pink."

We were all at the cemetery with Mama placing floral arrangements at Aunt Caroline's grave site. It was a sad and also a joyful occasion. As we placed the chrysanthemums, daylilies, phlox, and dianthus arrangements around Aunt Caroline's grave site, we cried when we thought about how much we missed her, and laughed when we recalled fond memories with her.

When we arrived at the cemetery, Mama had to coax frightened Rashaunda out of Lily's car. Mama assured her that no dead bodies would rise up out of the graves like in those scary movies she liked to watch and chase after us.

After we finished up at the cemetery, Lily and I were taking Mama to the bank to deposit the insurance check. Once it cleared, Mama not only planned to give my sisters and me the money Aunt Caroline had bequeathed to us, but she was going to send Cedric and his wife some as well. Daisy told Mama the last time she talked to her that Cedric and his wife had gotten behind on some of their bills.

Ivy was packing up her car and heading back to Durham the following morning. She'd taken my advice about being truthful with Allen regarding why she'd called off the wedding. Allen, she said, apologized profusely for being "insensitive." He promised that upon his return to Durham he would sit his mother down and have a long talk with her, and tell her in no uncertain terms that the future plans for his and Ivy's wedding would be solely made by Ivy.

Ivy apologized to Allen for lying to him at first about why she'd called off the wedding and for keeping secret her acceptance of a new job. Her immediate plans once she returned to Durham: meet with the program administrator with the Justice Project about the position she'd accepted; contact her sorority sister, the wedding planner, about helping her plan the wedding she'd always wanted: a fall wedding at Charity Chapel; and schedule an appointment with a chiropractor.

Lily was staying behind for two more days. She, Mama, and I were going to Reid's Monuments and Memorials to select a headstone for Aunt Caroline's grave site. After it was erected, Mama planned to plant peonies there like she did at Daddy's grave site.

Jasmine hadn't said when she was leaving, nor did

she appear to be in a hurry to get back to Charlotte, that is, not until her phone call from Kenya before we left the house for the cemetery.

Prior to Kenya's call, I had overheard Jasmine talking loudly on her cell phone in the backyard. I looked out the kitchen window at her. She said to whomever she was talking to, "I'm not gone do it! Uh-uh, no! I hate it for him! *Hate* it! Maybe his babies' mama can help him, 'cause I sho' ain't!" After hearing her "babies' mama" comment, I figured she was talking about Maniac. When she came inside, I asked her if she was all right. She shrugged and said, "Yeah."

Kenya's phone call threw brooding Jasmine into a state of depression. Kenya told Jasmine she was having a "great time" with her dad and Miss Yolanda. They had taken her to Carowinds after church yesterday, and the day before she and Miss Yolanda had a "girls' day out." They went to the salon and got manicures and pedicures and later had dinner at the Olive Garden. Jasmine cried all the way to the cemetery after talking with Kenya. She said Kenya sounded so happy.

We were placing the last arrangement of flowers at Aunt Caroline's grave site when Jasmine said, "I have an announcement to make."

We all stopped what we were doing and looked at her.

"This morning, just before we left the house, I called CHA," she said.

"What? Who's that?" Mama asked.

"Charlotte Housing Authority," Jasmine said softly.

"Okay," Mama said slowly.

Jasmine continued. "I—I submitted a verbal thirty-day notice to vacate my apartment."

"You did *what?*" Ivy asked.

Jasmine repeated herself.

"Hallelujah!" Mama shouted, throwing up hands.

"Jasmine, are you serious?" I asked, as tears filled my eyes.

Tears filled Jasmine's eyes too. She nodded and they rolled down her cheeks. Lily and Ivy ran over to her and hugged her. Smiles were on everyone's face, except Rashaunda's. She was clearly bowled over by Jasmine's announcement.

Jasmine walked over to Rashaunda and threw her arms around her. "I'm not gone lose my children," she said.

Jasmine's plans: Use some of the insurance money to get an apartment. Since she had no credit, Lily volunteered not only to go to Charlotte and help her find a place, but to cosign on a lease with her as well. Jasmine's second plan was to seek employment and enroll in cosmetology school. She said she wanted to be a nail tech. Plan three—maintain a civil relationship with Lorenzo in hopes that he would forgo plans to pursue custody of Kenya, and last but not least, she and her daughters would start attending church as a family.

Mama shouted a good while after hearing that. "That's wonderful news, baby!" she cried, hugging Jasmine. "Wonderful news!"

"And we're going to do everything we can to help you," Ivy promised, hugging Jasmine again.

"Yes, we are," Lily said, smiling and nodding.

Rashaunda's bewildered expression had now changed to sadness. Her mood brightened when Ivy asked her if she wanted to ride to Durham with her for a few days. Her mood got even brighter when Lily told her she would have her daughter, Sabrina, take her shopping for summer clothes.

"Rashaunda," Lily said, walking over to her, "we love

you. You know that, don't you?" she asked, smiling down into Rashaunda's face.

Rashaunda nodded.

"You may not have a father like Kenya, but guess what?" Lily said, smiling.

"What?" Rashaunda mumbled as tears filled her eyes.

"You got us, honey. And we love you a bunch."

"Yes, we do," I said, walking over and throwing my arms around Rashaunda.

Everyone else gathered around Rashaunda and covered her with kisses and hugs.

As we were about to leave the cemetery, Mama looked down at Aunt Caroline's grave, then looked heavenward and said, "Sista, the girls talkin' 'bout sending me to Alabama to see some of Augustus's folk. I reckon I might just do that. 'Sho wish you were here to go with me," she said, as tears filled her eyes.

"We'll go with you, Mama," I said.

"Yeah, we'll make it a family trip," Ivy said.

Mama looked at us, smiled, and said, "That would be nice. Before we do that, let's go to Arizona and see Cedric."

"That sounds like a plan too, Mama," I said.

Epilogue

Violet

One month later

I was flying back to Phoenix to spend the July Fourth holiday with Mama, my nephew Cedric, and his family. Severe nerve and bone damage resulted in him losing his right leg. Disheartening to say the least, he vowed that he would not let it get him down.

Jasmine moved out of the projects into a cute three-bedroom apartment. Our housewarming gift to her was furniture. Mama purchased a dinette set; Lily and Ivy purchased living room furniture, and I furnished Kenya's and Rashaunda's bedrooms. And not only was she enrolled in a cosmetology program, thanks to Lily's connections, but Jasmine had landed her *first* job. She was a part-time clerical assistant at the Department of Social Services in Charlotte. Rashaunda was enrolled in a summer enrichment program and Kenya was spending the summer between Lorenzo and Yolanda's home and Jasmine's apartment.

Ivy's plans for a fall wedding at Charity Chapel were going along smoothly. Her sorority sister was helping her with the details. Beatrice tearfully apologized to Ivy for her offensive behavior and asked for Ivy's forgiveness.

True to her word, Ivy began seeing a chiropractor for her back problem. She also reduced her hours at her office and was able to renegotiate her responsibilities with the Justice Project.

Upon Lily's return to work, the first thing she did was tear up Sandra's termination papers and begin making amends with her colleagues by being more approachable and deferential. She said things had been a little awkward, but she was determined to be a better supervisor. She wanted to be liked and respected by her employees.

It still remained to be seen if Colette was going to make good of her threat to sue Lily and me. She, Evangeline, Miss Emma, and more than twenty of their family members were at the church business meeting to cast their vote for Reverend Bobbitt as pastor. In a vote of thirty-three to thirty-five, Reverend Cherry ended up garnering the winning votes. With his role as Charity Chapel's new pastor, one of the first things he did—since he would be officiating at Ivy and Allen's wedding—was phone them and ask that they come in for premarital counseling.

Warren and I celebrated our first official public date at the new Golden Corral in town. Over dinner, I spoke candidly to him about my desire not only to marry, but to have children. He smiled at me and said, "I was wondering about that, because I would like to have more children." Later, while sitting out on his deck gazing up at the stars, he asked me if I'd like to go to the Caribbean for a few days.